DISCERNING
HER SHADOWS

BOOK ONE IN
HER STORY

A NOVEL

TARA WEBB

Discerning Her Shadows

By Tara Webb
Copyright © 2021 by Tara Webb

eISBN: 978-1-73655-370-1
Paperback ISBN: 978-1-7365537-1-8

Cover, map and branch design: Darcy Farrow
Poem: Alyssa Durham
Editor: Nicolette Beebe

TO MY DOMINIC

Because you remind me daily to love myself, especially
in the midst of my own shadows

SERENITY
LAKE

LEVANDER
CASTLE

MOUNT
FERMONT

BARRIER BEFORE DESERT

TUHKA
VILLAGE

MOUNTAINS
OF COR

REIS
SEA

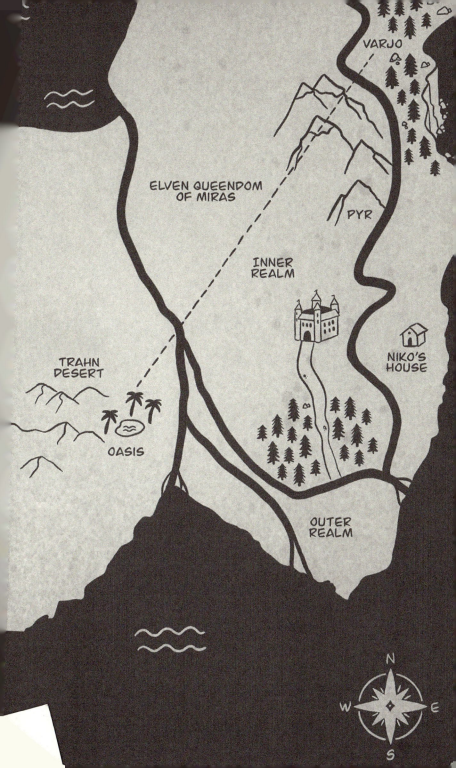

DISCERNING HER SHADOWS

Look at the fire burning in her eyes
Notice how the flames flicker
Layers peel back as she sheds their lies
Blooming lotus flower
Beams of energy flow in a fibonacci spiral
Dragons from within begin to dance
Listen to them closely as they chant:

LAM

VAM

RAM

YAM

HAM

AUM

OM

Her power is beautifully galvanizing
You can see her with clarity now
She is you
Kundalini Rising

-Alyssa Lilly-

CHAPTER ONE

Stick to the shadows. It was Ashlynn's daily mantra.
Stick to the shadows and she would be safe. Stick to the
shadows and all would be well. She tried, but her
curiosity made it hard to stay focused. Keeping her eyes
centered on Sebastian's back helped her remain attentive.
He was so good at keeping out of sight, just like
everything else in his life. The way he weaved in and out
of the thin birch trees made his footing and balance seem
superhuman.

"Stick to the shadows, Ashlynn," he called back to her.
"Father will be on the attack so stay hidden unless you
are needed!"

Ashlynn rolled her eyes at her cousin's command. She
didn't need him to remind her of something she could
never forget. She picked up her pace. The forest swam by
as Ashlynn propelled herself toward the castle. She tore
through the brush, pushing past her physical limit and
tapping into her mental one. Running as fast as Sebastian
was difficult. Her shorter than average legs hindered her
ability to keep up. Her tightly fitted dress restricted any

strenuous movement. The exact thing that someone who was always in hiding tended to avoid. However, it was a requirement for the ladies of the castle to be bound in such attire, and Ashlynn was in no position to argue. She was expected to keep up without a complaint. This time was no exception.

Up ahead, Sebastian jumped over a low hanging branch. His hair swayed in the breeze as if the wind were tousling it. His good looks were an added bonus to his perfect life. Most people with his warm features—chocolate eyes, short, brown hair, and medium height—would be considered average. Yet for Sebastian, it came across as handsome and understated. Her older cousin was the epitome of princely perfection. Everything came easy for the heir to the throne of Levander. From the moment he awoke to when he fell asleep, Sebastian was pampered and cared for like a prized stallion. His precise dictation and generous demeanor filled out the image of his elegant life.

A step behind, and always his shadow, was Barcinas. Barcinas was taller than Sebastian, and full of muscle. His robust stature couldn't hinder his speed if it tried.

"Yeah, stick to the shadows this time. We don't need another problem," Barcinas echoed.

"We can't run any slower, Ash," Sebastian hollered,

dodging another branch.

"I'm doing my best," she muttered to herself. Arguing with her overconfident cousin would only waste her breath, and each inhale was precious at this moment. A dark figure running on her left and keeping stride caught her eye. "Sebastian!" she yelled. "We're being followed!"

Barcinas's head pivoted to locate the figure while simultaneously increasing his speed so he could protect Sebastian. Barcinas was in charge of keeping Sebastian safe, and anyone who meant to harm his charge and lover would regret their decision.

The being following them was a beast. As Ashlynn ran, she kept an eye on the blurry creature, doing her best to stay upright and moving. Its eyes came into focus as they locked on Ashlynn. The intensity and intrigue made her stomach lurch into her throat. "It's a panther," she announced. "You go ahead. I'll distract it." She paused to take a breath and placed her hands on her knees for support.

"No! We have to stick together," Sebastian called back, the agitation blending with pure exaggeration in his voice.

"Just leave her," Barcinas yelled to him. "She knows the way, and we have to hurry. We won't make it in time if we wait for her!"

Once again, his words cut her, though he wasn't wrong. "Then by all means, your royal annoyance, run on ahead," Ashlynn panted.

They didn't wait for her to finish her sentence before picking up their pace. Sebastian was nearly out of earshot when he yelled back, "Remember, Ash! Stay hidden in the shadows when you get there!"

Her cousin disappeared with Barcinas trailing behind him. She pushed her sweaty hair out of her face with her plump fingers as her dark wiry curls pooled around her cheeks. Her head felt too small for the amount of hair she had. Ashlynn searched for the panther in the dense brush, but each breath made it harder to see as a pain grew sharp in her side. Her ridiculous dress made it difficult to breathe. It felt like she was intentionally tied tight to be an easy target for any predator, and she was sure a loose pin stabbed her ribs. She scratched at her side, but it only dug the pin in deeper.

A hearing had been called by the king that involved her aunt, the Queen of Levander. She needed to be in the throne room for the interrogation looking pristine and proper or the consequences would be disastrous. She hadn't been told the details, but Ashlynn knew it was precarious when King Theodore called a hearing. Each usually ended with someone leaving in chains or worse.

4

Ashlynn needed to ensure nothing happened to her aunt. She didn't have any other family left except her aunt and her two cousins. Unless she counted the king, and she never did since he barely considered her family, much less human.

The forest was poorly lit as the sun had lowered past the tree-line. It would be too dark to follow the path soon, and she was in more danger the closer it got to sunset. She scrunched her eyes and peered into the woods one last time, but the beast was gone. Either she had been seeing things or the panther had shifted its path for a better view. Neither thought was reassuring, but she didn't have time to think on it.

Ashlynn took one huge gulp, shook her head to clear her mind, and forced herself to steadily jog. Her feet felt like boulders with seaweed attached to them as legs. Sebastian was right. If she didn't find a way to pick up her speed, then she wouldn't make it in time, and that prospect was scarier than actually being there. Ashlynn trudged on, watching her feet instead of the path to be sure she didn't trip. A quick glance up made her realize she had veered from the trail.

Ashlynn halted and groaned out her frustration. It was a simple task to stay on the path, but she had a way of getting lost when her mind blurred from stress and exhaustion. One look around revealed she had been stuck in her thoughts far longer than she realized. The path was no where to be seen. Her mother's crescent-shaped necklace shined around her neck. It did this when Ashlynn needed its instruction the most. "Yes, Mother." She sighed. "I seem to have gotten turned around. I just need a quicker way back," she grumbled.

The silence of the woods usually calmed Ashlynn, but today the quiet unnerved her. Holding her necklace for support, she decided to walk farther into the forest instead of retracing her steps to find the trail. Her mother's necklace must mean there was more ahead than she realized, even if that didn't make any sense to her. Each step crunched from the fallen leaves, and she cringed at the sound. Walking quietly with so many around was impossible. Another crunch resounded, except this time it came while her foot was still raised. She froze. Every piece of her screamed to run, but an unexplainable sense of calm emanated from her core. This feeling had only come a few times in her life, and she vowed to adhere to that instruction as her life typically depended on it. Time slowed as Ashlynn waited.

Crunching leaves persisted until the hair on the back of her neck tingled. The sensation of eyes behind her had her holding her breath. Slowly, she turned. Nothing.

Looking to the forest floor made her giggle. A red squirrel studied her curiously. She knelt down to see the creature up close, and it skittered away. A dark outline approached out of the corner of her eye. Alarmed, she swished her head around and fell, causing the back of her dress to get smeared in dirt and leaves. She would definitely have to stay hidden when she arrived in the throne room.

She sighed. "Could this day get any worse?" As if in response to her question, the panther emerged from the brush with its piercing eyes locked on her. They made her skin tingle. Being so close to this beast was intimidating, while also intriguing. The beautiful dark brown coat of the panther reminded Ashlynn of her own hair. The panther's bright gold and brown eyes locked onto Ashlynn's burned caramel ones with muted gold flecks. The similarities made her feel as if the panther were a spirit sent to guide her. She heaved herself off the floor as the enchanted being raced off in a different direction. Brushing herself off, she followed it.

A few minutes later, they stopped in a clearing. The panther was quick to lose interest in her as it lounged near a small boulder covered in fallen leaves. A familiar sensation of knowing signaled to her that this boulder was more than it seemed. She had tried to explain this odd feeling to others, but every time she did, her words turned to mush. As if something prevented her from speaking about her secret connection.

Ashlynn shuffled to the rock and gathered the burnt red, gold, and brown leaves. Dropping them onto the forest floor, she rested her hand on the cool surface of the boulder. A pulse beat beneath her touch. She was sure it was just the blood pumping in her body from the miles of running. Her body was getting weary and needed to rest before venturing on. She put her back against the rock to settle herself when it trembled violently. The pulsing of the rock behind her caused Ashlynn to jump. She turned to find that a small opening had materialized out from where the boulder once sat.

It was big enough for one person to squeeze through and pitch black aside from the worn steps. Peeking at the panther, Ashlynn wondered if this feline had led her here on purpose.

"Look, I appreciate you guiding me to a strange hole, but I really need to get to the castle," she explained, rolling her eyes at how ridiculous she sounded for talking to a panther. The panther must have thought her talking was funny, too, because it seemed to grin. "Please tell me, in some way that I can understand, that this is a short cut." The large cat opened its mouth, and yawned, and then sauntered over to her. Ashlynn gulped but held her ground to prove she had faith in the beast. The panther didn't pause though and kept approaching as if nudging her toward to the hole. "Yes, I get it. You want me to go down the hole." Her fear turned to intrigue once she realized the animal had never meant her harm. The panther continued to advance, this time baring its teeth. Ashlynn had no choice but to oblige. "Just so you know, if this doesn't lead to the castle, then I am never trusting a dangerous, unknown animal in the woods again!"

She took one more look behind her at the hole and strode, with slow, deliberate steps, backward into the hole. Before descending entirely, she glanced toward the magnificent beast to find it had disappeared. Ashlynn swiveled around fully, but couldn't find any evidence of the creature. Unsure how to find the original path, she chose to take the one before her, hoping it would lead her to the hearing. Breathing the deepest breath she had all day, she peered farther into the dark. The opening closed, trapping her inside without a way out. All she could do now was take the path and hope she made it in time.

"Well, this seems safe. I guess a hidden tunnel in the middle of the forest makes perfect sense," she muttered. "Then again, imagining a panther corralling me here is probably not the oddest thing I have done."

Stick to the shadows had become stick to the dark tunnel. Her necklace produced a bright, golden glow in the black abyss that surrounded her. In the distance, she faintly heard horns announcing the start of the king's trial. Ashlynn ran, energized by the desire to arrive ahead of Sebastian and before her aunt was hurt, hoping it wasn't already too late.

CHAPTER TWO

"How kind of you to join us, Sebastian," King Theodore bellowed from across the throne room. His voice echoed, causing every face to turn toward Sebastian. There was a slight shift in his eyes as he searched for someone. It annoyed the king, which wasn't too different from any other day, except his furrowed brow meant he was expecting someone else to show their face. King Theodore licked his lips. "I was beginning to wonder if you had any inclination of being useful today!"

Sebastian stood at the entrance, his hand griping his sword at his side like a crippled person who used a cane for stability. The ladies and gentlemen of the court adjusted themselves to give him a clear path to the throne. He strode through the quiet room to where his parents sat as they presided over the meeting. Bowing to his father, he muttered an apology.

Hiding between the columns near the throne, Ashlynn's secret spot in the shadows, guaranteed her a front seat to the action without being noticed by the king. The hidden forest entrance had ended behind a dusty, old portrait of the previous monarch, King Theodore's brother. It was the perfect way to sneak into the proceedings, silent and unseen. She thanked the Goddess for the panther guiding her to a shortcut and vowed to listen to it without question if they ever encounter each other again.

King Theodore terrified even the bravest of men in the kingdom. While his swordsmanship was excellent, he thrived on tearing down a person with his words. Watching them crumble beneath his remarks ignited his thirst for blood. And once they were defeated in heart, he called for their death.

The King of Levander was taller than most, but his round belly made up for the extra space between his head and the floor. It was easy to become enamored with his soft brown hair and scruffy beard, if one discounted all of his other unattractive features. With a round face and generous smile, he gave the impression of being a kind and understanding king. But the people of Levander knew better. When he unleashed his steel grey eyes and harsh voice, they knew his enamoring smile would turn sinister. It made them wish to be anywhere other than in his presence.

That intimidating sensation was all too familiar when those piercing eyes landed on Ashlynn. She was never needed unless the king wished to make an example of someone. At that point, nothing could save her— not even hiding in the shadows nor her lover's high ranking position. That is *if* Tiberius chose to intervene.

She glanced around the room to search for his lopsided grin and long, golden locks, but instead caught Sebastian's eye. He was kneeling in front of the throne, commanding her with a stern brow to stay hidden. His perceptive stare had a tendency to spot her reckless impulses. This time, however, she had no desire to show herself. Barcinas was bent beside him, his black hair full of curls and green eyes probing anyone who dared a glimpse. Which most didn't. Those eyes found her. He smirked as she stepped back into the shadows to better hide herself.

The king dismissed Sebastian and Barcinas with a flick of his hand and turned his full gaze on Tiberius. "Bring in the prisoner and traitor to my throne!" he thundered, grabbing his goblet of wine.

Tiberius nodded as a tress of blond hair escaped his low bun to caress his lips. He surveyed the crowd, glancing in her direction, as if sensing her presence, then stalked off to obey his master. Her uncle babbled to the crowd, but her mind couldn't focus. She kept going over that last look from Tiberius, deciphering if he had seen

13

her.

"Ash! Ashlynn!" a familiar voice whispered behind her.

Ashlynn jumped as a thin hand landed on her shoulder. She spun to see Odessa's russet colored hair framing frantic eyes as her cousin gripped her arm.

"What are you doing here, Odessa?" Ashlynn whispered back. "Aren't you supposed to be with the royal family in the front?"

Odessa narrowed her eyes like the loving sibling she had never had. "I knew you'd be hiding in the shadows. I had to find you! Father would be in a rage if he thought you didn't show up for his little display today. My brother gives terrible advice. You should be front and center so Father doesn't think you've disrespected him."

As Ashlynn stared at her younger cousin, she thought about the many times Odessa had looked out for her with the intention of dissuading her father's attacks.

"I will stay right here. If he chooses to call for me, I can make myself known, but this way I can get away undetected if he doesn't. You don't have to worry about me," Ashlynn promised, putting her hand on Odessa's face. "Now go out there and show Sebastian how to properly address your father."

Odessa snorted and squeezed Ashlynn in a quick hug before flitting off to make her entrance. She turned her attention back to the charade. A man kneeled in the middle of the throne room. The shackles barely stayed on his scrawny wrists. Clumps of dark brown hair poured over his face, covering any discernible features. His clothes were drenched in blood from a recent whipping. Something inside Ashlynn fluttered with familiarity as she observed him— yet she couldn't place him.

"You have been brought forth to answer for your treasonous actions," King Theodore announced. "You are also accused of conspiring with the Queen in an attempt to overthrow me by seducing her."

Ashlynn scanned the crowd as a quiet murmur spread. Odessa was positioned at the entrance, waiting for the right time to appear while Sebastian had placed himself near the front of the room with Barcinas behind him. A quick glance at her aunt to gauge her reaction made Ashlynn smirk. As usual, Queen Arya was regal and motionless when dealing with her husband. The sunset from the side window made her silver robe shimmer with orange and gold, which accentuated her auburn hair.

The only one smiling was Marcus, the king's closest advisor and Barcinas's adopted father figure. A growing queasiness befell her each time she encountered him. Others saw him as reserved, but a slimy feeling permeated Ashlynn whenever she was near him or heard

15

his voice. Just another intuitive feeling she couldn't explain because Marcus had only ever helped her.

Marcus placed a hand on the Queen's shoulder to offer moral support. The slight movement from her aunt to free herself from his touch was something most wouldn't recognize since they chose to focus on the prisoner instead. Yet Ashlynn connected the anger in her aunt's eyes with the frigidity of her maneuver. The room grew quiet as Queen Arya stood to address her king. "My dearest, you know these accusations against me are baseless. You have always been my truest love." Arya reached her hand out to the king.

He looked across the room without reciprocating her affection before pausing to deal with her. "Yes, my sweet. I only jest at your inclusions. Of course you would never debase yourself with this ruffian," he sneered.

A sigh spread through the audience as the queen inclined her head. "Then, my dearest, let me vouch for this man and the attempts to frame him as a traitor," she continued.

The king stopped her by standing to glare down into her eyes. "No. I think you have said enough. You are no longer needed in these proceedings," he responded, plopping back down into his puffy, silk cushion as if standing were too much for him to bear. His dark red colored robe matched the blood covered blouse of his prisoner.

Queen Arya nodded again, curtsying to her sovereign. As she turned to leave, Sebastian seethed while Barcinas subtly restrained him. She shifted toward Odessa for guidance, and her cousin's stare pinned her in place. As the Queen glided down the throne in the direction of the door, the prisoner released a chuckle that rippled through the silence of the hall.

King Theodore narrowed his eyes. "Do you have something to say?"

The man glanced up, launched a half-crazed grin, then muttered, "You rule out of fear. You have become weak."

The entire court froze in fear of the accusation this man had thrown out. Arya stopped right behind him, turning to give her last curtsy to the king before leaving.

Ignoring his wife, he shrieked, "You thought to come back into this kingdom and demand what you so freely gave away? My delusional brother, you are the weak one!" Gasps morphed into whispers over his reveal. The king continued as he ignored their surprise. "Where is Ashlynn?"

Fear trickled down her spine as if she had been doused with cold water. Ashlynn took a deep breath to prepare herself for the walk toward his throne. Clearing her throat, she stepped forward out of the shadows to address the king. "I am here, Uncle."

Once more, the crowd parted, except this time it was out of fear and disgust rather than admiration and desire. This march was dreaded as each step brought her closer to her captor and overlord. It was as perpetual as her daily mantra. She made her way to the side of the prisoner with hesitancy. A glance to her aunt, who was still behind the king's brother, made her throat go dry. Aunt Arya must have known something terrible was about to happen because her face resembled the white marbled floor on which the blood dripped from the prisoner.

She wanted to run from the king and scrub away the sensation of his eyes exploring her skin. Yet, she knew from past experiences that it was better to endure his assessment than to intensify his anger by ignoring him. He was the king after all, and she had learned that choosing the latter only increased the severity of her punishment. Even when Ashlynn hadn't done anything wrong, he seemed to find the littlest details as an excuse to discipline her. It was a toss up most days between seeing if her face angered the king, or if her absence agitated him more. Not knowing if she should hide or

18

present herself made each decision even more taxing. Unless, that is, he specifically called for her to show herself.

His eyes drifted to Arya briefly. "It seems that your niece disrespected the Crown by being absent during these proceedings," King Theodore said, sneering as he spoke about her.

She curtsied to her uncle but observed a current pulsing in his eyes. Lowering as near to the ground as she could, she responded, "I do not wish to contradict you Uncle, but I have been here the entire time. I thought it best to stay out of the way as you interrogated your prisoner." She kept her eyes lowered, hoping he would get bored of her and go back to directing the scene without her being center stage.

The king looked on his niece with severity and disappointment. "Always like your mother, aren't you, Ashlynn?" he remarked. "Sabah thought she knew better than me, too. Always twisting my words around."

Ashlynn heard only the pounding of her heart crescendoing into her ears as she tried to breathe out the rising panic. Anytime the king mentioned her mother, he grew irate, which bled into his decisions.

"I guess she won't be twisting anything since she's dead," the king continued with a deep throated cackle.

Ashlynn tried her best to stop the words that tumbled from her lips, but they had an intention of their own. "You mean since you killed her," she spurted out.

Silence emanated from the king. Then, another chuckle. "Yes, Ashlynn. If that makes you feel better, yes. Since I had her killed," he amended, keeping his eyes pinned to hers.

His admission made the room spin and the air stale. Ashlynn couldn't breathe anymore, no matter how many times she opened her mouth for air. Her uncle had never admitted to killing her mother. This announcement was meant to unnerve her— and it was working.

"Tell me, Ashlynn. Since you know so much, what do you think of my brother's accusations? Do I seem weak to you?" The king widened his grin to show yellowing teeth behind his cracked lips, wetting them again like a starved dog licking its jaws while staring at fresh meat.

Her legs shook as she continued to hold her curtsy. She stole a glance at the prisoner next to her. Although he was beaten and starved, she couldn't connect this person to the portrait of him that hung in the gallery. Something about his dark chocolate eyes seemed different from those that had stared back at her when closing up the passageway. Shifting her gaze back to her king, she mumbled, "No, Uncle. I do not think you weak."

"I should hope not. Since he speaks lies as well as committing treason to my throne, he shall be killed." The King chuckled, but no one in the room followed suit. His hearing was beginning to bore his audience, and Ashlynn knew she needed to make an exit before he turned to her as an extra source of entertainment.

"If it pleases you, may I take my leave, Uncle? So you can proceed with your punishment?" She swallowed, almost choking as her spit got caught in her dry throat.

King Theodore stared at her for a few moments, as if fighting with himself about how to answer. Rolling his eyes, he grumbled, "Go."

Ashlynn had a difficult time breathing, much less thinking, as she struggled to stand. Her legs wobbled when she turned to escape, noticing her aunt frozen in her curtsy with her chocolate eyes wide. Before she could even manage a step, the crowd gasped. Remembering her dirty dress made her breath hitch in her throat.

"Oh, Ashlynn," the king sang.

She turned to face him and spotted a sickening, malicious grin emerge across his face. Immediately, she realized her mistake of turning her back to him and dropped to the floor. Her legs were almost too unsteady to hold her. "I apologize, Uncle. I forgot."

The King of Levander surveyed her like a lion studying

his prey before pouncing. "Yes, yes. I know. But I can't let it go unpunished now, can I?" He licked his lips, as if savoring this moment of fear before announcing his retribution. "After all I have given you, the ability to keep your face toward me when you leave my presence is a simple request that even you should be able to remember." Spit flew out of his mouth as he spoke, engaged and fueled by his excitement. "I shall have to remind you how lucky you are to be alive and living in my home. Plus your dress is filthy. We can't have anyone suspect I allow disorder in my kingdom. Seems like another discipling should set the record straight. Prepare her!" the king hollered, each word getting more labored. He acted as if he had drunk an entire case of wine and was suffering the effects.

"Theodore!" called the prisoner next to her. His voice hoarse, but strong. "Brother. You go too far. Do not continue down this path. I know you would not wish harm on Ashlynn if you were in your right mind."

Another gasp reverberated through the room. The crowd stood frozen in amazement and hunger for more.

"Silence, Kerst! I denounce you as my brother!" King Theodore pointed his quivering finger at his prisoner. "You believe I am weak? I will show you who is weak! Archers, prepare your arrows," he hollered.

"No, Theodore. I was wrong," Kerst replied softly. "I believe you are sick." He turned to Ashlynn and gave her a sad smile. "Step out of the shadows, Ashlynn. It's time to wake up."

"Fire!" bellowed King Theodore.

Arrows whooshed through the crowd and plunged into Kerst. He twisted toward his brother, as blood bubbled up over his lips, and whispered, "I will always love you." He tilted forward, his body thumping against the marble floor like a crate of meat being delivered from the butcher.

CHAPTER THREE

The crowd stayed silent. Tiberius rushed forward to check his pulse. Her aunt hadn't moved from her spot behind the now dead man. She was rigid in her curtsy, waiting for her husband to release her with blood splashed across her silver dress and pale skin. Ashlynn understood in that moment how easily the arrow could've missed the king's brother and hit the king's wife instead. King Theodore, smiling from his recent show of power, nodded his head toward her. Queen Arya stood to glide out. Tears bubbled up in her aunt's eyes, threatening to release. Only Ashlynn knew the repercussions of those tears escaping. Sebastian took her aunt's hand, with Barcinas following behind, as Odessa sauntered into sight to distract her father.

"Looks like I missed the excitement, Father," Odessa said, as she flitted her gaze the throne. She curtsied low as her father chuckled.

While Sebastian was the heir to the throne, Odessa was the light in her father's heart. Only she could calm him when he succumbed to his rages. Most outside of the kingdom thought that a princess spoiled by her father would be conceited. Yet those in the kingdom attested that Odessa was the kindest and most sincere person anyone could ever meet.

She was the spitting image of her mother— long flowing hair that covered her slender and graceful body. Her lavender-grey eyes stopped anyone in their tracks. And she knew it. Odessa used her beauty to beguile her father, even as he disgusted her to her core.

"Odessa! I am so glad you missed that debacle. Thank you for being so attentive," he replied.

"Father," she cooed, "I think there has been enough bloodshed today. Don't you think we can let Ashlynn off with a confinement to her room perhaps, instead of this disgusting exhibition of violence?" She batted her lashes and pouted her lip, Odessa's usual tactics for persuading her father to agree. There was just enough conniving spirit in her to prove she was the king's daughter, except she used her privilege in a much different way. Ashlynn admired Odessa's courage.

The crowd buzzed with anticipation. A scene had been set for entertainment, but their hunger for retribution hadn't been satiated yet. Ashlynn could feel the balance tipping slightly as she waited to see which way it would land—in her favor or in the courts.

"Maybe we could release her now, Your Highness," Marcus suggested.

King Theodore raised his hand to silence his advisor and held out his other to Odessa. "I care about your thoughts, my dear. But today your cousin needs to remember her place. She seems to have forgotten."

Odessa stepped forward to object, but Marcus intercepted her gesture by giving her a warning glance. She froze. Even Marcus knew when the king was too far gone to see reason. He reminded Odessa to keep her space during those instances. Nodding her head, she walked to the dais, stood beside her father and faced Ashlynn. "Then I will stay here with her until her punishment is completed."

"You are too kind, my daughter. Your cousin does not deserve you," he snickered. "Tiberius! Bind her!"

Tiberius walked forward and held her eyes with his as the brown in his light blue shifted from gentle swirls to sinister darts. She sent him a plea, like every other time before, for understanding or gentleness. Or even for the protection he promised so long ago. Yet just like those past experiences, he ignored her and bound her hands in their ritual of loyalty versus morality. How she could sleep with him after being beaten was a mystery to Sebastian and Odessa that they frequently brought up. Even she began to wonder how long she would wait for him to remember his promise. Ashlynn moved her eyes to survey the crowd as they watched the finale unfold. Once again, their desire for blood had won out. She heard the rip before she felt the chill. Tiberius had slit her dress from the top of her spine down to the lowest part of her back. Snickering from a few made Ashlynn want to blush and hide from revealing her bare skin, but she held their eyes and glanced around. She wanted them to know that she wouldn't feel shame for this. Not now and not ever again.

"I think thirty would be sufficient for today, don't you, Ashlynn?" the king said. "Is that enough to make you remember next time?"

Ashlynn peeled her eyes from the proper ladies and gentlemen around her to stare at her king. "Yes, Uncle. It will be a mirror to my inner state and will remind me in the future of your power and rule," she muttered, hoping her response appeased him.

King Theodore gazed down on his niece with a crazed look that no longer belonged to him. Odessa held her eyes. Ashlynn sensed every ounce of love and support her cousin sent her way.

"Thirty lashes, with no healer," he said, each word becoming more labored. "And if she doesn't cry out, then reduce it to twenty-nine," he said, laughing as he held his full belly with one hand and his chair with the other for stabilization.

Clearing her mind, anger began to replace fear as clarity overruled her oxygen deprived brain. Tiberius thrust the bit into her mouth as she shifted her mind to tranquility. She was done. This had gone too far. To give her this punishment for such minor mistakes was cruel and she would no longer play his game. Her body shook as her heart raced at the thrill of her newfound courage. Ashlynn spit the piece of wood out of her mouth for the first time ever. She glared at the king with such intense fury that she felt as if her rage burned her up inside. Directing her anger at him, she barely noticed when his face changed from smug to doubtful. "I won't cry out. I will no longer let my weakness and fear define me," Ashlynn declared, still staring at the king but directing her words to her audience. At her declaration, her necklace glowed dimly.

King Theodore didn't move. Her words had struck a chord with a few in the crowd. Tiberius jerked the whip up and back down without warning or hesitation. Ashlynn felt it slice her skin, cutting open her old wounds again and again. Yet this time felt different. This time she had a new strength and power rising inside of her.

Ashlynn held to her silence by biting on her lip through an exhalation, forcing herself to swallow her scream. Each slap produced blood on her back. In return, Ashlynn drew blood in her mouth by sinking her teeth into her bottom lip. For years she had withstood this abuse as her plight in this life. She had grown accustomed to being nothing in others' eyes— flinching at every sound or tiptoeing past doors to walk unseen. Ashlynn became invisible because her visibility was her torment. But something in her had snapped. She felt alive and more aware. The words spoken to her by the king's brother hadn't made any sense. Except now her need to hide was replaced with a desire to fight.

Ashlynn didn't know who she was or who she had been. She didn't even think about what her future held after this stand. All she knew was that she could no longer endure. She would thrive or she would die trying. Because she was dying on the inside from just surviving. Her necklace warmed her chest as the glow brightened, a sensation it had never produced before. It was as if her mother was showing her approval and solidarity as Ashlynn chose to let her strength shine through for all to see. Now she was certain nothing could hold her back.

Tiberius released the final lash, and Ashlynn heaved her timidness, doubt, and insecurities onto the floor, visibly flinching at the pain of her own awakening. The crowd, mistaking her action for weakness, held their breath for a sound to escape her.

But none did. Because nothing was left.

"Twenty-nine," Tiberius said, lowering the whip at the same time she fell to the ground.

The king lifted from his seat, his eyes stuck to Ashlynn as her breathing rose and fell in a labored rhythm. She held onto the strings of her consciousness as she raised her eyes to her uncle. Fear tore through his manic veil as he watched her rebellion form. The world around her had shifted. It was time for her to figure out what she wanted and how to save herself. And maybe, just maybe, she would be able to protect others in the process. A soft hand on her head allowed Ashlynn to breathe easy as she listened to the calming voice of her cousin. "You are done, my love. Rest and let me take you from here."

Ashlynn took one last look at the dead man next to her. His hand, inches from her face, dripped with blood. She gazed into his unseeing eyes, so similar to her own, before closing hers. One good thing came from this display. The king's power had lost its hold and now Ashlynn saw what others couldn't when she looked at him. Odessa picked her up and carried her out of the room to safety— without another glance at the throne.

CHAPTER FOUR

Ashlynn woke to muffled voices and a soft lulling as someone rubbed her back. She laid still a bit longer so no one would notice she was awake. The last thing she wanted was to deal with others, so she breathed in the scent of the lavender and calendula oil. A smell she could recall anywhere. This was the oil her aunt had used the first time she had been whipped. Since then, it was the only thing used to soothe her lashes.

The hands massaging her were soft and petite. Odessa had taken over the role of washing and comforting her once she realized her father forbade a healer. The king had been astonished in the beginning years to see Ashlynn walking around a day or so after being whipped. Her wounds healed faster than most, and she didn't understand why. The king did not like to be surprised though, so he prohibited any healers from taking care of her.

Being Princess Odessa meant she was able to subvert her father's declaration without much consequence. While Odessa wasn't considered a healer, Ashlynn sensed a greater awareness in her cousin that even Odessa didn't know. She had the most soothing hands and demeanor of any person Ashlynn had ever met, including her aunt. Most knew she had a natural affinity with helping others and was known for giving tonics or oils away to those mentally, physically, or emotionally ill.

Ashlynn had always imagined this was what it would feel like if her mother were here instead. But she would never know. She blinked away tears, hoping her emotion wouldn't give her away.

"You can't fool me," Odessa whispered. Ashlynn peeked at her. Her younger cousin stared back down, giving her a sad smile. "You caused quite a stir the other day, and I have not seen cuts this extensive on you since," she paused. "Well, I don't remember wounds as deep as these in all the time I've taken care of you."

Ashlynn assessed her body. The whippings were the worst she had endured. Remembering the searing pain each lashing created reminded her of the fire that had stoked inside. Her wounds were tender and she was nauseous at the thought of her blood mixing with the king's brother's. Yet Ashlynn knew that one more day of rest would have her back to her normal self. It would be her longest healing time yet, but she couldn't be upset that it was still only a few days. Although her skin would never be the same. She didn't realize the foreshadowing of her words when she told the king her marks would be 'a mirror to her inner state'. These scars she would wear with pride as a reminder to herself of the strength she felt when she stood in her own power. Her necklace warmed on her chest, and Ashlynn wondered what her mother had to do with this new ability to heat. It being a gift from her mother had always lead Ashlynn to believe it was her mother communicating with her. But now, she wasn't sure. She lifted it between her fingers to better study it, to see if it would reveal more. But it didn't.

A silhouette appeared above them and Ashlynn met the eyes of her disapproving older cousin. "Oh, Sebastian, I was wondering when you were going to show up to berate me," she murmured.

"Well, I would have been here sooner if I could have gotten into the room!" he spit out, eying his sister.

Odessa didn't turn around to respond. "She needed rest, Seb. You weren't tending to her. These are the worst I have seen in a long time and disrupting her yesterday would have—"

"She could've been killed, Odessa! Ash, do you realize that? Father could've killed you! He was farther gone than I have seen him in a long time. You have to—,"

"I have to what, Sebastian? Not make any mistakes?

Keep quiet every single time he insults me and my parents, much less every minuscule thing I do? I have to cower in fear? Does that work? Because I see you do it, and you don't seem much happier. So what precisely would you suggest, oh wise cousin of mine?"

They glared at each other. A dreadful silence engulfed the room.

Ashlynn rolled her eyes. "Yes, I should have been more careful about my attire. Or made sure to show him the utmost respect, even as it kills a piece of me every time I do. I know that I messed up, Seb! But it would be nice if you were on my side for once."

Pain spread across Sebastian's face as if he had been punched in the gut. Yet, the emotion disappeared as soon as Ashlynn noticed it, causing her to wonder if she had imagined it in the first place. Sebastian shook his head, and all she could see now was disgust for her.

"Of course you are disgusted by me instead of your father's actions. You are a hypocrite, Sebastian," she yelled.

His eyes locked on her, as if they were peering into her mind. She fidgeted in the bed, staring down to ignore his unrelenting gaze and anger that rolled off him.

"I just wish you trusted me, Ash," he said back.

She stared at him, too shocked by his response to

articulate a rebuttal.

She heard him mumble before walking out of the room, "I would never intentionally hurt you like that lover of yours. I always fight for you. You just never notice it. I will see you at your birthday party tonight." He closed the door with a soft click before she had a chance to respond.

Her birthday party! She had forgotten that it was tonight being out of commission for a few days. Ashlynn covered her face with her aunt's down blanket and tried to slow her breathing and heartbeat. Her head spun from everything that had happened. And even now to her fight with Sebastian. As she thought back to her words, she realized that she had tried to hurt him. She wanted him to feel some ounce of her pain and hoped that shoving it down his throat would help him digest the bittersweet bite she choked on daily. That was her intent, at least. Instead, it just left him uninterested in trying a morsel. Ashlynn sighed, and let her tears fall. No one understood her battle. Sebastian rarely seemed to mind his words when they argued. And it was even rarer for him to apologize first, if at all. She knew she would have to be the one to seek him out and mend any holes. And to know that she had to handle this situation and prepare herself before the party tonight just felt like too much. It was all too much. Tears poured from her eyes as her whole body shook through sobs.

"Oh, my dear," Arya declared as she glided over to the side of the bed. Odessa made room for her mother, who was an older, wiser version of herself.

Where Odessa was loving and gentle, Arya was motherly and warm. Her embrace was full of laughter, vanilla, honeysuckle, and security. These were the arms that hugged her when she had fallen and scraped her knee, when she was slapped for tripping over her skirts, or when she was pushed against a wall and touched because the king had announced her as 'available' the day of her first bleeding.

Every piece of shame, anger, and untouched sadness came pouring out. She couldn't stop crying. Her tears rolled down her cheeks as she shifted through her grief and frustration from over the years. The new voice and courage she had found yesterday felt like a distant dream. The spark had been lit, but her tears and doubt were like the breeze blowing on a cold night. The whole time, Arya held Ashlynn while Odessa massaged her injured back—her two rocks. After a while, her sobs turned to sniffles as her pounding heart calmed to a light thump.

"What did I do to deserve this?" she whispered.

Pulling away from her aunt, Ashlynn wiped her face on

the blanket. Her hands fiddled with its edge. They trembled and caressed it, tracing the pristine seam in hopes it would soothe her embarrassment. Showing her emotions was rare, even in the presence of those she trusted most. It was difficult being the one who controlled their anger and sadness. Even her happiness was pushed down for fear of it being taken away.

"Don't do that, Ash," Odessa whispered back. Ashlynn ignored the comment, but Odessa pressed a hand to her face. "It is okay to express how you feel! It is okay to be sad or mad and just not understand any of it. You are not perfect, Ash."

Ashlynn focused on the plum mixing with the teal of Odessa's eyes. Every swirl emanated love and understanding. She took a deep breath and nodded.

"You are right," she declared. "I will no longer hide how I feel or who I am. I can't bear the weight anymore." She gave Odessa a hug then hugged her aunt. "Thank you both for all you have given me. Today and over the years."

Arya wiped a strand of hair from Ashlynn's face. "My dearest niece, thank you for being raw and open with us. You are such a blessing in our lives."

Ashlynn tried to hide the skepticism that flooded her eyes, but her aunt saw through her uncertainty.

"Never doubt my words or your importance, child. And to answer your question," she said, pausing, as if trying to find the right words. She sighed. "Nothing. You did nothing to deserve any of it and there is nothing wrong with you. You are not weak or worthless for crying because of this injustice. He is, for inflicting it."

The only sound that could be heard were the birds chirping outside the window, unaware of the corruption in the kingdom.

"Let me start some tea for us," Odessa said, getting up from the bed.

"You and your tea," Ashlynn joked. "You would give it to a chicken who had just outrun a fox if you could."

Odessa chortled at the thought. "You can't deny that my tea has magickal qualities, which may or may not include apparitions," she reminisced, warming the water in the kettle over the fire.

Ashlynn sat on the edge of her aunt's massive bed, her feet barely touching the floor. Ashlynn felt like a little girl every time she sat in it. She pulled the blanket around her shoulders to cover herself from the chill. Recalling the sound of Tiberius ripping her dress made her cringe. As if reading her mind, her aunt placed a new dress beside her. This one was simple, similar to all her other dresses, but the expense of it would have fed a village family for a year. Ashlynn hated getting dressed up almost as much as she despised the king, but she played along for no other reason than to avoid even more pain.

She reached for a different topic to hide her embarrassment yet again. "Aunt Arya, that man in the throne room yesterday, King Theodore's brother, where did he come from?" Ashlynn felt like there was more to the story about his arrival and sudden death. Her aunt shifted from the bed to a nearby chair. "I didn't know he was still alive," she pressed, feeling like she had to find the answer to something stirring under her skin.

Ashlynn observed outrage that transformed into sadness as her aunt sat in her chair. She blinked, but those emotions could not disappear so easily.

Arya cleared her throat. "The grave, Ash. He came from the grave. He has been considered dead for the last 20 years. A few days ago he arrived making brash claims. The king had no choice but to address him and his statements."

"But why did he show up now?" Ashlynn asked.

Arya shrugged, glancing away. It was obvious as her aunt absentmindedly twirled a loose string on her dress that Arya was not keen on answering questions about this mystery man. Her aunt was meticulous about her appearance, from her auburn locks hanging without a hair out of place to her polished silver flats. A small thread would have been trimmed, not twisted. Yet, Ashlynn couldn't place the uneasy sensation that something was amiss about the prisoner. His unmoving brown eyes with blood dripping down his arm replayed in her memories. It gave her a chill as her mind shifted her own face onto his dead body on the floor instead. She gulped and focused on calming her rapid heartbeat, using it to remind her that she was indeed still alive.

Odessa sat down beside her mother and handed out the steaming tea. "I heard that he was the older brother and that he gave up his throne to father."

"Why would he do such a thing?" Ashlynn mused. She took a sip of the mint tea, Odessa's special blend, burning off the first layer of her tongue.

"It's hot," Odessa warned with a smile.

Ashlynn rolled her eyes with a snort.

"He gave the throne to your father because he claimed to love someone else more. He said he wanted to protect her from the royal life. The only requirement for abdicating was that Teddy would leave them alone. The two of them seemed to always have some sort of rivalry going about whom was better than the other," Arya continued silently.

The girls glanced at each other as Arya moved

through the past with her eyes. Odessa nudged Ashlynn.

"Um, what happened next?" Ashlynn muttered.

Arya focused back to the present. "The agreement lasted a few years, until they had a fight. He went against Teddy in a decision, only to find out he didn't have sway with the nobles anymore. So he disappeared, and we heard a few years later he had died."

"Did he say why he came back?" Odessa asked.

Arya fidgeted, uncomfortable with the whole conversation. "He said that Teddy had broken his promise, so he broke his. And that he came back to claim what was his," she said, rising from her chair.

Odessa and Ashlynn widened their eyes at the information she had revealed.

"If only he had been successful," Odessa mumbled.

Arya's voice rang out over them louder than either of them knew she could speak. Her dark eyes were large and raced around the room. "Your father is the king, Odessa," she said with vigor. "You would do well to remember that. Long may he live and reign!"

She eyed the girls as they reciprocated the required response, "Long may he live and reign!" Her eyes flickered to the door before she sat down again. "Ashlynn, is your dress ready for your birthday party tonight?" Arya asked, as if the previous conversation were a hallucination.

Ashlynn studied her tea, trying to not roll her eyes. "Yes, my tight, fluffy, turquoise dress of death is ready. I tried it on before everything happened," she said.

Odessa nodded as she sipped her tea. Her birthday had never been a big deal to anyone but her aunt and cousins. The king only recognized her existence when it benefited him, which usually meant torment for her. Ashlynn was torn between excitement at the thought of being celebrated and fear from not knowing the king's actual intentions with throwing the party.

"It's probably just another way to humiliate me," she mumbled. Neither her aunt nor her cousin denied her allegation. "I should make up with Sebastian," Ashlynn said as she rose out of the bed. Arya and Odessa gaped at her. "What? Did I miss something?" she asked.

"I will never understand it, Ash," Arya said. "Your wounds were the worst I have seen in a very long time, from anyone I have encountered. Yet you get up and walk around as if they were an itch less than three full days after they were inflicted."

Ashlynn blushed as she tugged the dress up over her hips, not caring if it tore. All of the emotional, physical, and mental pain inflicted on her disappeared faster than anyone understood. She alone knew that her pain didn't actually vanish as her aunt and cousin thought. Instead, it seeped beneath her surface as a protective barrier against the world. She tied her bodice with intention. "Well, it's a good thing I can get up. One of us has to take the high road, and we know Sebastian isn't the type," she said.

Her aunt mentioned her unexpected movement after each punishment, and Ashlynn could never tell if her aunt was surprised or scared of her unnatural ability.

"Ash, stay in the shadows for a bit longer today, please," Arya begged, sounding like her son. "You never know how Teddy will react if he learns you are up and about already."

Ashlynn inclined her head, overcome with appreciation and love at the warning. It was funny how that same phrase came across as kind and thoughtful when spoken by her aunt but sounded deprecating when Sebastian said it.

"Were you close to him?" she dared to ask. "King Theodore's brother, that is."

Her aunt's eyes bore into Ashlynn, yet her mind was far away. "Yes. A long time ago, he was my dearest friend." She sighed.

"For what it is worth, I am very sorry. I know that pain of losing someone dear to you, and I am sorry it has been inflicted on you," Ashlynn said.

Arya smiled at her. "I am sorry, too, sweet one. More than you could ever know."

Ashlynn glanced to Odessa before heading out. She now knew the importance of making amends with those she cared about. She had very few in her life whom she could trust, Which meant she had to be the one to heal this relationship. Anger bred resentment, and resentment grew into loneliness if not tended. And that is what she feared most— being alone.

Closing the door behind her, Ashlynn allowed herself to breathe. A devilish smile tugged at her lips. It felt good to be able to walk around in spite of her uncle's desire to keep her bedridden. Her aunt's unknowing revelation had showed her that the king was more scared than she had realized. He had feared the return of his brother enough to kill him. And she was determined to figure out what else he feared so she could release his grip on her. Her thoughts danced around the words of his brother again, except this time a certain one lingered in her mind— sick. Kerst had called him sick, and for some reason, Ashlynn's intuition told her it meant more than she had originally thought. Maybe this was the key to gaining her freedom. The thought made her giddy. But first, to find Sebastian and mend their relationship. Only then could she craft her new subversion.

CHAPTER FIVE

The day was in full effect when Ashlynn trudged out of the castle. In the past, she had laid low after being disciplined, but today was different. She was determined to find Sebastian and make things right between them. Plus, she no longer felt like hiding out for something that was not her fault. Tiberius had called it "licking her wounds" the first time she locked herself away. She shook her head at the thought of him. Ashlynn wondered if she could still desire him after all that had happened between them. He had stopped choosing her, so she had stopped choosing herself.

Her mind wandered to their last escapade. His body on top of hers while she breathed in his sweaty musk that stuck on him. Her fingers pushed through his golden curls, unwrapping them from his pulled back 'in command' look. She enjoyed running her hands along his hair. Although he seldom let her. Their last time began like every time before, playful and seductive but ended abrupt and cold when he had finished. He made an excuse about having to get back. As usual, she believed him. Ashlynn wondered how long she had rejected the truth in front of her. She could only hold onto her memories of the old him for so long. The kind, protective boy she once knew had slowly been replaced by an uncaring ass, and she sighed at the realization that Tiberius was showing signs of following in the king's cruel footsteps.

"Well, look who is walking around already," came a demanding, nasal-sounding voice ahead of her.

Ashlynn had wandered into the middle of the courtyard and rolled her eyes at her carelessness. While engulfed in her thoughts, she had forgotten to stay in the shadows. It seemed her desire to subvert the king had made her forget her daily mantra. Ashlynn turned toward the voice and blushed all over. To her right Marcus stood beside Tiberius. Both were watching her like a fox would study a rabbit, as if they were deciding her fate in that moment.

"I guess her lashes weren't as strong as you thought, Tiberius," Marcus joked. The sheen of his tied back, oily, blond hair shone in the sunlight, while his putrid green eyes sent swirls of nausea through Ashlynn's stomach.

Tiberius laughed quietly, sending her a hard look. He hadn't always been the one to dole out her punishment. One day he was her friend, and the next he was her abuser, promoted to head guard seemingly out of no where. Ashlynn had felt betrayed that her uncle stooped so low as to use their relationship against her, but over the years she had come to expect anything from him. It hurt even more that Tiberius willingly followed his orders. While he had begged for forgiveness from her that first day, a small rift was created in their relationship. Ashlynn forgave him every time because she thought she needed him more than he needed her.

In the beginning, he went easy on her. But things only got more difficult when the king found out that he had taken the orders lightly. Ashlynn had been able to walk around, as if her maltreatment hadn't happened. The next lashing she received, which occurred the following day, was one of anger and disappointment from both King Theodore and Tiberius. From then on, he blamed her for being the reason he had to perform those corrections.

"If you would just try harder to listen, or if you were a good niece and praised the king, then maybe you wouldn't be whipped and this disruption in our relationship would cease," he explained.

Something nipped at the back of her mind, insisting that she did her best on a daily basis, and his words were senseless. But she had been weak and too scared of him leaving her. So she would eventually give in and agree, if only to ensure one more time with him. He was her drug, and she hadn't known how to break free.

"Yes, dear Ashlynn. How are you able to walk around so easily?" he asked.

Ashlynn held her head high and said the first thought that came into her mind. "I guess you aren't as strong as you thought, Ti."

She nodded to Marcus and hurried off. Her body raced with exhilaration from speaking her mind. Marcus's laughter radiated around the courtyard. Her heart pumped faster and louder as if she could fly. Twirling as the wind breezed past her, Ashlynn held out her arms and closed her eyes, pretending she was soaring high above the clouds and trees. She had never had the desire to fly before, but today felt like the beginning of a new her.

She barely made it out of the entrance of the courtyard when a hand grabbed her arm, twisting her around. Her head spun as she was pulled to the side of the entry where an enormous tree covered part of the gate. She kept her eyes shut, but everything spun.

"What is wrong with you?" Tiberius asked.

Ashlynn peeled her eyes open to see him standing in front of her, his anger surging to the surface. Even with the recent memory of his abuse, Ashlynn struggled to focus on her reasons for being upset with him. He bewitched her with his sky blue eyes, which twinkled with flecks of brown each time he laugh, while his smile curved to one side. Now, though, his eyes held hers in unyielding restraint with his lip snarled. In contrast, the other side of his mouth was set in a firm line and marred by the scar beneath his beard, wearing a story he had never revealed.

"You embarrassed me in front of Marcus! He will tell King Theodore that I have been going easy on you again, but it will be my hide that pays this time," he said, pushing his long, golden hair out of his face. Those golden locks never seemed to stay tied back. The sheer volume of them, mixed with his rippling muscles and fierce glower, reminded her of a lion ready to pounce.

Ashlynn looked at him— at all he was and had ever been to her. This last whipping whirled to the forefront of her mind and wiped his enchantment away. "Maybe I would get to whip you!" she threw back, surprised at the venom in her voice. He stared at her, then reached for her arm again. Except this time, she was ready. She sensed his reflex before he moved and pulled away with triumph. His eyes widened with surprise. She had never dared to resist him, and he didn't know how to handle her defiance.

"What has gotten into you, Ashlynn?" he demanded.

She breathed deeply to steady herself. "I'm surprised

you even noticed. You are usually caught up in yourself—"

"See! This is what I mean!" he interrupted. "Why are you trying to make me out as the bad guy?"

"Maybe you are the bad guy, Ti! Have you ever thought about that?" she yelled.

He stepped back. "I don't know what is going on with you, but I cannot have you messing up my life with one of your tantrums."

His words hit her as deep and thorough as the arrow that punctured the prisoner yesterday. Except his blood had poured out while hers pooled inside, causing her vision to fuzz.

"My tantrums? Do you know how conceited you sound right now? You whip me like an animal and expect me to crawl back to you as if you didn't do anything wrong!" She stepped back to steady herself on the tree trunk behind her. Its energetic pulse blended with her heartbeat, helping her stay present.

"You never said anything before. Why now? Where is this coming from?" Tiberius raised his hand and traced his mustache as it formed into a short beard, as if he saw her as a puzzle to figure out. He studied her intently and she felt as if she were coursing through his mind.

Ashlynn glared at the guy she had given everything to. He had promised her she would never be alone, had given her so many dreams when she forgot they existed. Now she knew he had never meant those words. It was up to her to find out who she was and what she really wanted. "Thank you for not believing I was worth anything. Now I understand that I can climb out of this pit of nothingness I allowed you to put me in," she said, smiling at his confusion. "What has changed is I have become loyal to myself, instead of to others who were never faithful to me. We are done, Ti."

Taking a deep breath, she pushed off the tree and followed the long way around the outside of the courtyard in her quest to find Sebastian. She added Tiberius to the list of people who feared something enough to hurt others in their desire to have control. Her necklace warmed at the thought, and she wondered if Tiberius would fall under Kerst's description of sick as well.

CHAPTER SIX

Every place Ashlynn sought for Sebastian came up empty. Either he was avoiding her, or she didn't know him as well as she thought. Her body habitually led her to where he should've been. Following the worn stones, her head stayed down. Not out of fear though. Cutting Tiberius off had emboldened her to walk on the edge of the shadows. It wasn't much, and she occasionally chuckled at the image, but it felt like a huge step to her. No, Ashlynn was no longer scared of the king and what he could do to her. Death was inevitable. He had beat her down to a shell of herself, nearly destroying her soul in the process. Physical death would be far less painful than the inner one she had almost endured. Her eyes focused on the well-known paths, but her mind drifted in search of answers to questions she had forgotten were there.

Voices pierced through her thoughtful roaming. She glanced up, her mind focusing around the corridor. With the distraction of her thoughts, Ashlynn had wandered to an area she had not intended to be. In front of her stood the doorway to Marcus's apartment. It was one of the most dangerous places in the kingdom. Gulping down her surge of fear, she crept closer to the door to see if she heard Sebastian talking with Barcinas.

Two voices, each significantly different from the other, were muffled behind the thick door. Those she heard weren't from of Barcinas and Sebastian, or even Marcus. When she pressed her mind, she recognized one from a childhood memory that felt warm but fuzzy. It belonged to Oren, the wisest and most respected person in the kingdom. Even King Theodore exalted his status by avoiding Oren's sanctuary unless he was desperate for advice, which rarely happened since he assumed he knew everything.

"It wasn't wise of him to show up like that," Oren was saying. His voice was gruff and deep, yet it had a melodious feel that could rub someone like sand or ease them into revealing their truest desires. She couldn't remember meeting Oren, yet she felt a sense of understanding and connection to the sage.

"He was always prone to rash decisions," the second voice replied. It had a distinct lilt that reminded Ashlynn of the storytellers who travelled to the city during the king's birthday. The feminine voice spoke with a confidence that Ashlynn hadn't heard from many, if any, of the ladies around the castle. Most lowered their voices and eyes because they were either too scared to be noticed or preferred to be considered demure. This feminine being had none of those habits thought notable by the strength and compassion she put into each word. Ashlynn could get lost in her voice, which is exactly what happened.

Lingering a bit longer, she listened to them talk about Kerst and their memory of him. Their words spun a web of information in her mind, connecting new questions with old answers. She needed to go to her room to process it all. Maybe something would give her a clue about the king's weakness. Her name floated through the keyhole like a hook tossed out into water. Kneeling to the floor, she put her ear to the hole and listened.

"She has to find out soon. If the sickness spreads, then she may not find a way out," the feminine voice said.

Rumors circulated that Marcus was a bachelor with a lover or a concubine. The ladies of the kingdom claimed no one wanted to marry him. In truth, no one had seen him with any one of the fairer sex except the queen. The court loved to gossip, and he was primed for it being the wealthiest, most powerful, single man in the kingdom.

"Give it time, Daia," Oren said. "Ashlynn is waking up. She'll understand soon enough and be ready before she even realizes what is happening. Maybe even sooner than we know."

Her heart raced and her body shook. Pulling back from the hole, she pressed her back against the wall to steady herself. "Two people I have never met are talking about me as if they have known me all of my life. I don't understand," she mumbled to herself, wiping her sweaty hands on her satin dress. Unable to restore her breath and soothe her heartbeat, she pulled her legs up to her chest and held them in her arms. Both eyes closed, she worked to calm her pulse. Just a moment to pause the whirlwind inside of her, and she would be on her way. She needed to leave.

"What are you doing?" came a voice.

Ashlynn yelped as she jumped, hitting her head on the stone wall. She rubbed the back of her head as she looked at Barcinas towering over her. His arms were crossed with a broad smirk plastered on his face "Dammit, Barcinas. You scared me!" she whispered. "I am leaving." Pushing herself off the hard floor, she grabbed his large arm and tugged him away from the door.

He looked back as the voices inside quieted. "Were you eavesdropping? Ashlynn Forrest, eavesdropping on Marcus's private suite! I can't wait to see what—"

"You are not going to tell a soul, Barcinas!" she countered. "I was only resting my legs from searching for

Sebastian. And now I am leaving."

He gave her a look of pure control. She put every ounce of steel and confidence she had into her eyes as she stared back, but Barcinas had perfected his gaze and assertiveness over the years. Ashlynn dropped her eyes with a sigh. "Please, Barcinas. Don't tell anyone," she begged, twisting her hands around each other.

"He won't say anything, right, Barcinas?" came a voice she didn't expect.

Ashlynn gulped, closed her eyes, and slowly turned to see Oren and Daia. The old sage was massive in stature and towered over both of them. His figure created a shadow over her as she looked up into his milky eyes. The rest of his features were indistinguishable in the candlelight.

Barcinas ran his fingers through his short curls and spread a forced smile onto his face. "Right, Mama Daia. I wouldn't dream of telling anyone."

Ashlynn gaped between Barcinas and the two figures in the doorway. He had called her Mama Daia and listened to her instruction without argument. She didn't know what to think of their relationship or what to expect from being found.

"Barcinas," Daia called, "please escort Oren out into the courtyard. I would like a few words with Ashlynn before she rushes off to prepare for her big night."

Ashlynn froze and gulped again. Daia didn't seem angry from the tone in her voice, but she wasn't positive how she would react when they talked alone.

"Do you really think that is a good idea?" Barcinas asked, his body stiff and voice stilted.

"I think it is a perfect idea, Barc," she replied, placing a hand on Oren's back. She leaned in to whisper something into his ear before giving him a kiss on the cheek.

Oren ambled next to Barcinas who reached out his hand to aid him. "I look forward to seeing you soon," he predicted with a large teeth grin. Then he headed outside with Barcinas as his guide.

She was left with Daia, who stood in the doorway waiting. With a final glance at the sunlight pouring in from the door as it closed, she swallowed her fear and turned toward the suite. It was time to face the repercussions of her actions, and Ashlynn was ready for her first test of courage.

CHAPTER SEVEN

Daia's appearance was different from most of the women around the kingdom. Every curve was full and fit her body perfectly. She was much darker than others around here as well. Ashlynn had always thought of herself as dark skinned compared to her cousins and others around her. However, next to this warm beauty, Ashlynn felt pale and saturated. Daia's hair hung down to her waist with luxurious curls encompassing her entire body.

"Come in, Ashlynn. I am pleased you found your way to me. I was wondering how I could get you to meet me," she said, moving to the side of the entrance to let her in. The accent in her voice was unique and yet familiar. It reminded her of a moment in history she couldn't quite place. All Ashlynn could do was stare at her in wonderment.

"I know it is surprising to hear us talking about you. It would be a pleasure to answer any questions you have. But first, sweet one, you must walk in out of the corridor." Her eyes shifted nervously to behind Ashlynn, as if waiting for someone else to appear from around her.

Ashlynn pulled herself out of her mind and into the suite. As soon as she was in, Daia closed the door and locked it.

She giggled at Ashlynn's worried face. "Oh, Ashlynn. Please don't be alarmed. I am not going to kill you and eat you for dinner. I prefer for us to not be disturbed as there is much for us to talk about and very little time to do so."

Ashlynn expelled a breath, and the tension from her body soared away with it. She wasn't sure what else to do, so she studied the chamber. Few could attest to being in Marcus's apartment, and she wanted to examine every aspect to later dissect with Odessa. Oh, Odessa would be furious with her for not being more cautious after Aunt Arya implored her to stay hidden. But maybe she would be appeased with juicy tidbits about Marcus's private life. The windows were large and open as the sun shone through without any hindrance. Bright tapestries covered the walls, with a rich rug caressing the floor. A few chairs sat in the corner of the chamber, but the floor was devoured by cushions. The entry room was warm as a fire burned to her left in the grate. Ashlynn felt safe and comforted, which struck her as odd considering this was her first encounter with this woman.

"Now come sit with me so we can converse properly," Daia instructed.

Her voice was authoritative but enriched with love and affection. Ashlynn obeyed and positioned herself on a cushion across from the fire where she could fully examine Daia as she busied herself with tea preparations, confident with her movement. How a person could exude that much confidence and femininity was beyond Ashlynn. Her presence filled the room, and the quiet was serene. She did not need to chatter to fill the silence. The bright pink of her dress, which was wrapped around her waist creating a precise depiction of her curves, sparkled with little golden bobbles around the seams. This was not a typical outfit worn in the kingdom, and she wondered where this exotic looking being was from. A hardness lined Daia's face that mimicked her own. Often times, when alone in her chamber, Ashlynn wondered if her own trials created the lines and rigidity in her own face. Seeing it on someone else made her curious about what this woman had been through to appear so strict. Yet her words and actions were directed with warmth and intention.

Daia handed her a cup of tea that smelled like cinnamon and ginger and offered a seat on a large cushion in front of her. Lifting the cup to her nose,

Ashlynn inhaled the most intense aromatic spices she had ever smelled.

"You look like your mother," Daia said.

Surprised to hear these words, Ashlynn spilled her tea all over her dress. Thankfully it wasn't scalding hot like Odessa's. "Oh dear," she stumbled, "I am so clumsy. I am very sorry. Please, let me clean it up."

Daia held up her hand to stop Ashlynn's rambling and got up to find a rag. Ashlynn sat back stunned at Daia's reaction. She had experienced pain from the smallest of mistakes, yet this woman acted like it was not a big deal.

"It was an accident, Ashlynn. That is all. I alarmed you and should've better prepared you for the fact that I knew your mother. Well, both of your parents really," Daia said, handing her the rag.

Ashlynn dabbed her dress dry and squeezed her hands so tight that her nails drew blood.

"But does that mean that you should be berated for an accident? No, it doesn't. Remember that, sweet one. Now, let us start again. My name is Daia, as you have already learned from your time in the corridor." Before she could make excuses, Daia continued, "No explanation is needed. You were where you were meant to be, that is all. I knew your mother and your father before you were conceived. You remind me of both of them. I have called you in here because," she paused. "Well, I needed to see you. Marcus informed me of your unfortunate abuse at the hands of the king, as well as your recent dismissal of a certain young man's affections."

Ashlynn stared dumbfounded. Only a few hours prior had she ended her relationship with Tiberius. If Marcus already knew, then that mean the whole kingdom knew. Tonight was going to be even more awkward than she realized. She groaned.

"Oh, I am sure it is frustrating to know your secrets are not a secret anymore, but you have to know that Marcus is an expert at knowing what goes on in this kingdom. He is a better spy master than even the king's own man," Daia revealed. "He specifically warned against contacting you. I think he was somewhat worried about my influence or knowledge, and I would have to agree that he was right to be. I think it is time for you to know what he wishes would stay hidden." A sly smile covered her face, and Ashlynn couldn't help wondering why Daia freely gave her this information. "Marcus and I don't see eye to eye on quite a few things. I also do not keep my opinions quiet. Now, what you overheard from Oren and I is crucial to the survival of this kingdom. However, I wasn't sure you were quite ready to hear what I have to say. Until, that is, I heard Barcinas say your name in the corridor and we opened to find you there. Waiting for us as if you were magickally led to my door."

Confused, Ashlynn gaped at Daia as her mind reeled with curiosity. She felt better about eavesdropping, but that release was replaced with this catch in her chest about details meant specifically for her. Sitting across from Daia in Marcus's apartment was surreal. She hadn't expected this when she woke up today.

"Before I start explaining, I must ask you one question. Have you experienced anything similar to what Oren described as 'waking up' recently?" Daia paused and sipped her tea.

Ashlynn's mind spun with questions and uncertainty. She wasn't sure she could trust this woman, yet her inner intuition urged her to open herself to what Daia was offering. Although she wasn't quite sure what that even was, Ashlynn took a gulp of breath and chose to follow her intuition. "I am not sure I understand the term 'waking up', but I have experienced a sensation where my eyes have become uncovered, and I am able to observe without fear blinding me."

Daia's eyes flashed with gold and her smile grew. "That sounds exactly like you have woken up, sweet one. It is different for everyone, but what you have described is the first stage of realizing that things are not as they seem. That is the most important lesson you will learn on this new journey. Now, do you have any questions? We need your mind undisturbed before we begin down this path of awareness."

Ashlynn nodded, too stunned to speak.

"Then ask without fear of judgment or retribution. I feel as if I needed to add that last piece in there," she said with a gentle smile.

"How do you know Marcus? I mean," Ashlynn stumbled to find the right words, "how are we sitting here in his rooms? Are we allowed in here? And how did you meet my parents. Also, how do you know so much about me?" She blushed as the questions rushed out, unaware that they had bubbled up begging to be answered.

Daia raised an eyebrow as she smirked. "Those are questions with extensive answers, and I will do my best to address them succinctly. First, would you be surprised if I told you I am Marcus's wife?"

The idea of Marcus— pale, skinny as a twig Marcus— with this luxurious woman was incalculable. Yet, Ashlynn could tell by looking into Daia's eyes that she was speaking the truth, and that she only spoke the truth. All of it.

"How did he manage to capture your hand?" she asked in amazement.

The richest laugh she had ever heard flowed from this magickal person in front of her. Ashlynn opened her mouth, as if trying to breathe in her joy and security for herself. How glorious it would feel to be that certain of herself, except the thought abruptly died, because Ashlynn couldn't imagine the sensation.

"That is the one story that I can't tell you," she said. "We have very little time to talk about things that are more important. I wish I could give you that story, not just for your own healing but for those you are destined to meet. Maybe one day you will learn it."

"Oh, you mean we have little time because of the party tonight," Ashlynn asked. "I keep hoping it will get cancelled. I don't really want the king to throw one," she admitted. "Oh, please come! You are invited. You can be my special guest!"

Daia's smile broadened, while her eyes saddened. "You are such a jewel. How blessed your mother would've been to know you. Thank you, Ashlynn. I met your parents before the war with the Dragons. We were companions working on an important mission. I only know you from what Marcus and Barcinas tell me. I do not leave my rooms very much, you see. I am actually not allowed to. The king fears me and my knowledge, which is another reason I have not attempted to contact you. I respected their demands to stay locked away because of my own reasons. But that is also another long story." She paused to take a sip of her tea. "Now, you must know that there is no going back from what I am about to reveal. So, if you have any hesitations about what you might learn, then now is the time to walk away."

Ashlynn glanced to the door, deciding between this final chance to stay locked in her fears and stepping into something that felt bigger than herself.

CHAPTER EIGHT

Her necklace warmed on her chest and she grasped it. No, there was no looking back now. Smirking and thinking of her desire to free herself from the king, she answered, "I am ready."

Daia's physical presence shifted as she seemed to take on other energies. Ashlynn didn't even know what that meant, but the answer seemed to come as she observed this change. Yet, she couldn't make herself feel scared or anxious. The otherness that filled Daia was magnificent and old— even older than Oren. Her eyes turned black, and Ashlynn felt brave sitting there. If this meeting had happened a few days ago, then Ashlynn would've left immediately.

"As you have noticed," Daia whispered, "I am connecting with my guides. These ancient spirits from other worlds, and from our own world's past, are the ones who have been waiting to speak through me to you. They told me to wait and knew when you would be ready."

The aching in her voice rooted Ashlynn to her spot. She nodded to show her agreement, but locked her arms around her legs for consolation.

"There has been a message waiting for you over the years. Recently it has been itching to get out and contact you, but you weren't ready. There are many hidden messages and meanings around us, and your reality is about to transform."

Daia's sentences were riddled with a force that punted against Ashlynn's skull. It felt like the enlightenment about to be revealed was something she once knew but had forgotten.

"When you were young, you were taught of a war that happened before you were born," Daia began. "You were told that higher beings tried to eliminate the Humans, and we fought back to protect our lives and our future. That is all untrue. You will learn more about this soon, but what I have to tell you is that your mother was a rescuer. She fought to protect those higher beings. Not because she was a traitor as so many would like to label her. Her and few others like her. Your mother and these other women defied their king, their friends, and even their family by saving a group of beings who have only ever given us knowledge and love. Due to the actions of a younger King Theodore and those of that time, a sickening curse spread throughout the kingdom."

Daia paused at this moment to take a long breath. She

sighed out a sound that pealed like the tears of a mother losing her child. Ashlynn noticed Daia beginning to sweat as she experienced a sadness and anger released from the spirits and beings connected with her. Once, when Ashlynn was very little, she had heard a fairytale of an ancient witch who connected with something called guides, and Ashlynn had assumed the story mean ghosts or visible creatures. Yet, in reality the guides only affected the person with whom they were in contact and were entirely invisible. She saved that understanding as a tidbit to share with Odessa later. They had both always wondered.

"You might have noticed this sickness," Daia continued, "but excused it away with justifications thrown at you for your ill treatment. Kerst was right, although he didn't originally want to believe it. The king is sick. He is the sickest of all, and soon his sickness will get so deep that your entire kingdom will turn to darkness. But there is a light shining out of this darkness. You! You have a journey ahead of you as you figure out how to heal our kingdom. It will be dangerous and will challenge everything and everyone you have ever trusted and loved. It will also grow you and give you the brightest future. One that you could have never seen for yourself," Daia said with a passion that brought tears to Ashlynn's eyes.

The thought, the image Daia created, made Ashlynn's heart ache. The decision to go after the king to free herself was easy to reconcile, but she had only joked at helping others in her quest. This task thrust at her felt heavy, but the weight wasn't uncomfortable. She somehow felt as if it had always been there, but was just another piece that had been hidden from her.

Daia was caught up in her words and connection and continued without noting Ashlynn's lost focus. "What I speak of is dangerous. You are now in peril for having this awareness. Know that your mother, oh sweet Ashlynn, your kind mother was brave and determined to the end. Sabah fought for you with her last breath. Remember, she died not because the king had control over her life, but because she would rather die than for you both to become slaves to the system that had enslaved so many before you."

Ashlynn couldn't see from the tears that began to pour out of her. Hearing her mother's name in relation to her new path was comforting and overwhelming. All of it was overwhelming.

Daia's eyes changed back to their creamy brown. She took Ashlynn's hands and pulled them to her heart. "Sweet one, you are so brave. You have much to give.

Trust in yourself always. After this, you must venture to Oren's hut on the top of Mount Fermont. That is imperative. He will be able to give you more to help with this mission. Take Sebastian and Barcinas with you. They must travel with you, not only for the light that will shine brighter when joined together, but for their safety and growth as well." Then she kissed her hands and placed her own on Ashlynn's head. "May you seek the truth, know the truth, understand the truth, and speak the truth from here on out!"

Daia stepped back and lifted Ashlynn off the floor. Ashlynn was stunned by the message and her blessing, as well as all that had happened. She tried to process it when Daia ushered her to the door. "You must leave now. I wish we had more time, but I fear time is shorter than I expected," Daia said.

Ashlynn gaped at the woman, who had seemed full of life, as she now appeared drained. Daia held her hands one more time as they stood in the doorway but leaned on the frame for stability. Pulling a piece of paper out of her dress, she handed it to Ashlynn. "Here is a note from your mother. She wrote it to you when she first agreed to help us. May it give you answers and peace as you find your way. Keep it with you always. Lastly, you have to know that the necklace you wear is a key."

Ashlynn placed her hand on her necklace and rubbed it.

"Your mother gave it to you so you would remember her. Although, I doubt you could ever forget her. But she also gave it to you as the key that would guide you and help you unlock the door without a lock. Now, I have one last request."

Ashlynn focused on Daia's eyes to steady herself from all of the information and direction she had received.

"Please give him this hug for me, and let them both know that I did it for them. And that I love them. You will know who I mean when the time comes." Daia held her in a deep embrace for a few moments. Time seemed to stop as they stood there, hugging each other in the doorway.

Daia pulled away and pushed Ashlynn out into the corridor. Ashlynn twirled around to say goodbye, but Daia spoke first. "I will see you one last time, sweet one. But please don't act like you know me. For your own safety and for the safety of a brighter future, treat me like a traitor," Daia warned.

Ashlynn agreed to these commands with a slight nod, her brain too full to comment, but vowed to herself that she would ignore them if that time did come. Gliding away from the apartment, she turned around to check once more. Daia stood strong and full of purpose with tears pouring down her face, while her hair blew in the wind. Ashlynn would always remember that moment. In the years to come, when she thought back to that image frozen in her mind, she wouldn't recall there being a breeze. Welcoming the weight on her shoulders, she felt more equipped to expose the king's sickness.

Hurrying back to her chamber, she slammed the door behind her. Finally, she was able to crumble to the floor and let her tears fall. So much had happened, and Ashlynn was engulfed with the immense knowledge and encounters of the day. While she hadn't enjoyed her predictable life, it had been secure, in an unsurprising, miserable sort of way. She understood at a young age that uncertainty was dangerous, especially since she had the least amount of control over her own life. Or so it felt. The letter hung in her hand, but she stuffed it away to read later when she could better focus. She couldn't process her mother's words yet with everything she had just learned. Ashlynn hugged herself on the rug next to her door and sobbed. All she wanted was to nap and reset. So she stayed on the rug and fell into a restless sleep.

That is where a dream found her— curled up against the door with her arms around her legs in protection.

Ashlynn slept deeply, yet lucidly. She could still sense

everything around her. Much like an animal when it rests in the wild, she was asleep but aware that something crept through the dark and could attack the moment she dropped her mindfulness. Her awareness tingled as she felt the dream invade her mind. Its quiet maneuvers permeated without hesitation. Ashlynn's mind fought back, so instead of restraining her, the dream took form.

In front of her dream self stood a massive dragon with scales the color mauve and eyes as dark as her hair. She tiptoed back terrified, but the dragon continued to stare at her, like the phantom panther in the woods had. That intense stare pinned her to her spot without attacking. Her foot, paused in midair, stepped off into open space behind her, and she turned around to see an endless ocean full of soul crushing waves. Ashlynn faced the dragon's snout and ivory teeth, anticipating the need to jump over the cliff to save herself. Yet the dragon stilled, glaring at her. She felt an odd urge to approach it, like someone nudging her forward. So she gave into her instinct—noting that it may be the last decision she made. Ashlynn stepped toward the majestic and terrifying beast. Right as she got close enough to feel its breath, the dragon reared up and roared.

The sound pierced her ears, making her eyes water. She fell to the ground and covered herself with her hands as her only defense. A massive gust of wind forced her onto her stomach, pushing her face into inky sand. Ashlynn glanced as the Dragon flew over her. She laid herself parallel to the ground and gazed across the cliff. The dragon's wings twinkled as if covered in sparkling dust. Ashlynn could've sworn it was magick, but she had never seen any before for comparison. Ahead of the dragon was a cluster of black and blue smoke swirling together.

The two contrasting beings faced each other, one poised to attack and the other to defend. Ashlynn took a deep breath to calm her pounding heart and choked on the smell of rotting eggs and dead fish. She gagged, holding back her vomit, which attracted the attention of the dark energy.

It lunged for her, slithering in through her ears as she closed her eyes and held her breath from the foul odor. It penetrated her body, overtaking her subconscious. She felt it stretch out tentacles through her veins while engulfing her brain. Ashlynn shivered as she lost consciousness in the physical world as well as in her dream state. It fought her determination by dragging her into the watery abyss below.

She stopped struggling and gave in to the virus—this intruder, captor, and soon to be victor. Ashlynn desired nothing more than to be done. She was finished with the fighting, the daily struggle, and just the overall feeling of worthlessness. She wanted it all to end— and so it took her down to end it... and to end her.

A roar shook her entire dream and physical being. It reverberated up her spine to the base of her skull like another whip across her back, reminding her who she was and what she was fighting for. She reached a hand out of the water and grabbed hold of the dragon flying above her. Grasping its massive claw with both hands, Ashlynn clung to it with every ounce of strength she could muster, letting it lift her out of the abyss and out of her dream.

She awoke still on the floor. Except now she was stretched out with a limb in each direction. Ashlynn pulled her arms around to hug herself as she sat up on the rug, rocking back and forth. She shivered and tried to breathe in calmly, but her first intake reeked of that gut wrenching mephitis in her dream. She rolled over and heaved up every memory. Ashlynn kept vomiting as more and more of a black and blue substance squirted from her mouth. Every breath in stunk and caused her to hurl again until she was dry. She was finally able to breathe, yet her body trembled from fear and overwhelming rawness. As she reached toward a nearby chair for a blanket, Ashlynn was propelled back into her mind.

She felt the dragon roar inside of her, echoing in the distant dream as it created a fire so intense that Ashlynn could feel her physical body burning. She wheezed with each inhalation. Sweat poured from every crevice. It seemed as if her whole body were crying and releasing. Finally, it all stopped.

She sprawled herself out on the floor again, intentionally taking up space. A noise above her caused Ashlynn to stare at the ceiling. A dark energy swirled in a maelstrom of smoke and blackness. Writhing in panic, she remembered the drowning sensation. Ashlynn knew she had to destroy the parasite before it attacked her again. She breathed her deepest breath yet and exhaled, as if instinctively expecting that to be enough to blow it away. Except instead of breathing out air, she breathed out fire that singed the energy throughout. It dissolved into falling ashes around her, coating her entire body in soot. Ashlynn sat up to see if any traces of it were left. She pushed back against the wall, scared that breathing fire meant she was becoming sick like the king. Choosing to ignore the dark swirls on her skin and her raw throat, she rose to rinse.

There was a knock at the door and she opened it to Odessa's bright smile. "Why are you covered in ash? Is that vomit? Ashlynn, are you feeling okay?"

Ashlynn nodded, unable to speak from her parched throat.

"Good! But your party starts in two hours, and you aren't even close to being ready!" She rushed in, leaving the door open.

The dread and reality that her party was finally here sunk beneath her skin. She barely had enough time to prepare as she pulled herself out of her dream world into her real world of being the king's puppet. No, she was in charge of her own life, and she finally felt ready to announce it to the kingdom. Wiping sleep from her eyes and taking a gulp of water from the pitcher next to her bed, she grinned. "Let's get ready, then. But tonight I want to wear a dress that shows off my scars." Odessa's eyes went wide at her statement, but a grin emerged across her face. "I want to see the smirk on your father's face disappear when he remembers my words from the other day. When he realizes I will no longer take his abuse." For once, she couldn't wait to curtsy before the king. She laughed at the thought and closed the door to dress with manipulation and intention.

CHAPTER NINE

Odessa stood behind Ashlynn covering her eyes. In a fluid gesture, she pulled her hands away and pushed her to the looking glass, whispering, "Open your eyes."

Tentatively, she peeked through her slitted lids. Ashlynn had chosen her outfit— a deep burgundy, off the shoulder, satiny gown that was cut low in the back and flowed straight down to the ground— but she had let Odessa tamper with face and hair. Her dress was one of her mother's favorites, worn the day before the king sent for her to be killed. Ashlynn had never worn it, but had occasionally taken it out of the closet to study it, gently rubbing her fingers over the fabric with care. Her room was her mother's old place so it held pieces of a woman she never got to know properly. The moment she decided to show her scars, she thought of this dress, and it was everything she had wanted this moment to be.

She was no longer that stumpy, thick girl with frizzy hair. Her dress accentuated her curves, making them flow instead of clumped together. Her brown eyes were gentle instead of intimidating. Her hair fell in weightless curls that softened her usually hard face. Odessa insisted that she wear her hair down for the party tonight. Usually Ashlynn pulled it up and away, so as not to draw attention to herself.

When she pointed that out, while being plucked, twisted, tightened, and sculpted, Odessa laughed. "It's your party, Ash. Of course you will be noticed. Might as well make them envious."

Ashlynn rolled her eyes, but a tiny spark lit inside as she imagined what others would think when she stepped out looking like an entirely different person. What she beheld in the looking glass was so shocking that she forgot to be scared. Instead she gaped, wide-eyed and aghast, at the beautiful woman standing in the mirror. She hardly recognized herself, which was probably the best outcome for such an ostentatious event.

Hoping to slip into the party without being noticed by the king, Ashlynn slid into the room through the side door. The ballroom smelled of wine and sweat. So many bodies touching in a small space disgusted Ashlynn to an aggravating degree. Despite her aversion, it was obvious that the king had let the staff decorate for her party as if a royal from another kingdom were arriving. The beige room was covered with gold cloth that hung from the arches and twisted around the columns. Even the golden goblets and glasses were brought out for the occasion. The extravagance was alarming and Ashlynn felt as if there were a hidden agenda to this ostentatious event.

Caught up in the beauty around her mixed with the ludicrous number of people from the court, she didn't notice Marcus until he was upon her. His white coat with silver adornments, the required outfit for the men of the court, made his dirty blond hair and lanky figure appear out of place. He bowed and gave a genuine smile at her. The moment he peered into her eyes, the sincerity corrected into a shocked expression. It was difficult for her to not giggle at his silly, frog like features with wide eyes and mouth agape.

"Ashlynn, I didn't recognize you. The king will be most interested to see you like... this. Let me escort you over to him," he said, grabbing her arm before she could deny his request.

Ashlynn felt like a prized bride being shown around to potential suitors as Marcus paraded her up to the king. King Theodore probed her over with lust and hate-filled eyes. They intermingled so fast that Ashlynn couldn't tell which he really felt. She bowed and immediately turned to Sebastian to ask for the first dance. He eyed her and took her hand. While they were still in an argument, she knew he would never make her suffer his father's attention. Gliding her through the crowd as smooth as if he were skating on ice, they kept to their silence.

"Thank you for saving me from your father," she muttered. Sebastian, dressed in the same attire as Marcus yet looking majestic, stared past her head to the space behind her. He did not acknowledge her statement, but instead danced as if he were doing the king a favor instead of her. "I was searching for you all day. Where were you?" she asked, but he chose to not answer. "Sebastian, please," she whispered, "I am sorry for how I spoke. I was hurt, both physically and emotionally. I just wanted you to see my pain and I—"

"It's okay, Ash," he muttered, still avoiding her eyes. "I am... I apologize for how I acted when you woke up from your whipping. Even Barcinas said I was hard on you."

She knew how difficult it was for Sebastian to apologize. Acting surprised at his admittance to lighten the mood, she gasped then smiled back. "Yeah, you were. But you were looking out for me the best way you knew how. And I appreciate you for that. Even if it was a bit hurtful and misguided."

Glancing down into her eyes, he sighed and didn't respond. Ashlynn peered out among the sea of twirling faces, ready to bolt into the shadows the moment they stopped dancing. She needed to take a breath and regain her composure.

"Smile, Ash. You are radiant tonight in your mother's dress. Nothing can go wrong," he said.

She wished she could believe his promise, but something in her knew it was too good to last. Sebastian stared into her eyes as her mind tumbled back to the little boy who would sneak into her bed at night with Odessa to hold each other in hopes that the terrible monster in the castle couldn't find them. To show him that she was trying, she gave a toothy grin.

"That's better. Now they won't think you're trying to kill me," he joked.

Ashlynn narrowed her eyes but caught herself grinning with genuine pleasure. They bowed to each other as the dance ended, and she hurried off to find a drink. Hiding in the shadows, she sipped her wine and watched everyone else have fun. It was difficult for her to turn off her desire to separate herself from the people of the court, even if it was her special day. Odessa seemed to be enjoying herself the most. She was dancing with some prince from a kingdom across the Reis Sea. He shadowed over her both in stature and in character. Ashlynn couldn't help laughing every time he stumbled. Odessa, the gentle, understanding teacher, walked him through it.

He walked off to find drinks when the dance ended, and Odessa sauntered to Ashlynn giggling.

"He is a bit unique, wouldn't you say?" Ashlynn murmured.

Odessa studied him from the shadows and smiled. "Yes, he is. But he is also kind and seems... real."

"Well, Odessa, I would hope you were dancing with a person instead of a ghost," Ashlynn snorted.

Odessa nudged her and smiled at the thought. She watched him stroll back across the room to her with their drinks in hand.

"Princess Odessa, thank you for a wonderful dance. I am afraid I have to leave soon, but I wish to have one more with you, if you would permit," he said bowing.

Odessa looked at him, flattered, but tried to hide it by fanning herself.

"How kind of you, Prince Rohan. I would enjoy that as well. However, I cannot leave my cousin here all alone. This party is for her, you know, so it would be rude of me to abandon her... again," she justified.

Ashlynn raised her eyebrow at the comment but kept her mouth shut when she noticed Odessa cut her eyes at her. Prince Rohan turned his attention to Ashlynn now. With soft eyes, which were unlike the rest of him, and an honest and open smile, he replied. "I understand entirely,

Princess. Let me offer my best friend as a dance partner for her," he said.

Ashlynn stuttered a rejection to his offer, but Odessa clapped her hands together and grinned. "What a pleasant solution! I am sure Ashlynn would be pleased. Isn't that right, Ashlynn?" she said.

With the prince's eyes on her, all she could do was nod. Prince Rohan headed off to inform his friend while Odessa pulled her out to the center of the floor.

"Odessa, what are you doing?" she asked as they prepared for the next dance.

"I'm giving you the best birthday party, Ash! You were miserable sulking over there," she jabbed, lining up beside her.

"I don't sulk!" Ashlynn shrieked, yet somehow Odessa seemed to not hear her.

The music started again as Rohan took his spot in front of Odessa. Ashlynn turned to face her new dance partner, but her eyes caught Barcinas kneeling in front of the king. Marcus was leaned over whispering into King Theodore's ear. Watching him carefully, she took a step back from the dance lineup. The king's brow grew sterner but his smile and eyes gleamed with joy. Why would he seemed pleased while his countenance showed rage? It didn't make sense to her. He mouthed something back to

Marcus, who nodded with a sly grin and walked out of the room. Dancers bumped into her as she stood in the middle of the floor frozen.

As if feeling her eyes on his back, Barcinas turned to find her eyes. His face look resigned but his own eyes seemed distraught. Visibly sighing, he shrugged his shoulders and mouthed, "Sorry."

Daia. The king knows we talked. He betrayed Daia.

Ashlynn gasped and took a step toward him. But right as she moved out of the way of the dancers, someone grabbed her hand and twirled her around.

"Looking for me, Ash?" Tiberius whispered.

"Let go of me, Ti! I have to stop him!" she cried out, but he acted as if he hadn't heard her over the music, clutching her hand and lower back tightly so she couldn't pull free. Tears pooled in her eyes at the thought of Marcus confronting Daia while Tiberius danced her further away from the dais.

CHAPTER TEN

As she twirled around, Ashlynn felt her small amount of control fall away. She began to succumb to hopelessness when her necklace warmed. It surprised her, reminding her who she was now by bringing her out of her daze. "Why did you do that, Ti? I have to find him!" Ashlynn yelled, searching for Barcinas in the crowd of moving bodies.

Tiberius narrowed his eyes. "Have you already moved on so quickly, Ash? You have a party thrown for you, and you are suddenly of high-class?"

"If you knew anything about who I truly am, then you would never think such a thing!" she hissed.

She jerked away, but he squeezed her arm as tight as a healer's bandage meant to limit the flow of blood. He would leave another mark on her skin just to stay in control. Ashlynn couldn't pull away without making a scene, and she wanted to avoid that as much as possible. Stealth would be the best way to locate Daia before she was brought in front of the king.

"Look, if it makes you feel better, then I will apologize

for being so rude during our little squabble! Does that end this silly show now?" Tiberius muttered.

"Show?" she screeched. Guests noticed them, so Tiberius dragged her to the side as she continued. "How dare you! You are intolerable, Ti! You blame me for the whole situation and instead of actually apologizing for your actions, you make it seem like I'm the crazy one! That wasn't an apology. That was a deflection, you ass," Ashlynn spat.

"Well, Ash, you are the one tramping around in a fancy dress that doesn't suit you," he barked, his voice angry and full of jealousy. "With your hair down to attract males like a bitch in heat and color smeared on your face in an attempt to conceal your plainness. Showing off your scars as if you are proud of being beat. Maybe you enjoy it more than you reveal."

Ashlynn stepped back. He did his best to stand tall and confident, but she saw through his façade each time he swayed. He was drunk on wine and rage. For the first time since they had become lovers, Ashlynn didn't desire him. Instead, she felt sorry for him. She stared at him blank faced and chose to never again let him see any emotion. Whatever it took for him to walk away and leave her alone. Tonight and forever.

Her silence cut the rational cord in him. Rage formed

in his eyes as he turned into an unyielding beast who desired authority. Tiberius grabbed her and pulled them to the corridor outside the ballroom. Twisting her arm, she tried to yank away but couldn't get free. The back wall rushed to meet her spine as he shoved her behind a curtain. She opened her mouth to scream, but he slapped her before a sound could come out. The hit caused her to collapse, dazed from the intensity and pure vengeance, as her cheek burned like charred wood in the dying embers of her fire. Pinning her full body, he licked her neck. Ashlynn was disgusted at herself for letting him get this close.

"Do you like it when I'm rough, Ashlynn? Maybe I wasn't rough enough earlier. Is that what it was? Did the whipping warm up my favorite part of you and make you scared of me? Don't you worry. I have been assured time with you soon, and I will be sure to give you what you didn't know you wanted," he promised.

Tears tried to spring forward as he pressed her against the wall, but she swallowed them back—refusing to let him see them. She had never given him any reason to think she enjoyed being whipped. She struggled to escape his suffocating grip, unable to give in anymore. Feeling her squirm, Tiberius held her throat, which pinned her head back as well. With a determination to win, her nails clawed at his exposed hand.

"Say it, Ash. Tell me this is what you have always wanted. You knew you weren't good enough to be held, loved, or savored. You knew your body craved this. Isn't that right?" he said, staring into her eyes as he waited for her response. He reeked of overindulgence and stale wine.

Ashlynn had just enough gumption and breath to spit in his face. It caught him right below his eye. He loosened his arm to wipe it away, giving her just enough space to head-butt him as hard as she could. Tiberius fell back and howled. Ashlynn maneuvered past him to escape, but he grabbed ahold of her hair. Those beautiful curls she adored earlier had become a tool against her. She choked out a scream as he seized her throat again.

"You are sick, Ti," she sputtered. "I didn't see it before, but I can see it now. You will never have me fully."

He held her eyes. "I don't want you fully. I never did. But your body will be mine," he rasped, gripping her breast so tight that she whimpered.

Behind him, someone coughed.

Tiberius jerked around to see a shadow.

"I didn't realize a lady's denial was considered an invitation in Levander," the stranger said.

Tiberius hauled himself off her, surveyed the man full

on, and sauntered to him. Ashlynn could feel the tension between the two, and she wondered if Tiberius would fight him in his intoxicated state.

Tiberius stepped back and scoffed. "I'll see you later, Lady Ashlynn," he hissed without glancing at her.

Tiberius strutted past the stranger without further addressing him. Ashlynn covered her face in humiliation and adjusted herself. She rubbed her raw cheek and scratched throat, as if she had to be sure she was in one piece. She wanted to tear her dress off and scrub herself clean.

"Lady Ashlynn?"

She peered at the man. All she could see in the shadows were his dark blue eyes, the color of sapphires, shining in the deep water.

She had forgotten about him in her embarrassment. "Ashlynn, please. I am no lady," she murmured, securing her messy hair in a bun.

The man did not offer to help. He didn't even comment on the scene he had just broken up.

"Thank you, sir. I appreciate your help. What are you looking for in return for your kindness?" she asked wearily, wondering what favor she would have to give now.

He smirked with a shake of his head. "Nothing is

needed, Ashlynn. I was just doing what anyone else would have done."

"You must not know many people here then, sir," she sighed. "Because most would have let him finish."

He stood still a moment, almost as if he had to process her statement. Her words hung in between them like a bridge connecting two different worlds. "Let me rephrase that then," he muttered, taking a step toward her. "I was just doing what anyone else should have done."

"Sir," she replied, a bit louder. "May I have your name to thank you properly?"

Stepping into the dim candlelight, he positioned himself right in front of her. Which would annoy her in normal situations but chaffed her in this one. However, she held her ground to show she trusted him after his chivalrous act. It was too dark to see any of his features, but Ashlynn swore she saw his mysterious eyes illuminate as she gazed up at him. He reached out to touch her cheek, and Ashlynn stiffened. The man gave her a kind yet sad smile and pulled away before making contact.

"I am no sir, Ashlynn. And it is better if you don't know my name."

His eyes held hers and for a moment she got lost in his swirling embodiment of calm. They both gazed at the ruckus coming from the ballroom. When she looked back, the man in the shadows had disappeared.

Ashlynn slumped down to the floor and wept. She wiped her nose and eyes on her handkerchief, not caring if she smeared her makeup or not. Swallowing her embarrassment and finding her courage, Ashlynn stepped out of the shadows. Her party was over to her, and all she wanted was to go to bed. Even if she found Daia before Marcus, which she doubted was possible now, her strength waned from being mentally and physically abused.

She headed toward the stairs that led to her chamber, but her intuition told her to go to the ballroom first. Ashlynn wanted to disregard her gut, but with every step, the feeling pulsed louder inside of her. She had only ignored that feeling one time in her life, and since then, she vowed to trust her intuition over anything or anyone else. Swaying, she decided to walk back in to tell Odessa she was leaving. As she stepped to the ballroom, her necklace warmed for the second time that night. She caressed her crescent charm while she tugged forth her last bit of strength and bravery to endure the crowd once more, unashamed to display her bright pink cheek.

The scene Ashlynn walked into was drastically different from the one she had left. Everyone was up against the walls to form a circle with the middle open. Ashlynn pushed through them to see what was happening. In the middle of the ballroom were King Theodore and Marcus.

"Bring her in! We will handle this traitor right here!" King Theodore yelled.

Ashlynn hid in the crowd to watch the proceedings, hoping the king didn't ask for her. Out of the corner of her eye, Tiberius sauntered in from the courtyard entrance, half drunk and bruised from her head butt earlier, with a woman in chains. Her wrists and ankles were bound, and she wore a swollen lip with pride. The woman fixed her gaze up, and Ashlynn sensed time swirl around her. She could feel her blood in her ears, her heart speeding up, and the room closing in around her.

Daia.

Unconsciously, Ashlynn propelled forward, but a hand held her back. She turned to find Odessa gripping her hand, just like she had during the last interrogation, with Barcinas right behind her. She would not be able to approach without making a scene. There was no way Odessa was letting go, not this time.

She swirled back to study Daia as the scene unfolded. Her brown eyes, full of warmth and tenacity, stared ahead with a gaze as sharp as daggers and directed at both of the executors in front of her.

"It has been brought to my attention that you have reverted to your old, traitorous ways. You have pressed my hospitality for too long. I gave you leniency at Marcus's request. Even now he stands here at his wits end with you," King Theodore announced to the prisoner and the crowd. "A husband can tolerate an obstinate wife like you for only so long. Your time has come. You are a traitor, Daia! You fought against us in the war. That offense I was willing to forgive. Yet you continued to test my patience. Today you went too far when you approached a member of my household while being under house arrest and plotted to overthrow me. Even after Marcus warned you to keep to yourself!"

The guests murmured. King Theodore glanced around the crowd, smiling. He had his audience right where he wanted them. His murderous mob craved blood.

"If Marcus had not been alerted to your treason, then I could be dead right now. You thought to go behind my back to convince my niece into allying with you! Did you really think you could get away with it all?" he asked.

The king stared at Daia maliciously. Ashlynn gaped at the faces around her. Every person was drugged by the king's script. She wondered how no one saw past his deception and noticed he was sick. But she reminded herself of how her dormant state had fooled her the same just a few days ago. It was easier to stay asleep than to accept that you have believed lies your whole life.

"What is your response to these allegations?" questioned the king.

Daia smirked. Her beautiful hair pulled up and matted with blood from the cut on her lip. Ashlynn could tell as she searched the king's face that he had already decided her fate, and Daia knew it too. Her wounds were evidence. He wanted a show. For the people to think that he was being targeted, so they band with him against rebels. How could they not notice these desperate, fake trials? She prayed to the Goddess that Daia would find a way to get free.

"The past is catching up with you, Marcus. You will both fall hard and when you do, remember those of us who wouldn't bend the knee," Daia responded, her voice hoarse. "It is all an illusion, so remember to open your senses as you navigate your chosen path."

Ashlynn pondered those last words as Daia stared at her captors with glee and strength. Even now, bloody and in chains, Daia reflected the image of power. Marcus and King Theodore struggled to grasp and project this awareness themselves, and she knew how to trigger them with it. Daia gave her attention to Queen Arya.

Ashlynn's aunt eyed the woman in chains then briefly averted her eyes. "Do what you will. I am done," she said, walking away from Daia and subsequently solidifying her fate.

King Theodore laughed and yelled, "Take her away! She has lost her only ally. Now she dies like the traitor she has always been!"

Tiberius, realizing the king meant him, rallied his strength and jerked her out of the room. Daia didn't fight back, but chose to walk away with the poise and grace befitting a goddess.

Marcus was bent over whispering in the king's ear when he hollered, "Wait! Don't kill her."

Ashlynn gaped at the king, her fear subsiding for a moment.

"Instead," he smirked, "Marcus has a much better idea. Beat her, Tiberius, until she doesn't remember who she is. But don't kill her! We will give what is left of her to the Knarkes."

Tiberius nodded and Daia's face turned the color of the white marble but didn't say a word. Ashlynn heard her uncle laugh in the distance as her mind spun. Every piece of her was buzzing. She wanted to run out and grab Daia away from Tiberius. She wanted to fight for the last person who loved on her and gave her a sense of purpose. Daia's last command flashed through Ashlynn's mind. *I will see you one last time, sweet one. But please don't act like you know me. For your own safety and for the safety of a brighter future, treat me like a traitor.* She had known. She was prepared for what was about to happen and she chose to meet to explain everything.

Immense guilt and sorrow filled Ashlynn. Feeling responsible for her death, she could no longer take it. If Daia was going to die, then she would make them see the king was sick and lying. Or die trying!

Ashlynn jerked toward the center of the crowd, but before she could get anywhere Barcinas hauled her out of the room. Ashlynn struggled to pull away, but her body was too tired from Tiberius's beating.

"Let me go, you monster! I have to tell them. It is all your fault, Barcinas!" she screamed, her voice echoing in the corridor.

Barcinas held her tightly and dragged her up the stairs and into the queen's suite. She fought to get free as Odessa slammed the door.

"I have to get to her! I have to undo what you have done!" she yelled.

No one was listening to her, and she was tired of being ignored. Barcinas held onto her as Odessa blocked the door with her body, tears streaming down her face. Biting Barcinas's hand, Ashlynn struggled free and ran to the door when her aunt's voice stopped her.

"Enough. There is nothing you can do. It's over."

Ashlynn glared at her Aunt Arya. She had lost trust in the only person she thought she could trust after her mother was killed.

"You could have done something!" Ashlynn screamed. "You left her to die! You are sick and just like them!"

Odessa tried to step in, but Arya stopped her. "Ash, there is a lot you don't know. Please, sit down. I will tell you everything, I promise."

Ignoring her intuition for the second time in her life, Ashlynn gave into her rage. "Your inaction is as bad as their actions! You are not innocent in this, Aunt Arya! You killed my mother, and now you have killed Daia!"

"Ash," Barcinas interjected, "you don't mean that."

Whirling around, she slapped his face as hard as she could. "Do. Not. Speak. To. Me. This is all your fault!"

She recognized the heat swirling in her, like the dragon's fire from her nightmare had been unleashed inside of her. She hurt. Her skin burned and throbbed with the reality of her own failure. Ashlynn screamed in agony from the pain of being helpless. She screamed until her throat burned like the rest of her, and then she screamed more. When there was nothing left to release, Ashlynn huddled on the floor and sobbed.

"Come sit, Ash. There is much to say and very little time," Arya asked.

Ashlynn glanced at her aunt, who was standing as stoic as she had in the throne room at her mother's sentencing and in the ballroom. She glared at Barcinas thinking back to his ultimate betrayal tonight. And then to Odessa who guarded the door, eyes wide. Every fiber of herself wanted to bolt from the room, to run away from this woman who wouldn't make a fuss and the idiot who gave up his adopted mother. All of her wanted to hide away and never come back into the light again. Ashlynn used the last of her strength to stay and listen. She would give her aunt one more chance. But only because of all that she had done for her over the years.

Arya gave a small smile then said to Barcinas, "Find Sebastian quickly. Bring him straight to me. No detours or excuses, Barc. None. This is urgent. He has to hear this too. Everything changed tonight."

CHAPTER ELEVEN

A knock at the door brought Ashlynn back from her mental lockdown. She rubbed her hand raw from kneading her necklace. It brought her internal comfort when her external reality was far from comforting. Ashlynn shut down when Barcinas went to find Sebastian. She went into her safest space— inside herself. Closing her eyes, she imagined being back at her favorite spot by the brook. Except this brook was far away from a kingdom run by a dangerous king searching for her. The safe spot was hidden from everyone by thick brambles connecting rows of trees together to protect it from potential onlookers. Branches blocked the blue sky with a circle of light flowing down on her little rock. So she hugged the little girl inside of herself as she sat by that water, wondering why any of this had happened.

Another senseless murder tonight with more to come if she didn't find a way to stop the king. She had heeded the pull to uncover the truth and ignore the illusion. Tonight it had come tumbling down. Being awakened was useless if she couldn't protect those she cared about.

Overwhelmed by the accusations, lies, and murders, she swore that each treacherous act would be avenged.

While she had made her decision to stay and listen, her mind kept second guessing it. Stay and risk being captured for meeting with Daia. Leave without knowing important information. Back and forth. Like a bell swaying to sound its alarm.

Yet every time she had these thoughts, the voice of comfort and guidance appeared in her mind alongside her own. Trust her. Patience. You will know soon enough. And again, her necklace warmed. So her feet remained stuck to the wood floor.

Arya opened the door to let Sebastian and Barcinas in. Barcinas bowed to Queen Arya, and Sebastian kissed her on the cheek. Sebastian sat, comfortable in his world of naïveté while Barcinas stood behind him and studied Ashlynn.

She wanted to scream at his ease and rage at the ignorance. Her body and mind were heated and ready to attack when a cool hand on her shoulder caused her to flinch.

"It's okay, Ash," her aunt whispered. "We are in this together. Don't count us out so soon. Stay with us a bit longer, and it will all make sense."

Ashlynn felt the uncertain inferno that had grown in

her belly settle down. She recalled lashing out at her aunt, who took her accusations with grace and serenity. Making her body feel that pain once more, she realized that lashing out again would hurt everyone in the long run. As much as she wanted to give in to her lowest self, Ashlynn chose to stay calm and focused. She needed to hear what her aunt had to say.

As Arya walked back to the door, Sebastian noticed Ashlynn hugging herself in the chair. "What's wrong with you, Ash? Get too many offers at the party?" he smirked.

The only offer she received was Tiberius's and it made her gag. Ashlynn swallowed every touch, caress, word, and vomit inducing insult Tiberius had inflicted tonight. Even Ashlynn didn't have the desire to attack back and relive those moments, or the ones that came after with Daia. She heard her aunt in the background commanding the guards to bring food and drinks for the night. Ashlynn couldn't process being hungry right now. The thought of eating made her want to retch, and she had to keep swallowing to calm the tidal wave of ejecta that threatened to surge out.

"Knock the code when you arrive, then do not let anyone in until I open the door again. Not even the king himself. Do whatever you must. I will handle the consequences if there are any, but this door will remain locked until you see my face," she commanded.

The guards at the door, loyal only to the Queen, must have expected these orders for there were no reactions. They accepted the bizarre statements with a nod and a bow. As soon as the door was closed and locked behind her, Arya addressed them.

"Sebastian, you have no idea what Ashlynn has gone through tonight. So if I were you, I would choose kind words instead of joking insults. Or you may not like the result," her aunt warned.

Ashlynn didn't know at whom to gape first— her aunt or Sebastian. No one could have prepared her for the horror and regret that flashed through Sebastian's face after his mother's reprimand. Yet, her aunt typically kept her thoughts to herself so speaking her mind to her son had surprised Ashlynn. Sebastian stared in disbelief as his world tilted. It was as if he sensed something was about to disrupt it all but could not figure out how or why it would happen.

A knock at the door startled everyone. Arya nodded for Odessa to unlock it. Her cousin brought over the tray, of small meats, cheeses, fruits, and vegetables—all of which made Ashlynn sick upon seeing— and locked the door. Barcinas moved to stare out the window into the distance. Except for him, they each took a seat in the circle.

"Why did you send for me?" Sebastian asked while simultaneously loading his plate and his mouth.

"To stuff your face, obviously," Ashlynn retorted, annoyed at his ease and unawareness.

Sebastian swallowed his words with his food. Ashlynn thought she noticed a small smile on her aunt's lips as she took a bite of mango, but she didn't care enough to find out.

"What I am about to reveal," Arya began, "is something very few know and will cloak each of you in risk."

"Then maybe we should ask Barcinas to leave since he can't keep his mouth shut," Ashlynn muttered, her eyes burning into his.

Barcinas didn't say a word, but Arya gave her a stern look before continuing, "Upon leaving this room, you may be hunted for this knowledge. Except for Odessa, who is safe under the presumption that the king adores her and has a plan for her. But the fate of this kingdom, and even your own lives Ashlynn, Barcinas, and Sebastian, lie within this knowledge. So, I am choosing to no longer hide it from you."

Arya's confession grabbed their attention. Even Barcinas, who stood near the window, peered over.

"Long ago," she said, "there lived beings with magick and immense power. These beings were solitary and only interfered with other species when asked to keep the peace or when others approached them for their knowledge. These beings were Dragons, and they were more glorious and majestic than you could ever imagine."

Something inside Ashlynn tingled as her mind flashed to the dragon from her nightmare. She felt the power in those words, as if speaking of the past would unbind the constraints around their fears. Sebastian appeared dubious at his mother's words, but Odessa and Barcinas were enraptured.

Arya continued. "For many years, there was peace among the beings of the land, all coexisting willingly. However, there were those who sought to take the knowledge from the Dragons because of their own fear and ignorance. The war to obliterate the Dragon's wisdom and existence is told to you from birth. However, winners write history, so you have only heard the edited version." She paused to let the meaning of those words sink in.

"So you're saying," Odessa asked, "that we have been lied to our whole lives? In what way? By whom?"

Arya frowned. "Each of you have been brutally lied to and betrayed by those who wish to keep the truth hidden, as well as those who have worked to protect it from being destroyed. I admit that I partook in that betrayal as well, but I did it to protect each of you. Even you Barcinas, because Daia asked me to."

She stopped to take a few breaths. Focusing her attention on Sebastian and Odessa, she weaved a tale more magickal and extravagant with every breath. "Your father had been king for a few years, and I had been recently married when Daia approached me." Barcinas stepped closer, but Arya didn't stop.

"She told me of the plight of the Dragons. She was the only one capable of interacting with them since so many feared their intelligence and beast-like appearance. Her closest friend was a dragon who had watched out for her since she was a little girl. Daia trusted me by revealing that King Theodore wanted the Dragon's ancient knowledge that was hidden. He was ready to take it by force. I didn't believe he would actually do it. Until it happened. Our race destroyed the Dragons out of fear and a desire to control. As the attack was happening, Daia and a few of her friends asked me to help them save the Dragons and assist her in preserving their race. Each of us and our children were meant to play a special role in keeping the Dragon species from dying out entirely to greed and corruption. I agreed. The king didn't know of this alliance. He was power hungry as he became ensured that his victory over these enlightening beings would reveal the location of their knowledge."

"Wait! Mother, are you telling us that you conspired against your husband, the King of Levander? You are admitting treason!" Sebastian whispered, fear circling in his eyes as he searched the room.

Arya sighed. "Yes, Sebastian. I am telling you I went against the King of Levander. But no, I did not oppose my husband. You see, my son, I wasn't married to King Theodore at that time. I was married to his brother, Kerst."

CHAPTER TWELVE

The room fell quiet. Arya kept still, allowing each of them to process her revelation. After what felt like hours of silence, Sebastian started chuckling. Odessa gaped at him as if he had lost his mind. Ashlynn rolled her eyes. Barcinas seemed to only pay attention when Daia's name surfaced. Yet still, Arya remained tranquil, allowing Sebastian to sort it all out inside himself. Finally, after a few moments of crazed laughter, Sebastian wiped his eyes.

"You had me there, Mother. For a minute, I thought you meant that you were married to the man father killed, the traitor he called brother. You almost got me," he said, dabbing his eyes with a large smile.

Odessa gave him a hard stare, muttering, "Seb, I don't think she is joking."

Sebastian switched between staring at his sister to gawking at his mother, his eyes begging them to contradict each other. But neither laughed with him nor explained away Arya's statement.

"That man? You were married to him?" Sebastian

asked, finally ready to believe this truth over the one he so desperately wanted to be true.

Arya held his eyes as she responded, "Yes, Sebastian. I was married to him."

Ashlynn, feeling the pain roll off her aunt, reached over to touch her. "Your closest friend, that's what you said to me earlier. Your closest friend was your husband. I'm so sorry," Ashlynn said, placing a comforting hand on her thigh.

Ashlynn understood how all of the secrets and pain that Arya had hidden deep inside had allowed her to understand Ashlynn's own sorrow over the years.

"You're sorry, Ash?" Sebastian yelled. "We just found out that she has been lying to us our whole life, and you comfort her? She deceived us!"

Sebastian stood and headed for the door.

"Sebastian!" Arya called. "I know you are upset, but there is more for you to learn. And if you walk out that door, then you never know any of it!"

Halting in front of his mother, he spat, "How do I know that's true? You've lied to me my whole life! Why should I listen to the rest?"

Arya stayed in her seat, holding onto her composure and serenity as she shook. "Because I know that deep down you have as much compassion as I do. You have felt something was off and want so badly to know what it is. If you don't trust me, then trust yourself. There is a part of you that wants to learn why the king causes destruction and death. Trust yourself, Sebastian."

The air was tight and hot, as if we were wrapped in bedsheets while asleep and were unable to escape. Odessa sat with her hands clasped, dealing with the reveal in her own discreet way. Ashlynn sat in her seat silently begging him to sit back down. Barcinas walked over to him and held out his hand. Without saying a word, Sebastian grabbed it and sulked back to his seat, as Barcinas stood behind him once again.

The room continued to feel stuffy and uncomfortable.

Sebastian glared at his mother, waiting for her to explain. "Well, go on. How can I be in danger from *your* mistakes?"

Picking up where she left off, Arya continued, "Kerst and I had known each other our entire lives. When he asked me to marry him, I hesitated because I didn't want to be a queen. Yet, I loved him enough to do it. For the first year we were married, I did all of the things a good queen was supposed to do. But I hated every minute of it. I wanted to be back in my small village, roaming the woods. He saw how unhappy I was, so we agreed to give up the throne to Theodore. We left the castle and found a little cottage where we could be ourselves and have our own life. It was pure bliss."

Arya stopped here, catching her breath as she strolled through the happiest memories of her life. Ashlynn suspected her aunt hadn't let herself relive those years in a very long time because the pain and regret from remembering them overshadowed the purity and intimacy formed during those pivotal years. Even then, Ashlynn wasn't sure how she knew those memories existed, except that her soul understood what others couldn't.

"Then," she said, holding her shaky hands to her heart, "we found out about Theodore's mission to destroy the Dragons. Kerst tried to talk him out of his crazy plan, but Theodore wouldn't listen. He told his brother that he gave up his chance to rule. It was then when Kerst realized something was off with Theodore. Kerst defied his brother and fought on the side of the Dragons. I was, and still am, immensely proud of him for standing his ground!"

"Against his king! Mother, you supported a traitor. It's like I don't even know you!" Sebastian said. His face was covered with disgust and fear.

"Sebastian, he was my husband! A noble man, brother to the king!" she justified to her seething son.

"He was still your king!" he countered.

"Enough, Sebastian!" Ashlynn yelled. She was over his self-righteous attitude and could no longer sit there as he belittled his mother for her past choices. "You have no right to judge her! You act as if your father is a kind and perfect king! You know damn well he isn't, and if you truly believe that, then you are not the cousin that snuck into my bed at night when he was little to hide from that same father. So get off your pedestal and listen to her!"

Everyone stared at Ashlynn. Sebastian blushed as he sat back in his chair. He was still upset, but Ashlynn could see that he decided to stay and listen out of interest alone.

Arya cleared her throat and sent a gentle 'thank you' smile to Ashlynn before explaining further. "We were standing up for what was right. When Daia came to me to ask for help, she brought two other women. Her sister and Sabah. Yes, Ash. Your mother was a part of this as well. Your father knew, but Aurik left the decision up to her. I didn't want to include my brother's wife, but Daia saw something in her, and nothing would dissuade her from those she had chosen. Aurik was gone with Kerst to fight. We didn't know if they were dead or alive. When Daia arrived with her in tow, I knew that Sabah and I were more alike than we both realized."

113

Ashlynn held her breath, remembering her letter waiting for her in her room.

"The night of the war, Sabah became more than my brother's sister. She became my secret keeper and my sister-in-arms. We formed a sisterhood of secrets meant to protect us, our children, and the Dragons we dedicated our lives to saving. Sabah and I believed Kerst and Aurik were dead, and we had to be sure their cause lived on through us and through our children," Arya dabbed her eyes with her handkerchief as tiny droplets threatened to pour down.

"Maybe Father was right. Maybe you were deceived, Mother," Sebastian said with pure confidence and blind allegiance.

Arya looked at him with kind, sad eyes. "My darling son. For your entire life you have tried to justify your father's actions. You fight an inner battle between what you feel is wrong and letting him be right because of the love you crave from him. But you have to know, your real father was the hero."

Sebastian stared at her and started shaking his head, as if begging her to stop the tilting he had felt earlier. It was indeed propelling his world upside down entirely.

"Yes, Sebastian. My first husband, Kerst, is your real father. The king doesn't know."

Standing from his chair, Sebastian walked to the window to turn his back to his mother.

Arya stayed seated but kept her eyes locked on him as she continued, "When he realized all of the Dragons were dead, he and Marcus threw a celebration and called for our band of secret keepers to him. He wanted Sabah and I to swear our allegiance to him. He had always desired me, so he announced I would marry him or suffer death. It protected you, Sebastian, so I agreed." She paused, still staring at him as if waiting for him to believe her.

"Sabah swore allegiance to him by becoming my handmaiden. I thought I could protect her too. I didn't realize how quickly the evil would infiltrate him. Daia swore to go into hiding by staying locked in Marcus's suite. As for Daia's sister, well, she had already left the kingdom following her given task."

Once again, silence covered them like a thick layer of dust stifling a room that hadn't been opened in years. The dust that had covered those secret places for Daia and Arya were opened. Air circulated and the dust rose. It felt suffocating at first, but Ashlynn knew they would be able to breathe again when the dust disappeared and the beauty of it all became obvious.

"Why did he come back 19 years later then? If he was thought dead, what changed?" Barcinas asked.

Arya shrugged. "Checking on his brother maybe? The king is sick. We do not know how it happened, or how to reverse it. But if a way isn't figured out, then this sickness will infiltrate the rest of the kingdom."

Sebastian turned to face her. Arya's eyes followed him. "Sebastian and Ashlynn, each of you must leave. You are no longer safe here once the king finds out that you know this information. He will begin to suspect with the knowledge that Ashlynn and Daia met. Plus, someone needs to travel with Ash to be sure she stays safe."

Sebastian stared at her stunned. Barcinas walked back over to the window with Sebastian.

She continued, "Odessa will stay with me to help hide your disappearance. The king would never hurt her, especially since she is his daughter and true heir, although he still does not know this. Sebastian," Arya said, walking over to him and Barcinas, "I am truly sorry for the rush of information, but you have to leave with Ashlynn."

"How can you tell us what to do after all you have revealed to us? We can't trust you anymore!" Sebastian exploded.

Arya stood facing her son, letting him erupt. "The king needs to be healed, Sebastian, and Ashlynn needs your help."

"You can feel inside of you that the king is sick. I know you can," Ashlynn said.

"Seb," Odessa whispered, going to him. "Please go. Even if you don't believe mother, please go. I don't want her to go alone. I will stay behind to distract him as only I can." Her eyes pleaded. "She needs help, and you need space from all of this."

Staring at his sister, Sebastian sighed and pulled her into a hug. "Yes, okay. You're right." He kissed her on the cheek. "It is my responsibility to save this kingdom, and I can protect Ash in the process."

"Oren said he would see me soon, so I guess we will head to him first. Daia seemed to think he had more information about the virus attacking the king," Ashlynn explained.

"Yes, Oren will have the information you need to find the answers required to heal the king before he does any more damage," Arya agreed.

Next to Sebastian, Barcinas nodded his head and put his hand on his shoulder. "I will go with you. We will do this together."

Sebastian grasped Barcinas's hand. "Ash, meet in my room around midnight. We will leave when it is darkest out." Then he stormed out of the room without a word to his mother.

Ashlynn was thrilled that Sebastian would be with her but annoyed that Barcinas decided to come along. "How can I trust you, Barc?" she asked. "Why do you want to help us when you reported Daia? What would Sebastian say if he knew?"

Barcinas looked at the floor and shrugged. "I didn't know Sebastian would be in danger. I want to help both of you. But only if you promise not to tell him what I did."

"You mean like you promised to Daia?" She glared at him, wanting to ignore his offer. But her necklace warmed, giving her the feeling that everyone deserved a second chance. "Fine. But I am watching you closely. One wrong step, and I will tell him."

He nodded, then he left as well, giving Arya a quick hug and Odessa a smile before walking out.

Arya walked over to her niece and pulled her into a deep hug. "I am proud of who you are becoming," she whispered.

Ashlynn breathed into her shoulder. "I'm sorry. For what I said earlier."

Arya held her closer without another word. Odessa hugged her older cousin with tears in her eyes. Ashlynn wiped them away and held her close.

"Watch over her, Odessa," she whispered. "That was a lot to reveal."

Odessa nodded her head. As she released her hold, Ashlynn stepped back for one more look. With a strength and confidence she didn't know she possessed, Ashlynn forced herself to walk out.

She slipped into her chamber for the last time and closed the door behind her. She sighed. It was all happening much faster than she had expected. Needing to feel clean after being touched by Tiberius, she began undoing her dress. Yet every button that came undone felt like a little reminder that her skin was tainted. Her breath caught in her chest, and her heart began to race. She needed to be out of this dress. Each precious second it took her to take it off made the room close in.

Grabbing for the nearest sharp object, a letter opener, she slit the belly of the dress open. From one side of her hip to the other, she tore. The sound of the rip opened the dress and gave her stomach room to expand. She was able to deepen her breath. But she couldn't stop there. Next, the opener tore through the thin fabric left from her chest to her belly button. The top fell away. She could breathe again. Laughter came from her chest as air pushed itself in. Shaking her body like a dog releasing tension, Ashlynn threw off all that happened tonight and let it fall away with the bottom of her gown. Her gown. No longer her mothers. And she had destroyed it.

On one hand she felt free, able to breathe as if a huge weight had been lifted off of her. On the other, she had destroyed her mother's gown. One of the few things she had to remember her by. Falling to the floor, she picked up the remnants and held them to her face. The smoke and wine from tonight permeated throughout the seams. It was as if her mother had been replaced. Anger took over, and she ripped each piece to shreds, leaving only strips lying on the floor as evidence that she could no longer go back. To her old perceptions, her ignorance, or to when her mother was alive. All she could do was move forward.

Searching, Ashlynn mentally and physically prepared for her journey in a few hours. She packed her bag with intention and speed. When nothing was left to pack, she rang for the maid to bring up warm water. Relishing in the heat pouring over her head, Ashlynn let her frustration wash away with the waterfall. After scrubbing her skin until it was pink, she climbed out of the basin, grabbed a cloth, and stood in front of the fire to dry herself. She stared at the silken mess on the floor and noticed one piece of fabric that shown brightly when the light from the fire hit it. Picking it up, Ashlynn felt a comforting energy radiate throughout her. A final token from her mother before she left. Her letter was still folded up on her desk next to her secret key to Odessa's room. She wrapped the fabric around the letter and placed it in her bag while stuffing the key in a pocket of her blouse hanging near the fire to warm. Trying to imagine her new journey, Ashlynn climbed into bed naked and ready.

CHAPTER THIRTEEN

The moon began her descent when Ashlynn awoke to a sound. Many would not have registered the shuffling of feet and silent yet muffled breathing of someone else, but years of living in fear had trained Ashlynn to be a light sleeper. She slowed her breathing to mimic the soft and shallow inhales she was hearing. She learned as a child that surprise was the best element when attacking to preserve your life.

She had fallen asleep on her side with her back to the door in her fetal position of comfort. Moving to check on her intruder would alert them to her ruse, so Ashlynn did the hardest thing one can do when scared and in danger. She kept her back turned away from the intruder and the door. She focused on the beautiful full moon through her slitted eyes and prayed to the Goddess they would leave without touching her.

The back of her neck tingled as she felt a presence behind her. All of her senses urged her to scream or run or even attack first. Yet that one small voice inside of her counteracted this fear by reminding her to stay calm and patient. She waited for a few more breaths. Her skin crawled when the breathing moved next to her ear. One more move and the person would be right over her. She attempted to calm her heartbeat one last time.

"I know you're awake," the voice purred in her ear. The quietest of whispers that sent chills down her spine while simultaneously propelling her heart into her throat. That voice— the one she had dreamed of and agonized over for years. "You can't fool me, Ash. I know you too well," he said.

She sighed, turned over, and scowled at the dark, shadowed face and breathtakingly sexy eyes of her former lover. The door had been left unlocked, something she never forgot. Yet her emotional evening clouded her sense of safety. That was the only explanation she could think of. She sat up and the blanket fell to her waist. A slight chill in the room reminded her that she had decided to sleep naked. Tiberius's eyes flowed from her face down to her chest. Her face grew warm as her nipples and shoulders prickled from the sudden chill. His gaze continued down to her navel.

His hungry eyes caressed each area as they lit with desire. Her necklace warmed as a reminder that she was more powerful than she realized. He could no longer hurt her, and she would fight instead of allowing herself to be subdued. Steadying her breath, she held her head high. "What are you doing here, Ti? You are delusional to think I would agree to still be with you after the way you have treated me."

His eyes dallied as he dragged them back up to her face. Her cheeks turned hot with desire and discomfiture. "I came to check on you," he hummed.

Those words came out quick and smooth. This Tiberius was in charge of his actions and words. She recognized the change from his inebriated, anger-filled tone, to his calculating, mask-off persona. An exhibition of the calm after the storm of emotion where he would act remorseful for a few days before putting on another mask.

Yet in all the time that they had known each other, Tiberius had never checked on her. Ashlynn sat on her bed, wondering what he really wanted. Gaining a boost of courage, she used her only form of leverage. Ashlynn stood out of her bed and walked intentionally to a chair near the fire. Tiberius watched her deliberate movement, taking in every step and sway of her bare hips. His eyes were unable to look away as she sat on the edge of the armrest to better position herself, legs barely spread. She wanted him to want her, to feel desired and be touched, to make him sweat and ache like she had for many years. Ashlynn desired to be the temptress this one last time. Because after tonight it was over and she would never debase herself with him again.

She breathed in the smoke of the fire to steady herself. Her entire body warmed, from the heat of the fire or from her courage, she wasn't quite sure which. It was a reminder that she was worth more than one night in the arms of her abuser. This time, she would be the one to walk away with the upper hand. A promise easily made but harder to keep.

"Ash, what are you doing to me?" his voice came out rough and full of hunger. "I know you want me as much as I want you. Come here, so I can tell you why I really came."

Tiberius parted his lips slowly, moving them into that seductive smirk that used to be her undoing. Ashlynn shook her head and stayed where she was, tilting her navel up a little to entice him more. "I told you we were over. Have a few good looks, and then tell me why you came because you will never touch me again."

The intensity in Ashlynn's voice stunned him. She had never spoken to him with such intention and authority. Knowing that he had clearly lost, Tiberius nodded and sat down on her bed. He rubbed his hands through his hair, unaware of the lust that attacked Ashlynn as she saw his golden locks fall to the side without care.

"I'm sorry, Ash. I am sorry about tonight and for all the times I hurt you physically, mentally, and emotionally. But mostly for never being there when I said I would. There is something inside of me that I have tried to control, but some days are harder than others," he mumbled, building up his courage to continue. "Tonight, I crossed a line. I gave into the beast within. I came to ask you to forgive me."

Ashlynn was speechless. Tiberius had stopped caring or apologizing the moment he got promoted to captain of the guard years ago. He became a man of commitment, doing and saying whatever he was commanded. She could feel his remorse with each word but being truly sorry didn't mean Tiberius would stay on this path of honesty and integrity. She wanted to believe in him again, but that would hurt her too much. Was he admitting to being ill, as well? She couldn't ask for fear of giving up her knowledge, her one source of protection against the king. Ashlynn knew she was different now and had to step away, or she would never get another chance.

"I forgive you. I have always forgiven you," she admitted. "I just don't trust you anymore. I can't. It hurts too much. I waited for you to remember your promise to protect me and be there for me, but it seemed as if I had dreamed up that version of you. Now I know you always knew and chose to not act on it. Thank you for letting me know. I can walk away without wondering what happened— you didn't find me worth your original promise."

In the dark, Ashlynn could see him slump down, his head in his hands. She reached for her robe and tied it around her. He looked up, eyes dark and full of self-loathing, deceit, and emptiness.

"You have no reason to trust me, Ash," he muttered. "I am here as a diversion. I am meant to distract you while the soldiers prepare to grab you. The king is upset about your conversation with Daia and wants to question you. Even now I am supposed to be tricking you."

Every feeling of forgiveness that Ashlynn had built up dropped out of her like a rock falling to the depths of the ocean. Her heart couldn't comprehend his words, while her head screamed at her to get away. All of her exploded as she processed his implications that they were coming for her. Ashlynn had to leave now, her body knew it. Yet she couldn't make herself move. She just stared at him. Her whole body shook. It took all of her control to untie her robe. Shaky hands reached for her skirt and blouse as her mind mulled over how long she might have left.

Ashlynn ignored Tiberius as he watched her dress, unable to say or do anything in this moment about any of it.

"Ash, I told you I was here to hide the fact that they are coming. I am supposed to lure you into bed through force or lust and ensure you don't leave," he paused. His insinuation didn't need to be clearer. She wasn't supposed to have a choice. "In about 10 minutes, they will throw open the doors and lock you in chains to take you down to the dungeon. They know you have information that will help you overthrow the king."

Tiberius stopped talking and stared at her eyes with the zeal of someone wanting to prove their innocence. The buttons on her blouse were slick in her sweaty and trembling hands. She tried to focus on them, while his words swirled around inside her head.

"Then, why are you telling me this? You could've done that before I was dressed," she wavered, unable to get the last one buttoned, eying him.

"Yes. I should have trapped you before now, but I am finally fulfilling my promise to you. I am having a rare moment of clarity. Something has taken hold inside of me, and it has taken every ounce of strength to subdue the beast inside," he said. "I want you to tie me up and leave before I hurt you again. Go and don't look back." He untied the rope from around his waist and offered it to

her.

Ashlynn didn't believe him. After years of abuse, his clarity came the moment she was about to leave. Something didn't add up, but if what he said was true, then she didn't have time to think about his explanation. He disgusted her and nothing could change that now. She secured the last button on her blouse, tucked it into her skirt and gazed at her old friend from so long ago who taught her how to let go in the midst of grasping for control. She tugged on her boots, hastily forcing her feet in without her stockings for protection. Taking the rope from his hands, Ashlynn did her best to tie him up.

"No one will believe I was able to tie you up," she said. "But, that is your problem, I suppose. Thank you, Ti," she whispered, standing back to study him.

"Don't thank me. This just gives you a head start. I will be after you as soon as they find out. And next time, the beast within won't be able to let you go. My duty won't allow it," he said.

The painful honesty of those words nailed it into her mind that this was truly the end for them. She kissed him on the forehead and put her head to his. They stayed together in this moment and held onto their shared memories— the happy and the painful.

She stepped back. "Remember that you are not bound

by your past decisions, only your current ones."

Tiberius glanced up at her and smirked. "If it were only that easy, Ash. You are lucky. You get to escape. I'm deeper in than you realize. I did choose this path, though," he said with a shrug.

Ashlynn picked up her bag and opened the door. She glanced back once more at Tiberius. He was tied up with his head hung over his body in the image of defeat, he had become the perfect portrayal of who she was and what she had been before finding her voice.

"Until we meet again, Ti," she unknowingly vaticinated and snuck out to meet Sebastian and Barcinas in Sebastian's room. The quickest way out of the castle, without being seen, was through the hidden tunnel near his room. They would have a head start. If she could get there without getting caught, that is.

CHAPTER FOURTEEN

The hall outside her chamber was quiet with the candles on the walls sparsely lit, creating a shadow of protection or risk. It seemed like someone wanted to divert people from choosing this path tonight. Ashlynn snuck around the corridors and hid in the shadows, utilizing them to her advantage. She saw Sebastian's door across the hall, but the dim light made it difficult. The eerie quiet of the corridor and dark lighting felt like a warning. She proceeded cautiously, checking around her shoulder with each intentional step she took.

Sebastian's room was at the end of this corridor in the castle. Next to his door was a window, which was usually left open to let in the breeze. Tonight, however, it was closed. She needed to get inside his room and sneak them out before they lost this chance.

Ashlynn knocked on his door and only heard a hollow thud. She twisted the handle, but it was locked. Sebastian locked his door every time he walked through it, whether it was to enter or leave his chamber. Ashlynn teased him about being paranoid. Annoyed that he wouldn't leave the door unlocked for her knowing she would come here, she chose to find gratitude instead in his desire for secrecy and safety in case the soldiers came to his room looking for her. Making a loud noise to wake Sebastian would alert everyone to her location. So she glided to Odessa's room instead, which was around the corner from Sebastian's.

She jiggled the handle, expecting it to be locked as well. When it didn't budge, Ashlynn pulled out her key to Odessa's room hidden in a secret pocket of her blouse. She always kept it on her for times when she needed to hideout in Odessa's room. Ashlynn fiddled with the lock. The moment it was unlocked, she slid into her room, clicked the door shut and re-locked it.

The room was dark without any light. Odessa had closed the curtain and put out her fire. Tapping into her childhood memories, Ashlynn put each foot down with purpose and silent force as she walked by recollection to the wall on her right where an elaborate tapestry hung. The tapestry was of no importance, or so Odessa claimed when anyone asked why it hung in her room. Only her and her cousins knew it hid a door. Ashlynn felt to the left of the cloth and caressed the hole to find the exact spot that would open the door. She checked her on cousin who could sleep through cannon fire raining down on the castle.

She pushed back the tapestry and pressed the switch into the stone. The wall in front of her swished open, blowing her dark hair back on her face. They had used this when Ashlynn slept over with Odessa and wanted to plan tricks on or test strategies with Sebastian. She glided through it to a path on the other side and peered back over at her sleeping cousin. As the door swished closed, Odessa opened an eye and grinned at her. Ashlynn sent her a wave as her heart ached knowing this would be the last time she would see her cousin for a long time. She put her forehead on the closed wall for a moment to collect her racing heart and then turned to the wall behind her.

Ashlynn stood in the little stone corridor between the chambers, dim from the lack of lighting. Ashlynn and Odessa checked it regularly and relit the candles in case they needed to escape. This path had been used as a route for the children of past kings and queens to leave the castle in secret. They used to fantasize about having to run and hide when they were little and even followed the path to see where it would come out. She smiled at the memories and leaned against the wall to press the other side open. Ashlynn grunted as she pushed into Sebastian's chamber. He hadn't used his door recently so she had to use all of her strength. She stepped into his room but halted upon noticing two bodies in Sebastian's bed. The back window overlooking the garden was open to the bright moon, but her eyes had become accustomed to the night.

She shook her head. Such an awkward way to start their journey.

Leaving the wall open for an easy escape, she snuck to the bed and stared at the intertwined bodies. Ashlynn blushed at the thought of them together and their vulnerability. Uncertain of how to proceed, she reached to wake them up. Barcinas's eyes flashed open, and his cocky grin spread across his face when he noticed her staring.

"If you wanted to join, Ash, all you had to do was ask," he said, propping himself up on his elbows. Barcinas's voice nudged Sebastian from his sleep.

Opening his eyes to find Ashlynn, Sebastian tugged the blanket up around him and yelled, "Ashlynn! What in the name of the Goddess are you doing here so early? We said midnight. You're an hour early!" Sebastian gripped the cover over him, embarrassed by his exposure and evidence.

Ashlynn wanted nothing more than to run out the door and hide, but she stood firm. "Well plans change when the king is after you!" She was too impatient to let him respond. "We have to go now. Tiberius said the guards were coming for me any minute," she said, her eyes not leaving his.

Fear permeated through him as he grasped her words and the reason for her appearance. Barcinas was already dressing and threw clothes at Sebastian. Sebastian was shocked and unable to move until a boot hit him in the face.

"Barcinas!" Ashlynn shrieked.

Barcinas glanced at Sebastian to check on him and smiled. "He's fine. Ash, what is going on? How do you know?" he asked. His trousers and shirt were already on, so he quickly and methodically packed their bags.

Sebastian had finally come to his senses and dressed — he put his trousers on backward.

"I'll explain later," she muttered, cocking her head at Sebastian's disheveled attempt at dressing. "We just have to go now!" Horns blared to alert the guards. It was the alarm for her capture, guards would be covering the grounds and searching rooms for her any moment.

Sebastian fixed his trousers but was tying one boot to the other, unable to focus. Barcinas knelt by Sebastian's feet to fix his mess before grabbing him and their bags as they ran for the path.

Shouts from outside the chamber rang as they fled to the hidden passageway for their way to escape. "Prince Sebastian! We apologize for waking you, but your father needs you," the guards yelled as they banged on his door. "Your cousin has disappeared and tied up the captain of the guard. Your father is worried you are in danger! Prince Sebastian? Please unlock the door. You must come help us look!"

They slipped through the opening and closed it tightly right as they heard the doors to Sebastian's chamber crash open. Ashlynn, Sebastian, and Barcinas did not wait to hear what was said. They scurried through the hidden corridor. Ashlynn knew the path as well as she knew the woods around the palace. They crept in silence for a few minutes and paused as the path diverged in front of them. She chose the tunnel that traveled below the castle, next to the sewage. No one would be able to hear them down here. Ashlynn briefly whispered to them as they walked about waking up to find Tiberius in her room, and the events that had unfolded so far.

"You must have some spell over him to make Tiberius let you go," Barcinas chuckled.

She blushed before her stomach churned at the thought. "We have to get to the stables without being caught and then make it to Oren's hut on the mountain. He is supposed to have more information to help us navigate this mission. We should be safe for a little while when we make it to him, but we need to keep this head start," she said.

"Oh, so you mean avoid the whole army, while sneaking into their central location for a ride out. Then, we outrun the fastest horses in the land to make it up a giant mountain that few traverse. Not a dangerous plan at all, Ash," Sebastian grumbled.

Ashlynn ignored Sebastian as they arrived at a hidden gate near the exit of the gated courtyard. Barcinas stepped up to look around and turned back with a smile. "We have company."

Sebastian breathed harder and Ashlynn narrowed her eyes. A hand reached through the gate to pull it open. The kind, intuitive eyes of her aunt peered back at them.

"I figured you would need a ride out when I heard my guards conveniently talking about an arrest tonight right outside my door," Arya said with a grin.

They crept out to find their favorite horses waiting for them packed with food and supplies. Ashlynn hugged her aunt and kissed her on the cheek.

"Watch out for each other. Remember, there are illusions all around you. Stay sharp and stay together,"

Arya instructed.

"Come with us," she begged. "How do we know you will be safe?"

"You don't know," her aunt whispered back. "You just have to trust that I will be. Watch over them, Ash. They need you more than both of them realize. Go directly to Oren's hut without stopping. We are counting on you three to figure out how to heal the king from his sickness so our kingdom can live in peace again."

Ashlynn sighed, nodding her head. Without time to argue with her aunt, she said a silent prayer to the Goddess that her aunt and cousin would stay safe while they traverse the kingdom for answers. She climbed onto her favorite mare, Seaweed— named for throwing Ashlynn into seaweed the first time she rode her. She scowled down to hurry the other two up and saw Barcinas already on his stallion, holding the reins of Sebastian's. Ashlynn could see the outline of Sebastian as he hugged his mother tightly.

"I'm sorry," he mumbled, barely audible above the wind. "I am still angry, but I love you, Mother. Keep yourself and Odessa safe."

Then he climbed onto his horse without another word. Barcinas led them out of the courtyard toward the back gate without being seen.

As they raced toward the mountain in the distance, Ashlynn heard trumpets blaring with the call for soldiers to mount their steads. They pushed their horses hard through the streams and bushes as they chose to stay off the normal path until they made it to the base of the mountain. The sun had started to break over the side of the landscape ahead of them. In the distance, they saw a cloud of dust as the soldiers charged after them on the main road. A strange beast she could barely see outran them, which gave Ashlynn the feeling that death was at their heels. They raced up the mountain moments before the guard broke through the tree-line. Only the creature saw them escape toward Oren. So Ashlynn pushed Seaweed faster, commanding herself to ignore the piercing, bloodthirsty eyes locked on her back.

CHAPTER FIFTEEN

The path around the mountain led them to a river within a few minutes of attempting the climb. The horses, tired from the physical exertion of racing there, dipped their mouths in for hydration. Barcinas pulled his horse away and urged him toward the path upward once they were finished. Everywhere Ashlynn looked she saw sand. She had never seen the desert, but the landscape around was close to her interpretation of what that terrain might yield.

The trail was thinning out, with enough space for one horse at a time. This made it tricky to travel without being seen since the trees were sparse. She thought she had noticed a forest on the mountain before they approached it. Yet now the trees were almost vanishing in front of them. It seemed peculiar, but there wasn't time to stop and ponder it. She wanted to be far away from the trail before the beast following them made it there.

"We need to keep going!" Barcinas yelled. "Stopping here will make us sitting targets. I don't know about you two, but I am not going back until I choose."

He rushed around the curve without waiting for them. Sebastian gazed in admiration at his lover for taking on the role of the leader, one that had never been entrusted to him being Marcus's lackey and Sebastian's shadow. Ashlynn rolled her eyes and followed Barcinas, content with someone else in charge.

An hour later, they reached another river. Their surroundings resembled the previous spot they had paused at. It gave Ashlynn an eery feeling that they had been here before, but one glance at the water made her forget her thought. She jumped down as Seaweed galloped to join the other horses to drink. Gazing out at the water, she studied the cool, blue reflection. The sand beneath her boots was white. She bent down to run her hands through it, the warm and soft texture made her ache to cool off. She was sweaty from the adrenaline rush. Her mind felt fuzzy while her throat felt parched. Looking at the refreshing pool made her throat feel even dryer. Her body headed toward the water absentmindedly as she craved the sensation of the wetness around her skin and over her head. She took a few steps in and relished the water pouring over her boots and up her legs.

"Ash! What are you doing? We have to get going!" Sebastian called out.

But she didn't want to acknowledge him. The stream called to her, like a sweet lullaby. Just one dip. Sip the water. It pulled at her. Rest within the waters. Relax your beating heart. She ached to become one with it. One step at a time as she merged herself with the summons.

The water was up to her hips now with her arms out in the air as if she had no other care in the world.

"Ashlynn! Stop! Get out of the water. Ashlynn!" Barcinas yelled as a loud splash rang out behind her.

Sebastian dashed after their horses to tie them up.

"Leave me alone. I want to be in the water. I want to float around and forget about the heat. To forget about it all," Ashlynn mumbled, stepping farther into the watery trench.

With each step her mind got fuzzier and more muddled. She could barely hear Barcinas or Sebastian screaming for her. Instead, she heard a gentle humming that spoke to her deepest core. It was seductive, yet alarming. Her body chilled with fear, yet her mind grew calm as she focused on the song that pulled her forward.

The water was at her stomach when Barcinas stomped in. She lowered herself in further, letting the water engulf her head and her mind. The moment her entire body went under, music exploded in her head and the river pulled her legs out from under her with a force so strong that she became like a leaf in a windstorm. She couldn't hold on, and she didn't want to. All she wanted was to be free of the troubles that awaited her on land. The water begged her to release herself forever into its grasp. She never wanted to go back, and the song that flooded every cell of her body confirmed that she was where she belonged for eternity. Suddenly, she flew backward through the water. She landed on the bank with a slam to the ground. Coughing, a hand slapped her face.

"Breathe, Ash. You are okay. Clear your mind and breathe," someone sounding familiar said.

She took a few breaths and stayed still. She heard the birds chirping, the rustle of leaves around her, the worried voices of Barcinas and Sebastian, and the horses neighing as they pulled against the rope that tied them to the tree. The warm sand beneath her felt soggy as water poured from every crevice. Ashlynn took one more breath and sat up.

"If you wanted to drown instead of being locked up, then let us know next time. That way we don't get drenched in the process of saving your life," Barcinas said, walking away.

"What were you doing? You could've been killed," Sebastian asked.

"There you go as you start raging into me because I made a mistake. I lost my mind to something I couldn't control," she said. "Mistakes happen! Help me up instead of berating me so we can leave here!"

Still annoyed, Sebastian reached down to help but stayed silent. She dried off as much as she could, dusted off the damp sand, and climbed onto Seaweed, who was still drawn to the water. The others waited for her, visibly annoyed. She glanced back at the water one last time and noticed extra prints along the bank. Something about them seemed familiar. Ashlynn jumped down and headed back to the river. Her thought before rushing to the water had been correct. But somehow, the river's song had washed it away.

"Not again! Come on, Ash! Get back on your horse!" Sebastian cried, reaching to grab her before she could go in again.

Barcinas stopped him. "This time is different. Look at the way she is walking. She noticed something."

Sebastian stared at him incredulously and in awe. "How do you know these things?" he asked.

Barcinas shrugged. "When you've studied people your whole life, you pick up the subtleties in movement. I had to be good at it. Marcus depended on me to," he paused, tasting the words before announcing them, "to preempt any attempts on his life." Sebastian gawked as Ashlynn trudged back to them.

"We have been here before," she said, pointing to the prints in the sand.

"How do you know it was us and not someone else?"

"There are only three set of hoof prints and they follow in the direction we walked. We made one big circle. I had a feeling this was true before I looked to the water. It's as if, this sounds silly, but it's as if the water did not want me to notice that we were going in circles," she said, mulling over the issue.

"It is warded," Barcinas whispered.

Sebastian and Ashlynn grimaced at him. He searched the area, taking in the landmarks. "Daia once told me a story of Oren when I was little where it explained that anyone wishing to seek the wisest man alive must come with a pure heart, or the path will lead them toward insanity instead. I always considered it part of the tale to make the seeker seem stronger and heroic. Now I see that it's true."

"So you're saying," Sebastian asked, "that we have to choose a path and hope it leads us to his hut, and be sure that we only have pure desires, or else we will be driven insane? What does that even mean, Barc?"

Rolling her eyes, Ashlynn strolled away from them to

145

search the area as Barcinas explained it to Sebastian again. She closed her eyes and honed in on her other senses, just like Daia and Arya had instructed.

Clutching her necklace, she reached into that spot inside of her that gave direction and asked for guidance. The seconds ticked by as she tried to wait patiently. Peeking open her eyes to check around didn't yield anything different though. Breathing out a sigh of frustration, she turned to head back to Seaweed. A bush snagged her skirt, and her necklace lit up. The bush was ordinary with no distinguishing features, yet the moment Ashlynn touched it she could see the path ahead of them clearly. She stepped back and looked at the trail with fresh eyes, noticing how this spot differed from the obvious area behind her. This spot was obsolete and full of thorns. No one would intentionally choose to go this way. It was hidden next to a boulder where most would not think to check. Ashlynn ran back to Sebastian and Barcinas who were still debating the logic of Daia's bedtime story.

"Did you find anything?" Sebastian asked in a flat voice.

"We have to stop thinking so hard. The path that feels right and seems the most logical choice to get up the mountain is what most would choose. Only those who have the patience to keep trying, and the idea to check for different approaches are more likely to find the path," she said.

Sebastian gaped at her like she had grown four arms. "That is probably the wisest statement you have made since I've known you," Barcinas said.

Sebastian growled out in frustration. "So, what did you find? You didn't answer my question."

Ignoring his attitude, Ashlynn responded, "I found a bush that called to me. When I touched it, it showed me the path before us."

"You felt called to touch a bush? Is this like the feeling you had when you decided to take a plunge of death?"

"Just follow me, for once, without making snarky comments, would you?" she gritted out.

Barcinas howled in laughter as he followed Ashlynn past Sebastian. "Death plunge," he chuckled.

They came to the bush, and Barcinas focused on it. He touched it, walked around it, and studied it fully.

"I don't see anything. Do you, Seb?" he asked.

Sebastian plodded past Ashlynn, mirroring Barcinas's movements. "No! This is stupid," he declared. "I agree that we need to follow a different path that is more conspicuous, but jumping into a trail full of thorns does not seem the logical idea to me!"

147

"That is the point. If we do what is logical we will never make it up there, and the soldiers will find us. They have to be at the base of the mountain by now! Please, just trust me!" she begged.

"I said I didn't see anything," Barcinas explained. "I didn't say I didn't trust you. I think we should follow this path, but let the horses go. They won't make it up and it will alert the guards to where we have gone."

"You believe me?" she asked, astounded.

"You seem to have a better grasp on feeling the enchantment around the place. I would even bet that the fact that you were drawn into the water means that you are more in tune than we are. But remember, it is all an illusion, so we have to be open as we navigate the path," he said. Ashlynn stared into his eyes and noticed a look of pride that she had never seen from Barcinas before.

"Daia said that before she was killed," she whispered. Barcinas grabbed their packs and released the horses before heading on. He didn't respond to her comment, and Ashlynn wasn't sure if he intentionally ignored it or hadn't heard her.

The path behind the bushes angled back down the mountain. While the path was covered in thorns, it had grown in width so that they would be able to travel side by side. The trees grew, becoming the forest she had seen while studying the mountain from afar. She checked with the others to gauge their reaction. To her it made total sense that this was the obvious path.

"This seems counterproductive," Sebastian muttered. "But since I know you will tell me that is the whole point, I will keep my mouth shut."

"Your comment seems counterproductive, Seb," Barcinas responded.

Ashlynn hid her smile and steadily stepped onto the path as she chose to follow her inner guide and ignore the desire to go back. Each step ahead felt like they were wading through honey, yet the scenery around her felt more inviting. Each turn produced more branches and barriers to fight through, yet the sky became clouded as the forest grew in height. It messed with her as she pushed herself to physically follow the trail while her mind knew it was the only way to go. Right as they wanted to give up, the area opened to a field of beauty.

They breathed in the fresh air and walked toward the open, sunlit pasture. The forest faded away behind them as the sun poured his rays over the flowers, insects, and travelers. Once again, the warmth called to her. She closed her eyes as it rained down, setting her on fire. The sensation was calming as it lulled her anxious mind. Yet she couldn't help comparing it to the feeling of being burned by the dragon in her dream. Her dragon. Peeking through heavy eyelids, she watched as Barcinas and Sebastian sat and rolled in the enchanting flowers, causing their sleep inducing pollen to rise. It became clear as they yawned and stretched out to fall asleep.

"Wait!" she cried, trying to project confidence into her voice as she pulled her body and mind from the glorious view in front of her. Grabbing Barcinas and Sebastian by their arms, she struggled to pull them back into the shadows. Weary and exhausted from fighting her instincts, she knew it was the only way to make it to Oren. Barcinas cleared his mind quickly upon being dragged. He propelled out of the blossoms, heaving a drooling Sebastian, who had succumbed to the illusion. "This field is hypnotizing. Just like the water was to me! We have to find the path that repels us!"

"Of course, the most beautiful field we have seen is a way to keep us stuck forever." Sebastian mumbled while sitting on a rock in the shade as his brain seemed to be working overtime to pull him out of his bewitched state. "Oren, you have one sick sense of humor."

As Barcinas snickered and helped Ashlynn search for the next path, she couldn't help wondering his true intentions and if she had perhaps misjudged him. Maybe he did want to make up for his mistake with Daia.

"I found something!" Barcinas called.

She trudged over to him. Sebastian popped up from the rock, sat back down, then jumped off again. He seemed to be unsure of his choice to sit down and feared the consequences of resting when everything could be a trick.

Ashlynn sidled beside Barcinas. He stood in front of a small, one person path that cut out of the rocks ahead of them. It led straight up the mountain, but not without treacherous footholds. Ashlynn held her breath and felt the tug to climb up those stones, fighting against the desire to run in the opposite direction toward the openness.

"Sebastian! We found the way up!" she called back.

"Let me guess. It is a tiny bridge over a huge ravine of razor sharp rocks," he said, peering at the path ahead. Sebastian sighed as his hand covered his eyes in frustration.

"No, just a treacherous climb up the mountain with the chance of tumbling back down to your death. But good guess!" Barcinas joked.

Sebastian rolled his eyes and gestured for them to proceed in front of him. The three of them ascended through the rocks. A few sharp turns later brought them to another open field. This one was similar in appearance as the previous one, except a massive tree stood in the middle. Ashlynn didn't get the feeling they had been here before, and wondered if the previous field was meant to trick them into not trusting this obvious one.

"Looks like we should follow the path that leads straight off the mountain next. That seems like the logical choice!" Sebastian muttered.

"Not a bad idea, Sebastian. Let me know how that works out for you!"

"Don't encourage him, Barcinas! Look, I think we actually need to walk through the tree," Ashlynn suggested, taking a step forward. Sebastian gawked at her like she was the one who had just suggested walking off the mountain. "I'm serious! It just feels right!"

"Then by all means, Ashlynn. Lead us through the tree," Sebastian said, ushering his hand out with a bow.

Ashlynn turned red and stalked toward the tree with the other two in tow. The flowers leaned in around her as she walked and her pendant glowed as she led with confidence. As soon as they got close to it, a hole appeared. On the other side was a hut and another river that seemed exactly like the one at the base of the mountain.

"I told you," she called out, running to the waterfront. Barcinas chased after her. Only Sebastian approached

152

the water hesitantly. A rock at the edge of the river held someone sitting very still. While the others dipped their hands in to cool off and replenish, Ashlynn faced the individual on the rock, showing respect to the old sage.

Oren was the most intimidating person any of them had ever met. Yet she didn't feel scared around him like she had when they were in the presence of the king or his closest advisor. Oren emitted confidence and knowledge. This made others revere him and his essence, instead of fearing who he was and what he would do. It wasn't readily noticeable while he sat, but Oren was massive in height. Yet his height was still not his most striking feature. For as dark as his skin was, his eyes were just as light. The stark contrast between his milky white eyes and his deep espresso color were accentuated by his lack of hair. Each of these factors combined created a formidable being full of compassion and wisdom. All of him felt comforting the moment he smiled and spoke. His smile was full of warmth and peace, and his voice carried you across the mountains into the Reis Sea.

"Welcome, Ashlynn!" The others jumped at his voice. "I see you finally noticed me Sebastian and Barcinas. Welcome to you, as well. You made it up the mountain. I am impressed," the man said. "I am Oren."

Ashlynn and the others stepped up to the rock and sat

down quietly. "Thank you, Oren, for the welcome. We have come for your guidance."

Oren gazed out across the stream. "I would hope so, Ashlynn, because few who make the journey up this mountain do so for fun."

Unsure of how to respond, they stared at each other in silence. Oren burst into laughter. He rolled around the rock cackling. Finally, he propped back up and projected his gaze out across the stream to the beastly shadow lurking on the other side.

CHAPTER SIXTEEN

The three seekers sat on the bank of the river while Oren sat on a rock on the opposite end. Sitting in his presence was like feeling the peace and love of the entire world. Ashlynn's heart felt full yet sad, as she thought of how the people of their kingdom had lost this connection with each other.

Ashlynn glanced at the other two to assess their reactions, but both had shifted their eyes over the water. She followed their gaze to see a mocha tinted panther drinking from the other side of the river. It wasn't the terrifying creature she had seen following them earlier. This was her panther from the woods. The feline was immersed in the moment and didn't regard them or anything else around her. This beautiful scene took hold of time, freezing their worries and stress by allowing them to be present.

She strolled to the edge of the forest and looked back at them with a heavy stare. Just as she appeared with grace and ease out of nowhere, the beast disappeared into the brush behind her, confident in her path and her surroundings. Each of them sat in the silence, fully absorbing the beauty that had now shifted to a memory.

"There is your guide, Ashlynn," Oren said.

Ashlynn gaped at him. Oren held her eyes and, studying him for the first time, she noticed his irises, too, were cloudy.

"You're blind," she announced.

The others shifted as Oren's laugh reverberated through the clearing. Ashlynn blushed.

"Yes, I am blind and that will be the first among many surprises that await you," he said with a smile.

"You told Ashlynn that the panther was her guide. What did you mean?"

"Each of you face significant changes to your path and mindset ahead, Barcinas. This specific animal was chosen to aid Ashlynn." Oren kept his attention on Ashlynn the entire time he spoke.

"Why did she choose me, Oren?"

"You already know the answer to that. You can sense the feminine power of that fascinating feline. You've seen her before. I know because she told me, and she is here to guide you."

"Wait. You're saying an animal talked to you?" Sebastian asked, rolling his eyes.

"Keep your eyes and ears open, Sebastian. There are

156

more fantastical sights awaiting you."

"We have heard that many times. We came here for answers. We need to know how to save my father from some disease. Not to be given more confusing metaphors," Sebastian said, rolling his eyes again.

"Then you are on the wrong journey. You will be sorely disappointed if that is all you seek." Oren's intensity and honesty pierced through their doubts.

The anger and betrayal rolled off Sebastian in a tsunami of energy. "I was lied to and forced to run because of the stupid choices my mother and birth father made! I might have chosen this journey, but I just want answers so I can get my life back! For everything to go back to normalcy."

Barcinas reached over to touch him, but Sebastian jerked away. He huffed off toward the water in a storm of frustration.

"You will get answers," Oren responded. "But first you have to ask questions. You cannot have an answer without a question burning to be known."

"All I have done since we found out about the stupid Dragons and illness is question myself. I wonder what is right and wrong. Or how I am supposed to be choosing the best path. I feel like all I do is question!" Sebastian shrieked.

"Yes, but you're not asking the *right* questions. Open your eyes and trust your senses. Knowledge is not obtained without persistence and patience," Oren guided.

The waters receded inside of Ashlynn as she gained more insight into their journey and her future. Whereas each bit of information shifted those tumultuous waves into a more methodical sway of confidence in Ashlynn, the reverse happened to Sebastian. His waves grew rampant and drowned him in his rage.

"What are the right questions then, oh wise one?" he muttered, bowing in sarcasm.

Ashlynn stared at him with a look that could kill.

Oren smiled, amused, "You are angry, Sebastian. That is understandable. But anger will not help you on this path. It will only lead you further astray. The answers will vary for each of you," he replied. "You are not on the same path, therefore your questions will yield different answers."

"We came here to find guidance! Your answers are like the confusing paths up here. Why can't you just tell us how to end this cursed illness and save my father and kingdom?" Sebastian cried, dropping to his knees. He pounded the dirt with his fists, expelling his uncertainty and sorrow into the ground. Sebastian needed someone, or something, to take away his fear. Ashlynn could tell the pressure was becoming unbearable for the prince who had always had his life planned for him. He had been respected and envied. Now he was a fugitive.

"Seb, you aren't being fair." Barcinas bent to put his arms around him, as if he were trying to hold the pieces of Sebastian together.

"Sebastian, the answers are all around you. I only talk in circles because your mind is resisting this change from your old way of living. Only when you give into what has happened and focus on the future will you truly be able to find what you are looking for," Oren said, giving the lost prince a soft, sad smile.

While Sebastian capitulated near the riverbed, Ashlynn focused on the wisest man, knowing this would be their last chance for pure knowledge without payment or recompense. "Oren, what do we need to know right now to move forward in finding these answers?"

Oren smiled. "That is a magnificent question, Ashlynn."

Sebastian growled in exasperation. Ashlynn covered her smile as Oren stared across the river. He closed his eyes, held out his arms, and slowed his breathing. His movements reminded Ashlynn of Daia when she connected with her guides the day they spoke. Yesterday. Time had already flown. She felt like they had been traveling for many days.

"The tide is coming in, just as it should. When it goes back out, this riverbank will be changed and gleaming with new treasure. This is the pattern of life, and the world around us. Change is the only constant. Even I do not know what will happen in the future. I do know that each of you play a vital role in the protection from the curse that plagues the Kingdom of Levander and the rebirth of this world without darkness overshadowing the purity of love and truth. You are called to bring the Dragons out of hiding. To reveal the truth and solution about the curse affecting your father and so many others in his kingdom. It is his own doing, of course. Everything you have ever known has exploded. You cannot go back to Levander or even to your past. That time before you knew these stories was only an illusion of normal. All you can do is move forward in your search, because if you do not, then you will surely succumb."

Oren's words rang in Ashlynn's ears and soul like the chiming of a clock to signal the start of a new hour. Sebastian shivered at the call to push forward. He hugged himself one more time then breathed out a sigh as he got up.

"I can tell you that which all know but everyone must learn and a secret that will confound, exhaust, and enlighten you," he said. "First, that which all know but everyone must learn. There is a curse in this land that must be cured. As you venture on this path of healing, remember that no one is as they seem. Not even each of you." He paused to lock eyes with each of them before proceeding. "Now, for the secret. One will be the key to all doors. One will lose faith in themselves and their beliefs. One is not seen and will find something they do not wish to see. When this has been repeated thrice, the one who has nothing and sees everything will give it all."

The finality of his words hung over them like a spell tying them to their destiny. The path ahead felt ominous and convoluted with this influx of information.

"I cannot tell you the cure to heal your father, Sebastian. Nor can I explain where the Dragons are hiding. I will say, they are important to this mission because only by finding them, and forming a connection built on trust, will you learn the cure. Your next step is to locate the Elves. They hold the knowledge about the Dragon's whereabouts, as well as how to access them. It is not an easy task to access the Dragons, so venturing to the Elves is the only way forward." Oren sat on his rock and smiled out at the water.

"Why can't you give us these answers if you know them? We came here because we were told you knew!

While you clearly do, you are just sending us on a wild chase after something you already know!" Sebastian hollered, spit flying out of his mouth as he paced.

While Ashlynn was annoyed with how Sebastian spoke to Oren, she couldn't help but agree with his statements. Birds in the tree behind Oren's hut sang a sad song as if they knew of what Oren spoke.

"If I told you, Sebastian, then nothing would change. You would have the answers and head straight back into the pit of darkness to shed light without the awareness of how to manage the flame. You would quickly be extinguished. No, you must learn through your own experience, young one."

Ashlynn stood up and dipped her hands in the water behind her. It was warm and inviting, but not like the enchanting river they has first encountered. She rubbed her hands on her face. The wet kiss on her brow and eyes rejuvenated her tired mind and helped clear her frustrations. "Can you tell us how to find them, then?" she asked.

"Alas, no. Elves exist outside of our daily flow of time. Their world is only accessed with consent from their queen. No, child, that is another task you must undertake to prove you are pure in your intentions to reach them."

They sighed at his response. Ashlynn squatted on the

162

ground to play with the wet sand, while Barcinas and Sebastian whispered to each other.

"Now, you all must leave," he finished.

Each of them stared with alarm at his abrupt announcement to vacate upon receiving knowledge and instruction.

"This is the third time I have heard that, Oren," Ashlynn sighed, throwing the coarse sand down and rubbing her hands together to clean off the rest.

"Then you know the importance of what I speak. There isn't any time to spare. The longer you wait the further the sickness spreads," Oren announced, checking over his shoulder. "Soldiers surround each known exit." He chuckled at an image none of them could see.

"Is there a way out that will help us avoid them?" Barcinas asked as he grabbed their bags.

"Of course. I would be foolish to not have an escape route," he responded. "Take the path behind the tree. It will lead you."

Ashlynn ran without waiting for the others. "Thank you for your help, Oren! May the Goddess see you safe until the end of this!" she hollered over her shoulder.

The other two sped after her, not wanting to be left behind. As she rounded the hut, Oren's voice echoed in the distance, "And may the Goddess keep you three safe

163

in your journeys as well."

Ashlynn searched for the path but the only one she saw led them straight off the mountain. Oren's hut was at the upmost point. Ashlynn silently hoped Sebastian didn't connect his previous comment with their predicament. There was a stump to the side she walked in front of and it morphed in height and width into a majestic aspen tree. Almost as if the tree had sped through the years of growth in front of her eyes. "Of course! It's an illusion!" she exclaimed. Sebastian and Barcinas ran to her but shook their heads.

"We don't see it, Ash," Barcinas admitted, "but I trust you."

She smiled at his unlikely words. Sebastian wasn't as accepting.

"Yes, okay. We don't have another option, and you've been right so far. Minus the death bath, that is," he admitted. "It's better than following the path off the mountain, I suppose. Although I did mention that earlier."

"You are so supportive, Seb. Have I ever told you that?" Ashlynn muttered, cutting him off as she stared past the tree.

"You have! Wait, are you being sarcastic?" he asked. She ran off chuckling before he could demand an answer.

164

CHAPTER SEVENTEEN

Descending the mountain was faster than maneuvering up it, as if the mountain expelled them downhill. Ashlynn couldn't explain the sensation, so she chose to not mention it. Being the leader wasn't part of what she imagined last night when she fantasized about their journey. It was daunting to make the decisions. Leading them to Oren had been exhausting, but it was exhilarating to finally be followed and appreciated. Once they made it off the mountain, Ashlynn could feel Sebastian's eyes lock on her back, awaiting her next decision.

"I'm not sure which way we should go, but Oren said to find the Elves. So, unless either of you have an idea, I say we continue east and watch for any signs along the way to direct us," she suggested.

Ashlynn cringed as she waited for their response to her first decision as their official, unannounced figurehead.

"Sounds good to me, Ash. We'll follow you," Barcinas said. Both her and Sebastian stared with their mouths agape.

Her mind fought with her gut as she wondered if he meant to mislead them or truly wanted redemption. Maybe getting away from the castle, and Marcus, meant Barcinas was finally being true to himself. She gave him a small smile, while narrowing her eyes.

Sebastian snorted. "Now that we have validated each other, let's go!" he announced.

Ashlynn faced forward, ignored his comments and led them away. They had made it a few miles when Sebastian stubbed his toe on a rock.

"This is so Goddess-damned stupid! We have no idea what we are doing. We will wander until we are found!" Sebastian hollered.

"Seb, you stubbed your toe. It's okay. Who knows, maybe we will be dead before they find us," Barcinas said, smirking.

"Real funny! That could be our reality! You don't know," Sebastian started, but Ashlynn didn't let him finish.

"Enough, Sebastian! Shut up, for Goddess sakes," she yelled.

"What is your problem, Ash? Missing Tiberius's abuse? Feel the need to yell at us instead?" he slung back.

Her eyes bore a hole into his as she channeled her

frustration into her words. "What is *your* problem? We are in the same position as you! Each of us are making this work while we figure it all out! You don't hear me or Barcinas complaining every second! What makes you think we want to hear it from you?"

Sebastian stared at her like a cannon fully loaded with the spark lit. "Neither of you get it! We are not in the same position. We never will be!" he gritted out.

"Wow. Cutting it deep, are we? Do you really have to flaunt your status now?" Ashlynn said, taking his jab personally.

"I know you're jealous of me, Ash!" he exploded. "You always have been. I bet you're so happy to see how far I've fallen! I found out that my mother betrayed me and my father. Throw in that he isn't my real father either. Suddenly, I have to run for my life because if the only father I've ever known finds out I'm not his real son then he will kill me!" He tore his bag off his back and threw it to the ground, kicking it a few times before continuing. "Your life didn't come tumbling down around you! You didn't just find out that you aren't the heir to the throne and don't have an actual claim to fix the issues your so-called father is creating anymore! No, Ash. You don't get it!" Sebastian was shaking from his confession. Tears streamed down his cheeks. He hastily wiped them away and kicked his bag once more.

Ashlynn studied her cousin. For the first time, she saw his pain. She realized this recent burden replaced his last.

"I am sorry that you feel so alone, Sebastian. That this left you bare and your life got harder because your princely immunity from hardship wore off. Truly, I'm sorry." She held his eyes. "But you're right. I don't get it. I have been jealous of you, but that doesn't mean I am thrilled to see your fall from grace. If you want to compare pain, then we can." The words tumbled out in an unstoppable waterfall. Too many times she had been silenced, and she could no longer hold it all in. "I may not understand exactly what you're feeling, but I have felt betrayed. Actually, I have been betrayed, lied to, and told my existence was inconsequential my entire life. Maybe that has given me more time to process and block the blows that have perpetually penetrated me. I am used to them, but that doesn't mean they don't hurt every time.

"Maybe it hurts more for you now because it is new. But pain is relative. I never got the chance to know my parents. I thought your father killed them out of malice! Now I know there is more to it. That there is a deeper well of pain and truth that I have to unravel."

The tears threatened to gush down her cheeks, but she pushed through. She couldn't stop if she wanted to. "I

168

was deceived as well, Sebastian. So was Barcinas and even Odessa! It may not be the same exactly, but we are all searching for answers!" She paused to be sure he heard her. "Help us figure out this problem, so we can heal ourselves, our land, and our people!" she screamed back at him. "We need to cure your sick father and hope that once we do he stops being an ass!"

Sebastian sat down on his bag, tears trickling onto his clothes. He stared up at her dry face and swallowed.

"I still know who you are, Seb, even if you don't. I will help you figure it all out. But only if you help yourself first," she said.

She took a few steps away, released the breath she didn't know she held, and gazed out at the vastness before them.

Barcinas sat down beside Sebastian and put his arm around him. "She's right, you know," he said.

She stood in silence for a few moments to give them privacy.

Ashlynn cleared her throat before asking, "Barcinas, what did Marcus tell you about the Elves?"

"I actually didn't hear too much. He grumbled about how controlling their queen is, but that is about it," he replied.

"I didn't know Elves still existed," Ashlynn wondered

169

aloud.

"How do we even know that Oren is sane? Many times father has commented on Oren's feeble mind the older he gets," Sebastian pointed out.

"Don't start, Seb!"

"Hear me out, Ash! I'm not trying to be negative, but just want to study every angle," he insisted.

The atmosphere remained stilted since his blow up and her retaliation.

"Even if he isn't sane, it is all we have to go on. Plus, your father thinks everyone is inferior to him, so I wouldn't trust anything he says," she pointed out.

No one else said a thing, so they continued east in silence. Their course was covered with trees as they stayed off the main road. There was not a set path to follow, so Ashlynn did her best to guide them by watching the sun to gauge their direction. She wasn't sure they were going the right way, and grew weary from the mental and physical exertion. But she kept her thoughts to herself, all while watching the mountainous terrain for signs.

"Barcinas! Tell us about your family. You know all about me and Sebastian, but I feel like we don't know much about you!" she encouraged.

He eyed them with uncertainty. "There isn't much to

tell. I am an orphan and Marcus took me in as his protege since he didn't have any sons."

He glanced at them, their faces expectant and eager. "The earliest memory I have is from when I was little, and Daia would cuddle next to me and weave stories about her childhood. When I was around seven or eight, Marcus had come back from one of his trips and saw me in her arms. The next morning, I woke up and Daia was gone. Marcus told me she left for a while. When I asked him why, he wouldn't tell me. Except that she hated being there. I didn't see Daia for a few years after that. When she did come back she wasn't the same. She smiled, but it never reached her eyes. She barely sat with me. Marcus had become my teacher and protector, and Daia didn't say much to me after that," he finished.

There was an awkward silence as Ashlynn tried to wrap her mind around the picture of Daia Barcinas had painted versus the woman she met.

"That doesn't make any sense. The Daia I met was kind and full of life. She couldn't be that heartless," Ashlynn insisted.

"You didn't know her," he said. "It was like she suddenly remembered that I was just an orphan instead of her son, and she got tired of playing with a little boy who wasn't her own," he retorted.

"I'm not saying you are lying! I just don't understand," she said.

"People act differently in secret, Ash. Even you should know that," he muttered, pushing ahead of her.

Sebastian glared at her and ran to catch up with him, clearly blaming her for being rude. The conversation appeared closed as they dipped back into an uncomfortable silence.

CHAPTER EIGHTEEN

The sun had begun his descent when Ashlynn sat for a short rest. Their first day on the run had left them exhausted and overwhelmed, not to mention the constant surprises they had to digest. She heaved out a breath and took a few gulps of water.

"We will need to find a place to stop soon," Ashlynn pointed out. "I don't think we should be on the road at night. I just have this feeling." Sebastian and Barcinas stayed silent. "I mean, I guess we can walk through the night if you both feel like we should," she said, hoping they would answer her.

"There should be a safe place to find a spot for the night up ahead," Barcinas responded.

"How do you know there is one nearby?" Sebastian asked.

Barcinas shrugged away the information. "Marcus brought me out here for some instruction a few years back."

"I'm sorry if I made you feel uncomfortable," Ashlynn said.

Barcinas stood and walked away without answering. Since he knew the way to the next village, Ashlynn let him take the lead again. They strayed from the dusty road to walk among the brush.

Stuck in her own thoughts, Ashlynn didn't notice when Barcinas and Sebastian stopped. She collided into them, stunning herself briefly. They ignored her as they stood staring out over a small ledge into the valley below.

Excited at the thought of resting, Ashlynn pushed through them to see the remaining distance to cover for the night. She peered out over the edge and saw the village below them, nestled into the valley. All that was left of the Tuhka village was ash, blackened land, and a distinctive smell that she had never experienced before and knew she would never forget.

"What happened?" she asked, stunned. She didn't know why she asked because no answer would suffice for the damage she saw.

"King Theodore sent his army to destroy the village last night," Barcinas whispered.

Sebastian and Ashlynn gasped. "Why? Why would he do that?" Sebastian begged, questioning every instance he had defended and trusted his father.

Barcinas held his eyes. "His brother was known to have support here years ago. The king wanted to make an example by burning them. While we were at Ash's party, his soldiers were here. Kerst's resurgence made King Theodore fear that once the villagers found out he had killed Kerst they would revolt."

The mountains protected them from most damage caused by nature, but they couldn't stop the king and his anger.

Ashlynn felt like someone had stabbed her in the heart. "While we were partying, their homes were being destroyed. How horrible." Tears poured down her face into the dirt, planting them as seeds for a better future. "Where did they escape to? Is there another village near here?"

Barcinas, pale from his earlier confession, gazed at her with such sadness that she fell to her knees, shaking.

"Barc, where are they?" she whispered.

Surveying the destruction, he whispered back. "They were killed, Ash. The soldiers were ordered to lock the doors and burn everyone inside. Anyone who tried to escape was beaten, tied to a stake, and made to watch their family and friends burn. Then they were burned as well."

Ashlynn didn't know she could feel such pain and agony. Compared to this, her own beatings felt like scratches. She stooped down and screamed, draining every ounce of anger, pain, and betrayal into that release. She clutched her stomach and sobbed. "We were laughing and dancing while this happened. It doesn't feel right," she stuttered between the sobs.

The tears flowed like streams in the forest heading downhill toward the sea without anything to stop it. Her mouth tasted like dust. Yet she couldn't reach for water knowing that doing so would end this pain. She wanted to prolong this misery, so their death would be felt and remembered until justice was served. She didn't know how she could get up and continue on knowing that so many had experienced deception at the hand of the very person who was supposed to protect them.

"Ash, Tiberius was upset by not being allowed to go. I remember seeing him angry that night, so I thought you should know. King Theodore thought Tiberius went easy on you when he whipped you, so he took away his leadership abilities for the night. He said he couldn't trust Tiberius to follow orders," Barcinas revealed.

Ashlynn could barely wrap her mind around what Barcinas said. The fact that Tiberius was saved from participating in this atrocity angered her more as she understood his rage at blaming her. She knew it wouldn't have made a difference anyway. His presence wouldn't have stopped them. He would have followed orders like he had every time he beat her, never questioning why or if it was humane. Tiberius was not the boy she had met when they were kids. The Ti she knew would've stood up for what was right. Now, he stood up for what was easy. She clutched her head. It all felt overwhelming.

Ashlynn wanted the pain to end. It felt like the revelations wouldn't cease. She noticed a hand on her knee and peeked to see Sebastian staring at the soot. This image of the village below was the physical embodiment of his father's reign—he destroyed all he came in contact with. His hand grasped hers as if she were the only lifeline keeping him present. She squeezed back sending him the love and belief she could barely feel herself.

"Why did you bring us here, Barcinas?" Sebastian mumbled. "You knew they had been sent here to destroy the village There are other paths east, and yet you brought us here. Why?"

Sebastian still stared at the village, unable to peel his eyes away. The question in his voice was full of accusation.

"I did think that we might find safety here since it's abandoned," he whispered. "But now, looking at it, I don't think I can stay here tonight. Or even much longer."

He waited for their response before continuing. When

none came, Barcinas sighed. "We have to keep going. Since we can't stop here we need to find a place before it gets dark. We will be in more danger tonight than any other night. We are still close enough for them to find us, and they will make ground while we rest."

Ashlynn was numb all over. She breathed deeply and held the smell of death, anger, and confusion inside of her. Her lungs burned and her head pounded, but she didn't ever want to forget this moment or this smell. Her body begged for breath. Ashlynn imprinted it all into herself, so she would always remember what she was fighting for and what she had to lose. Then she gave in and released it all, vowing to hold that memory in her being for as long as she lived.

Reaching into her bag, Ashlynn grabbed the burgundy strip of fabric torn from her mother's gown. Untying it from the letter, she picked up the nearest stick, placing her note in the secret pocket in her blouse with her key. She stood with the stick in one hand, the fabric in the other, and tied the fabric around the tip of it. The wind picked up the dark red stained tails of the satin dress, blowing them toward the village below as if it too felt the agony and anger. She put every ounce of love, hope, and peace into this symbol, imbuing it with the promise to right these wrongs and forever honor those who fought.

Ashlynn bent to the ground and plunged the stick into the dirt with all the power she possessed. The stick hit a rock as it descended, scratching her cheek as she tumbled into it. She covered the stick with dirt and sand to keep it stable.

"This is for you—for those who fought, those who believed goodness would win, and those who never gave up hope. This is for each of you," Ashlynn whispered. "May the Goddess take you back home where pain and sadness no longer exist."

Barcinas and Sebastian lowered their heads in prayer to give honor to those who had died. Ashlynn stood and wiped her tears. The dirt over her cuts smeared, but she ignored the burn as she walked on to find someplace to stop. Her feet carried a heaviness that made it difficult to move at all. Sebastian and Barcinas mirrored her footsteps with silence. Their previous chatter had been burned away with the victims.

After walking for a few hours, Ashlynn stopped abruptly. She no longer had the will to move on for the day. She paused in a shaded grove a few miles from the village and pulled out her bedroll. Sebastian handed her some bread from their packs as they sat and chewed their dinner in reticence. The world was dark around them. A chill lingered around their camp, but Ashlynn knew it wasn't from the sun disappearing. This chill came from the awareness of evil still thriving throughout the night. They bundled up near each other, too affected by the burnings to light a fire.

Ashlynn closed her eyes and heard soft breathing around her. Her tears and fear poured out, unable to contain her sadness any longer. The grief from her whole life flooded her body and overwhelmed her senses. She shook from the never-ending torment. A hand on her back morphed into arms that surrounded her, continuing to cry as she was unable to pause for a breath.

Sebastian held her next to him and rubbed her back. "I'm sorry, Ash. I was horrible. I have been for a while. I just thought I could make it better if I pretended along with him. But now I see that he never would've trusted me. The love I wanted so badly from him isn't worth losing those who already love me. I'm sorry that I couldn't protect you, but I am here now. I won't let him or anyone hurt you again. We are in this together. I promise."

Ashlynn leaned against him, letting his stability keep her grounded as the waves of grief assaulted her body. Slowly, her turbulent breathing turned peaceful as she descended into her subconscious.

CHAPTER NINETEEN

She fell into a dream as a bystander looking in on her past. Her subconscious halted at one unique memory, as if it chose this certain page from a worn book.

Around age eleven, she sat alone outside the courtyard, too embarrassed to walk back through it. Her younger self was focused on blaming herself for the punishment she had received. Little Ashlynn sat in front of the tree near the entrance, twirling a strand of grass as she dissected each moment of the torturous whipping. It was the first time she had been whipped and didn't know what she had done to deserve her uncle's anger. A boy around her age approached her, but little Ashlynn ignored him. He stared at her a few moments before sitting next to her under the tree.

"My name is Tiberius. I saw you on the balcony yesterday," he said.

She could barely look at him. Younger Ashlynn stared down instead, still twirling the grass between her fingers. Her hair, knotted in a braid, hung over her shoulder. That was the first day she chose to never leave her hair untied again. It had become a tool used against her when the king grabbed it to laugh into her confused eyes. She waited a few breaths, hoping he would disappear. He didn't. He seemed unconcerned with the probability of her disgrace tainting him.

"I wanted you to know that I think you are brave. The king was an ass yesterday," he said with confidence.

Her younger self gaped over at him in amazement. He smiled kindly and wiped a stray hair out of the way of her bruised lip.

"Thank you," she said, unsure of what else to say. "But you shouldn't talk like that. You could get punished too."

The boy grinned at her. "Don't you worry about me. King Theodore wouldn't dare touch me. He would regret what would ensue if he did. I will do all I can to protect you too."

Shocked by his kindness, she studied him for a bit. "How can you be sure he won't hurt you? And why are you willing to help me? You don't even know me."

"Because," he explained, showering her with his dazzling smile, "I stand up for what is right. It's in my blood. And, I think you are stronger than you realize."

Not sure how to react, she shifted her gaze back to the landscape around them. They sat there quietly, eyes fixed on the distant field.

Ashlynn watched her dream self and young Tiberius, unable to connect the little boy here from the sick man she knew today. Was he lying to her even then, or had his betrayal come later on? She gazed out to the field and gasped. In the distance, far enough to be hidden but clear enough to be seen, stood her panther. Ashlynn ran toward the beast, glancing back at her former self under the tree. The majestic beast sauntered to her. The moment they reached each other, the panther gave Ashlynn a soft lick on the arm. The roughness of her tongue startled Ashlynn out of her dream.

She jumped as the dark surrounded her. Sebastian and Barcinas were sleeping peacefully beside her. Turning to survey the trees, bright yellow eyes stared back at her with alarm. The panther was warning them that something was wrong. Closing her eyes to listen and holding her breath, she took in each sound of the orchard around them.

A twig snapped in the grove. She nudged Sebastian and covered his mouth before he could yell out. Seeing her eyes, he got up and woke Barcinas. Ashlynn glanced back at the panther, who waited in the brush. They listened, hearing only the silence of the night. Unable to release the dread from her dream, she signaled for the others to pack. They rolled their mats and tied on their packs. As they finished tying them around their waists, whistles erupted from behind them and they took off. Their eyes connected. Fear coursed through her as she sprinted. With the freshness of her past in her mind, Ashlynn propelled herself ahead without thinking of her speed. The voices got louder and closer behind them.

Ashlynn recalled Tiberius's message last night. *"This just gives you a head start. I will be after you as soon as they find out. And next time, the beast within won't be able to let you go."* The king found the perfect man to do his bidding. Each had an unquenchable desire to control her.

She yelled back at them. "Ti won't stop until he finds me! We have to find a place to hide!"

"There is a hidden cave out on the edge of the cliffs. Follow me!" Barcinas cried, dashing ahead of them.

Ashlynn tried to follow him in the bright night, but the tops of the trees blocked the moon's light. Sebastian ran right at his heels. "Why does it always come down to running?" she puffed. With every turn, she could hear Sebastian shouting directions back to her. Tripping over a root, she fell to the ground. She pushed up quickly, but it was too late. Sebastian and Barcinas were already gone, not even realizing she had been left behind. Studying the path in front of her, Ashlynn couldn't tell where to go. Everything was dark. "Sebastian!" she called, but quickly hushed when she heard a soft rustle in the bush beside her. Maybe yelling in the middle of the night while running from soldiers was a bad idea. "Barcinas? Is that you?" she whispered.

No answer.

Tiptoeing to the bushes, Ashlynn took a breath and pushed them aside. Two large yellow eyes stared at her. The eyes of a panther. Her panther.

"Oh, it's you." She sighed. "Where do I go? I've lost them." The panther looked at her again then prodded farther into the woods. "We will get lost," she argued to its back. But the beast ignored her. "Is this another time when I should follow you?" When no answer came, she heaved out a breath. Her necklace lit the moment she stepped off the rough path into the dense forest. Within a few minutes, the trail she had left was covered with stamping feet and voices. Her panther had saved her from being found. Now, to find Barcinas and Sebastian.

Stepping as quietly as she could, the panther led her around as a path morphed with each step. As they walked, Ashlynn heard the trickle of a stream near her. The sound was mesmerizing, and she had to remember to stay focused so as not to lose the beast guiding her. The woods opened to the very edge of the mountain ridge. She checked behind her to see that the trees shifted to hide their trail. It was as if the forest protected them. They switched off the path, and a small cave came into view. Barcinas and Sebastian were waiting for her, eyebrows bunched with worry.

"Where did you go?" Sebastian asked as he pulled her into an embrace.

"I tripped on a root when we were running, and the panther guided me here. She led me away right as the soldiers were about to find me," she said, checking back to thank the best. But once again, she had disappeared without a trace. Ashlynn took a sip of her water and surveyed the cave. A few steps in and she reached the back.

"They will be able to see us if they come this way," she said, her eyes darting toward the path that brought Sebastian and Barcinas here.

"Exactly. That is why I am going to run back out and hide our tracks," Barcinas informed.

"No! What if they catch you? We said we wouldn't split up!" Sebastian said.

Barcinas kissed Sebastian firmly and without reserve. Ashlynn searched each crevice of the cave as a distraction. "I am the fastest. They won't be able to catch me. Give me until early morning and if I am not back by then, go on to the Elves without me. I will catch up," he said to both of them.

"Barc, we aren't leaving you," Sebastian assured.

Barcinas gazed at Sebastian with sad, intense eyes. "Then I will be back before sunrise, so you don't have to wait." Without another glance he ran off.

Ashlynn and Sebastian waited, trying to stay awake, but Ashlynn fell asleep after a few hours. She woke as the sun rose on their quaint cave. The cave wasn't fully illuminated yet, giving just enough light for her to study the space around her. Ashlynn spotted someone approaching the cave.

The shadow's steps were deliberate and quiet, as if the intruder were sneaking up on them. She rose and pressed herself against the wall in one of the few lingering shadows. The person stepped into the entrance of the cave and froze. Ashlynn held her breath as the shadow stumbled and lunged for Sebastian. The figure landed on Sebastian's body, pinning him down.

CHAPTER TWENTY

Sebastian screamed, jolting awake from the pressure. Ashlynn froze as he tried to scoot out from underneath, but the person was larger than him. He struggled and tried to roll, but the person didn't move.

"Ash, help me. I think he passed out," he whispered.

She tiptoed and bent down to check for breathing. His hair was tangled from the dried blood covering it. Moving it aside, she gasped. "Barcinas!" She rolled him onto the ground. Sebastian crawled to him while Ashlynn grabbed her water to rinse his face. When she splashed water on him, he tried to move and groaned from the exertion.

"What happened? Are you okay?" Sebastian asked, rubbing his hair.

Barcinas stared at him, trying to swallow a few times before speaking. Ashlynn poured water down his throat. He gulped it down, coughing some back up.

"I'm fine," he managed to spit out. "I was out tracking them and covering our prints when one found me. Someone I have never seen before. He was stronger than me. I fought him, but he kicked me to the ground. My head hit a rock. I got back up and was able to hit him a few times. Somehow he pinned me to a tree and had his hands around my throat. Then he fell to the ground without me even touching him. It was as if someone shot him with an arrow, except without any blood or a wound. He just fell and convulsed. I went to touch him, but I heard others and had to leave. It took me all night to create a new path for them to follow, but we should be good for now." He shrugged.

"I'm glad you're back. Thank you for protecting us, and thank the Goddess for keeping you safe!" Sebastian kissed him. Barcinas turned red, as Ashlynn walked off to get him food and give them privacy.

"Give me a bit to rest, then we can be on our way," Barcinas said, yawning.

"We aren't going anywhere with you exhausted like this!" Sebastian exclaimed.

"I'm fine. I rested earlier. I just need some time to catch my breath. Plus, they will soon figure out we tricked them. I want to already be with the Elves when they do."

Sebastian took a breath to argue but realized it was pointless when Barcinas began snoring.

"He must be more tired than he thought," Ashlynn muttered. "I wonder whom he met out there."

Sebastian reached for his own water and washed the blood out of Barcinas's hair. "I was thinking the same thing. I know every soldier my father has employed."

He massaged the water through his hair, using his fingers to comb out the knots. Ashlynn watched the loving and careful movement of Sebastian's hands with jealousy. She was happy that he had found someone who cared for him, but her heart ached to be appreciated and desired.

"I agree with him," she whispered. "We need to keep moving. I hate to wake him in a few hours, but I don't want to be on the receiving end of Tiberius's anger when he realizes we outwitted him."

Sebastian nodded without taking his eyes off Barcinas. "I feel like something is off. Do you feel it too?"

"I feel something, but I'm not sure it's what you feel. That doesn't mean you are wrong. I just think it might be important to your path," she explained, mulling over his question.

Silence as Sebastian focused his eyes on a spot over her shoulder.

"I trust the panther to lead us. That's all I can say. The rest we have to deal with as it comes, I suppose." Ashlynn rubbed her eyes as the sun rose over the cliff into their little cave. Her body felt tight and tense, and she was sure she smelled. "I am stepping out for a stretch and to fill our water jugs."

Sebastian nodded while still gazing at Barcinas. "Don't take a death swim again," he said.

She swatted at him, but smiled to herself at his joking compassion. The path out of the cave twisted with every step she took. Ashlynn was sure no one would be able to find them. Reaching the end of the path, she checked where to go. Closing her eyes, she smelled the air. Taking deep breaths, she remembered the stench from the village and swallowed back the bile that rose. She opened her eyes and decided to take a risk. To the right should be the edge of the cliff, which meant left is where the water she heard last night should be.

She headed off the trail into the ever growing forest without a glance back. This forest was sparser than the one near the castle. The trees were larger and older, yet fewer of them remain. The branches covered the forest floor with dark splotches, making way for sunlight to peek through. The fallen leaves shuffled as Ashlynn crept around the ever expanding wood. Up ahead, a clearing appeared and she paused at the edge to gaze down the bank. Below was the clearest water she had ever seen. She stepped down onto the damp rock and submerged her hands in cool water. The other side of the bank climbed up to continue with magnificent trees growing smaller, younger, and denser as they progressed back toward the kingdom.

Ashlynn peered back down into the water. A rush of comfort settled over her. Her being felt connected to this place, as if she had traversed it in a past life. She focused on the curving of the stream, and a desire to follow it spread through her. Ashlynn sat in her spot and closed her eyes, imaging herself running through the forest around her. Except the image she saw in her mind wasn't of a her as a girl. Instead, Ashlynn envisioned herself as a creamy mauve dragon leaping over fallen trees as if they were mere twigs. She held out her arms, relishing in her winged imagination. Ashlynn felt more connected to this space, and she wished she could explore it more.

As her body stayed put, her mind soared with this dragon from her dreams as it flew over the forest, giving her a bird's eye view. She knew it was the same forest she was sitting in, yet it felt older and even more sacred than now. "Thank you," she whispered, crouching near the water's edge. Ashlynn stayed in this moment for as long as she could. Leaving would mean more responsibility, something she had always craved. Yet now, it felt restrictive and overwhelming. Having Sebastian and Barcinas follow her made her feel guilty at her lack of knowledge and own understanding.

The water caressed her legs and feet while she mentally left her body. It felt like an old friend comforting her on her role, knowing how challenging it was. Ashlynn smiled, relinquishing herself from her daydream. She bent to rinse her face and refill their jugs.

"Thank you for the love and fulfillment that will sustain us until we meet the Elves." She closed her eyes and breathed in the scent of fresh water.

"Ashlynn! Ash! Where are you?" came Barcinas's voice against the soft run of the spring.

"Ash! Answer us, please!" called Sebastian's anxious voice.

"Over here!" she hollered back. "Near the water!"

Her two companions ran toward her voice. Sebastian darted up and squeezed her tight.

"Are you okay? What happened? Why were you gone for so long?" he asked without waiting for answers. "You could've been found or killed! I didn't know where you were or when you would come back."

"Sebastian! I'm fine. I apologize for scaring you, but I told you I was going to get us some water."

"That was two hours ago, Ash! How long does it take to find the damn water and get back?"

"Two hours?" She raised her brows. "I was gone for

two hours?"

"What happened? Did you get lost?" Barcinas asked, a bit calmer than Sebastian.

"Not really. I just lost track of time relishing in the silent, peacefulness of the forest," she said, confused.

They studied her with doubt in their eyes. She hugged each of them, then she passed out their jugs as proof of her story. "Here. They are full, and now that both of you are here, we can grab our things and head out."

Ashlynn smiled sweetly at them and jogged back to the cave, wondering how it was possible for her to be gone for so long and not even realize it. Just another question to figure out as they set out to find the mysterious Elves. Multiple questions hummed in her body, urging her to go on and solve them. She was getting tired of the constant surprises.

They walked the entire day without guidance and stopped briefly to rest in the sparse shade of a few final branches. The view in front was drastically different from the terrain they had just left. Behind them, the shade from the tall trees had made the air feel cool. Even with most of the leaves covering the forest floor, the sun had not been able to shine his rays through the massive branches. Looking ahead it was obvious that the travelers would have little reprieve from the sun. Dirt transformed into sand while lush bushes morphed into tall, green plants covered with pointers. Cactus. The word appeared from the depths of a memory she didn't know she had, especially since Ashlynn couldn't remember traveling east before.

"This will be the last signs of vegetation as we persevere into the desert. Be prepared for intense heat," Barcinas warned.

"I am running low on food," Sebastian whined.

"Then stop eating it so fast! Barcinas and I have enough for another day or so! You should as well," Ashlynn shrieked.

Sebastian grumbled, but didn't say anything back. Their earlier excitement encouraged them to walk through the night. Yet their confidence faded as the mountainous forest tapered off into a desert. The Desert of Trahn. Few had successfully navigated and returned to tell of its miseries. Sebastian constantly reminded them of this perilous addition to their already death-defying journey. Ashlynn had decided to travel along the routes that were covered with overgrown branches to stay hidden from the soldiers. Without a way to buy provisions or find a place to stay at night, their outlooks and rations waned. The following day they still had no idea where they were going.

"We need to stop. We need to find a way to get food and replenish our jugs," Sebastian groaned.

"And our attitudes," she mumbled. Only Barcinas heard her and responded with a smirk.

"There aren't any villages near here," he commented. "Tuhka was the last one before the desert."

The thought of the torment and destruction that village encountered, along with the smell of death, permeated her senses. Ashlynn had to swallow a few times to suppress the urge to vomit.

"I don't know where to go now. The Elves have to exist, but I don't know how to find them. Do either of you have any suggestions?" She stared at them with desperate eyes. Barcinas shook his head no.

"They do still exist," Sebastian said. "They are just secretive and it is challenging to find them."

Barcinas and Ashlynn froze, gaping at him.

"Wait, you know how to find them? Why are you just now telling us this?" Ashlynn asked.

Sebastian shrugged. "I didn't think Oren was serious. He is known for his riddles and outlandish stories. I thought he sent us to figure it out, and something would appear to help us. Receiving guidance from them is one of the hardest things to do, even if you are an emissary. Queen Elspaeth made it difficult to gain access after the last war."

Barcinas scowled. "Nothing comes without work. Things don't just appear, unless you do something about it."

"I see that now, Barc!" Sebastian shrieked. "I honestly thought that we might be caught by now or that Oren's declaration to send us to the Elves was all we needed to contact them." He shrugged. "I didn't mean to hide it. I guess I doubted that this is where we are supposed to be going or doing right now. Everything has been confusing lately. To contact them we have to reach out into nature and be ready to undergo a series of tasks."

"How do we do it?" she asked.

They glared at Sebastian waiting for instructions. The sun beat down on their backs as he descended for the day.

"It's simple to contact them. You have to show interest by letting them know your intentions, which was why I thought Oren's intention to send us there might be enough. It's like a formal letter sent between kingdoms to ask permission to visit. You have to make a formal announcement. But hearing back is usually the difficult part," he explained.

The two gawked at him. "That's it?" Ashlynn yelled. Barcinas gritted, "How does it work?"

"Elves are in tune with the vibrations of nature. They can sense frequencies at a higher rate than Humans. Someone invoking their name for passage would gain access to them if they allow it. Then they would be able to send us the tests, or so my tutors explained," he replied, eyes downcast.

"So you mean something like this would get their attention?" Barcinas raised his arms to the sky and gazed up. "Oh Great Elves! We ask for entrance to your lands. And to not die on the way. Please guide us, great ones. We have much to learn from you!" Barcinas grinned at Sebastian. "Was that what you meant?"

Sebastian guffawed while Ashlynn rolled her eyes without covering the huge smile on her face. They needed a reason to laugh, and Ashlynn was grateful for Barcinas as the journey progressed. Normally, she would've been cautious of their volume, but they would be able to see someone coming after them in the desert. And if the soldiers did make it this far, then the three of them would be an easy catch without many places to hide. Thankfully their tracks were covered by the ever changing wind.

"Well, if that doesn't get us somewhere, then nothing will," Ashlynn joked.

They observed the sky and as far as they could see in

every direction for a message from the Elves. A few minutes passed before Ashlynn slumped down into the sand.

"So we tried," Barcinas said. "We knew it wasn't going to be easy. What else can we do, Sebastian?"

Sebastian shrugged. Ashlynn thanked the Goddess for Barcinas's positive mindset and encouraging attitude. She twisted her fingers through the sand, watching as it fell through to the other side. Anger surging to the surface, Ashlynn threw it with all of her strength. The wind blew it back in her face, which felt like the ultimate example of this entire journey.

"Every step seems to put us further away," she screamed. "I don't get it. We were so confident yesterday. I thought everything would start coming together. But nothing has happened! We keep wandering around hoping for a sign! What is the point? Oren said we had to find the cure but how would we know? To cure an illness you typically have to drink a potion or tonic. Or maybe we are supposed to learn an incantation to say over the king! But even then, will King Theodore let any of us close enough now that we have left? He would probably kill us before we got a chance!"

"Ash, we have to keep moving. If we don't find shelter before night, we will freeze. The desert gets cold once the sun goes down," Barcinas said, bending next to her.

Ignoring him, Ashlynn reached deeper into the sand to grab more. Sebastian and Barcinas watched as she let it sift through her fingers again. They didn't know what to say to help her. So they sat beside her, giving her support through their presence. Ashlynn became mesmerized with the flow of the sand as she repeatedly let it slide away and refill. They sat like that until the sun was almost gone.

"When I was younger, I would go to my secret spot in the forest to be alone. It was the only thing I could trust." Sebastian and Barcinas jumped when she spoke. They had become used to the silence. She continued on, not noticing their surprise.

"One day, I slipped out to that place. I sat on my rock and stared out at the water. I cried and rocked myself to release my fear and sadness. My tears hit the water and made ripples. Those ripples grew larger and permeated throughout the whole stream. At that moment, I felt like I was a part of something bigger. In my excitement, I reached down to grab a handful of water and it fell right through my hands. Like this sand is doing." She paused, as if lost in the past.

"I saw myself as part of nature. The water in my tears dripped into the pond, becoming part of a larger circle. I became connected to it all. Yet when I tried to bring it to me, it dissipated. That day I realized we have to immerse ourselves in nature to truly become part of it. My tears were a part of nature then, but I could not force nature into me. Only by releasing my control could I fully embody that ripple inside my own life." The three companions sat in the cool sand pondering her words and their journey.

Ashlynn sighed. "I forgot that lesson over the years as I fought for control in any aspect of my life. Even now I try so hard when all I should be doing is surrendering and becoming part of the energy around us. I can't make this sand part of me by grabbing and squeezing it. But I can put my hand through it and feel its heat and life source, blending my being with its healing energy. I can't make the Elves contact us or hear us. All we can do is immerse our souls in the flow of life and be ready when they do."

She sat in the warm sand as the air chilled. She sat with her eyes closed, breathing in the air and moment around them. She just sat. Because that was all she knew how to do. Meditating in her state was the only thing Ashlynn could figure would connect them to the energy of the Elves. The others sat with her and did their best to wait and be patient. And still she sat.

After a while of Ashlynn blending her mind and energy

with the others around her, she opened her eyes, gazed at them, and smiled. "Let's find a place to rest by trusting in our intuition and the energy of our surroundings to provide for us," she said. Ashlynn stood from her little perch and walked toward the rising moon, trusting herself more than she ever had before.

"Sometimes I follow her train of thought and think she is wise beyond her years. Other times I think she is half mad, and we are the same for following her," Sebastian whispered.

"Which do you believe now?" Barcinas asked, watching her lead with purpose.

"I don't know. Maybe both?" he replied with a frown.

Barcinas nodded, and they headed off after her. Ashlynn knew her idea was new, scary, and enchanting. While Barcinas and Sebastian didn't seem sure how to apply it, she appreciated their confidence in her. The travelers began to shiver. Ashlynn felt her sweat from their arduous trip turn cold without the sun to warm it. Neither Barcinas nor Sebastian wanted to be the one to suggest taking another break. Ashlynn trekked in silence as her way to focus her mind on the energy around her.

There had to be a portal or a path that would lead them the right way. If there was one, then it would be hidden as an illusion. Somehow this all made sense to her, and Ashlynn wondered if her attempt to commune with the energy around her had opened up new insight. While Ashlynn tuned into herself, Sebastian squinted ahead, focusing on a spot in the distance. The sun was just about to drop below the horizon, letting his last beams hit the sand before delivering the darkness.

"I see water," he shouted.

Barcinas and Ashlynn jolted as he dashed for the spot, giddy with the prospect of fresh water and a place to rest. Barcinas made it to the oasis first. It was a small spot with two palm trees casting a shade over the area. Ashlynn came up behind him laughing, but halted when she arrived at the oasis. While the new area contained palm trees in a perfect circle, the only visible indication that this place may connect to the Elves, the rest of the space was a replica of the desert around them. A few dry bushes with sand. Not a drop of water to be found.

Sebastian was a second behind. He pushed past them, then twirled around expecting to find a pool of water waiting. He spun in his spot, searching every corner of it for his vision.

"I know I saw it!" he yelled.

"It might have been a mirage," Barcinas said, unpacking his bag. "Either way, this is the best place to stop for the night."

He laid out his mat while Sebastian plopped down. Ashlynn, on the other hand, did not give up quickly. She focused on the spot across from her and closed her eyes. Peering into her mind's eye, she imagined the oasis with a pool of water filled with the fresh scent of rain.

"I can smell it," she whispered.

The others didn't hear her as she stared into the water of her mind. While she focused, Sebastian shouted, "It's here! Ash, you found it! What did you do?"

Ashlynn didn't respond. She couldn't hear him. She was in a deep trance-like state focusing her mind's eye on the water. She peered around the oasis with her eyes closed, imagining the palm trees and the space around her as an illusion. Each area in her mind combed for details that might be off. She glanced back once more between the gap in the trees and noticed a tiny hole. She breathed a few moments to focus. This time a fuzzy image appeared like a veil of water and air between this world and another. Ignoring the boys and their excitement, she approached the trees.

"Ash, open your eyes!" Sebastian called.

Ashlynn kept walking, letting her sense of knowing guide them. Pieces of her skin buzzed with the electricity of energy floating around her body. She arrived at the trees and stood there, breathing deeply. The wind changed directions as it swarmed from behind the trees. She could smell the dampness after a rainfall with the richness of cedar and mahogany. Her skin had bumps as cool mist emanated from this portal. Ashlynn heard the songs of birds, the chatter of squirrels, and the soft patter of raindrops falling onto a forest floor.

"Sebastian. Barcinas. I think I found something," she whispered.

The chilly air descended on their camp. They walked over to Ashlynn with their bags on.

"I don't see anything," Sebastian whispered. "What about you, Barc?"

Barcinas studied the spot intently, but shook his head. "No, I don't either. To me it just looks like two trees planted close together. We are staring out at the desert, Ash."

When her eyes were closed, she was able to imagine a large doorway created between the two trees with a milky white and silver swirl in a vortex of energy. It was a portal. Ashlynn opened her eyes but couldn't see the doorway as clearly with them open. However, she did feel a pulse coming from it. Ashlynn reached her hand out, and a jolt of electricity shot through her. Pulling back, she studied it. It appeared and felt the same, but her energy was anxious for more. She shoved her hand in the portal and it disappeared through to the other side. Sebastian and Barcinas gaped at her but stayed silent.

"This has to be it! I think the Elves have sent us this doorway to their world. At least, I hope it was them. Are you two ready?" she asked. They nodded, too surprised or nervous to speak. "Don't forget to keep your senses open and be wary of more illusions," she warned.

Ashlynn took a deep breath in and held out her hand to Sebastian, who grasped Barcinas's hand behind him. Releasing her breath, they pressed through the doorway into a massive rainforest covered in black from a crescent night.

CHAPTER TWENTY ONE

They blinked out into a different night than that
which they had left. Ashlynn glanced behind them and
saw the oasis had vanished. The rainforest around them
was lush and stirring with life. They sensed eyes watching
them and heard sounds of animals prowling through the
dark. The moon was only a sliver of her full beauty, so the
rays cutting through barely touched the floor.

Ashlynn shivered. "Being able to feel so much around
me is becoming unbearable. We need to get through this
forest to find the Elves. Maybe one of them can help me
center this energy," she muttered. Neither Barcinas nor
Sebastian responded. Ashlynn rubbed the middle of her
forehead as she massaged out the tension. Her headache
stayed centered between her brows. Lack of water and
sleep, in addition to the opening of her senses, was
beginning to take a toll on her ability to lead and be
present with Sebastian and Barcinas. She wasn't sure
how much more pressure she could take. Yet, in this
overwhelmed state, her body seemed to buzz with
excitement since stepping through a portal.

"Can you see anything? It's too dark and my eyes haven't adjusted yet," Sebastian whispered, almost too softly to hear.

"I see trees all around us with a few rays of moonlight peeking through. But I don't see a path or anywhere to rest," Barcinas replied equally as soft.

Ashlynn searched around them as best she could to find a trail. In the thrill of finding this entrance, she had forgotten that they needed a place to sleep. Her energy was full of a desire for adventure, but one glance at Sebastian and Barcinas dampened it. Sebastian grasped Barcinas's hand and kept his eyes scanning. Both looked overwhelmed. They needed to shut down for their body to process all that had happened. Though she was ready to venture farther, the boys wouldn't last long.

"Let's walk a little ways to see if we can find a place to rest for the night. We have time tomorrow to explore and figure out where to go. I think we will find plenty to eat and drink around here," she reasoned then muttered, "I hope at least."

A soft glow emanated from the inside of her blouse as her moon necklace produced a faint light to guide them. She pulled it out, rubbed it in thanks, and lifted it to see more clearly.

The other two agreed with their eyes to travel a bit.

They were still too nervous to speak louder than a whisper and followed her like a horse blindfolded crossing a river. The area they traversed was exactly the same as what they had seen upon arriving. Each massive acacia tree looked identical and every sound reverberated through the silent woods.

After walking for a while, Ashlynn stumbled into an opening. She tripped over a log, coming face to face with the mossy ground. The moonlight shone directly in between the branches, illuminating the clearing in a perfect sphere. It was as if someone, or something, had created this place specifically for them to pause. Ashlynn couldn't decide if they had done so out of goodness or malice. It was their only option though, so she made it count.

"We can stop here. The moss is soft enough to rest until the sun comes up. Then we can move on," she said, navigating them to the spot. Sebastian and Barcinas seemed blind to it until Ashlynn heaved them in. It was as if a ward had been created around this spot in the forest so that only those with an open mind would be able to enter.

"Thanks, Ash," Sebastian said. "I am worn out. It is as if that portal thing took all the extra energy I gathered at the oasis."

"The oasis! I left it there!" Barcinas huffed, covering his mouth in humiliation at forgetting to whisper as his voice echoed around them.

Ashlynn and Sebastian were alarmed by his sudden frustration. "What did you forget?" Sebastian asked.

"My mat. I put it on the ground since we thought we were going to stop there. When I walked over to see what Ash found, I grabbed only my bag," he groaned.

"Good thing the ground is softened by the moss," Ashlynn said with a shrug.

Sebastian squeezed Barcinas's hand tighter. "You can share mine tonight."

Barcinas grinned and gave him a peck on the cheek. They laid down the mat and pulled out their blankets.

"Good night, Ash. Please stick to the shadows and do not wander off without us. You might be entirely open to everything around here, but we still need you. And you need to stay safe," Sebastian warned.

"Okay, worry toad. I will stay right here with you two," she promised, wondering how he knew she craved exploring on her own.

They rolled over and cuddled together under the moonlight. Soon, she heard their snores and gentle breathing of slumber. Sebastian had made her promise she would stay here, but her mind was whirring with excitement. She couldn't explain it other than it felt like an electric current pulsed on her skin.

Ashlynn sat down on a rock and took out her jug. She didn't fill it up at the oasis earlier, so a few sips emptied it. Ashlynn set it down and studied the woods around her. The forest had a hue of green and turquoise mixed with a bit of pale light from the moon. Her little rock sat in the shadows while the boys laid in the perfect rays of moonlight. Ashlynn wasn't sure how the moon was able to expend so much light into one area when it was just a sliver, but she knew no other word for the light that covered them. It seemed like a protection had been cast around them from an unknown source.

Her hands fidgeted with her blouse as a sensation appeared under her skin. She itched as if tiny beetles crawled right below the surface. The current she experienced buzzing atop of her skin seemed to have dipped beneath her first layer.

Something tugged inside, but it wasn't her normal pull of intuition. This was stronger, darker, and messed with her head. It lured her out with a desire to satisfy a craving that she hadn't known existed. While the edges of Ashlynn's vision darkened, the center sharpened, as if she only saw that which she was specifically meant to see. The path lighted ahead as something drew her away.

"Great Goddess, protect them while I am gone," she whispered over Barcinas and Sebastian, her words connecting and weaving out of her like a spell.

The moonlight around them glowed brighter. Ashlynn smiled at the thought of this brightness surrounding them. She stood listening to the distant crying of a hopeless mother. Her body tensed as she took a step past the thin barrier of protection and into the expansive forest.

Ashlynn focused on her feet, specifically placing each on fallen leaves succinctly. With each step a mushroom lit beside her as a guide. Its luminescence was alluring and she felt as if all her problems would fade away if she stuck to the path. Aligning her breath with her movement to keep herself calm and focused, she trailed off into the dark forest. The crying continued and moved further into the center of the forest as she followed it. When she moved closer, the sobbing increased. The intense emotion behind each release cut through Ashlynn's heart like a sharp, quick slice with each exhalation.

She came to a spot in the woods, similar to the one Sebastian and Barcinas were protected in. In the middle of the grove knelt a woman hunched over her legs with her hands covering her face. Her back was to Ashlynn, and her body shook with each sob. Her long hair hung over her pale sea green dress. The bottom of the satin dress was tattered. A tinge of warmth permeated Ashlynn's consciousness, as if this woman were from a memory. Ashlynn crept into the grove. She heard muffled sounds.

"It isn't enough. I am not enough. How can I protect her if I can't even keep myself safe?" The woman's voice seemed to come out of Ashlynn's mind instead of a few feet away.

"I know that voice. I have heard it in my dreams since I was a child," Ashlynn whispered in disbelief. She made her way around to the front of the woman who appeared to have no idea anyone was watching her. Ashlynn closed the gap between them and knelt in front of her. The woman did not move from her spot. Her long flowing curls of chocolate covered her hands. The same curls that gave Ashlynn her own tangled mess. "Mother? Is that you?" she whispered, scared to learn the answer. Just when she had a sense of unease, remembrance forced its way into Ashlynn in waves of sharp comfort. My mother!

The woman didn't react. Instead, she repeated the same words amidst muffled sobs. "I am not enough to save her. I can't even save myself. Why did you leave us?" she whimpered.

"Are you talking to Father?" Ashlynn asked, reaching

out to touch her. "Mother, I am here. I am safe now. You don't have to be afraid. I am alive."

The moment she touched the woman, her curls transformed from rich, velvety brown to a sopping wet mess that pooled over her face. Her hands, which covered her eyes, were drawn in fists with long yellowed nails cutting through her skin. Her soft, hazelnut skin turned grey and sagged with water flowing down. The being slowly looked up.

The face Ashlynn expected, the green eyes with fierce flecks of gold and rosy cheeks with the fullest lips showing the most loving smile, was torn and ragged as if the teeth of a great beast had clasped onto her face and dragged her for miles. The eyes were black and full of hate with that warm fleck of gold threatening to reach out and ignite Ashlynn on the spot. Even worse than all of this was the anger on her lips. No longer full of life and happiness, they were scarred and pale with a sneer of disgust running across them.

"Mother?" she asked as she slowly backed away. The creature transformed, causing Ashlynn's senses to resurface.

"Yes, child. Come to mother. Let me give you the same hug of death I suffered at the hands of your uncle," the now crackly voice cooed.

"My uncle? What did he do?" Ashlynn backed away. She had been deceived, lured away from her companions by this monster impersonating her mother!

"When I wouldn't give into his demands, he took me below the castle and tortured me and told me everything he would do to you. Then, he dropped me in these woods to die. I tried to find my way back, but I couldn't get out. Soon the beasts throughout the woods smelled my blood. They found me and fought over what was left of me. I was pulled back and forth by my hair. I ran again, but they chased me. One knocked me over and grabbed hold of my arms with its jaws. Another was close behind and pulled me away. Right as we got to the edge of a cliff, another beast attacked. I was pushed over the edge, into the water below. I drowned as the waves rocked me to my final sleep," it replied, gazing up at Ashlynn with eyes like a predator.

Ashlynn stared in horror at the story. Her words tumbled out as she unconsciously took a step to comfort this being. "You are not my mother!"

"How would you know? If I had promised to give you to him, then I would be free. It is your fault I am dead. I gave everything for a worthless daughter. All you did was hide and do what you were told! My life was not worth what you have lived. You will sorry be when I take back my life," screamed the voice as she stumbled closer, "from you!"

The creature reached out to grab Ashlynn, but she pulled back fully aware now that this creature worse than she had realized. She was facing a deadly Knarke. "I know you aren't! Get out of my head!" she yelled, more to the sky than to the creature as tears threatened to pour over.

"How do you know?" came the eerie, cracking voice. "I was dead long before you really knew me."

Ashlynn glanced around the grove and noticed that the trees formed a tighter circle, as if trying to keep her trapped here. She searched for an opening and spied one behind the being. Ashlynn gulped. She would have to run right at her and trust she would make it. "I guess I have to live with those consequences while you live with yours," Ashlynn said, focusing her energy on the slight opening and pausing in her retreat.

Her statement confused the being, making it pause its attack. "What consequences, child?" it spat.

"The one where I escape!" she yelled, running right at it.

The being let out a screech of fury and glided toward Ashlynn. She kept her path, slightly veering to the right as they almost collided. It expected this and reached out to grab her. Its nails scratched against Ashlynn's skin,

216

tearing part of it into ribbons. Ashlynn screamed in agony and dropped down to the dirt. Her body slid away from the being, who turned around to face her.

It let out a cackle. "You thought you could escape? Did you really believe I would let you?" it laughed. "Your soul will taste delicious. I have been in need of replenishing, and yours is vibrant, open, and full of adventure. You won't taste sour like most do when they die in terror. You are a challenge girl, and it will make you even tastier!"

The being was so focused on its meal that it didn't see Ashlynn gather her courage and energy. Putrid blood dripped from Ashlynn's arm, burning the ground when it dripped. Ashlynn realized that if she didn't run soon, then she wouldn't make it back. She pushed up to the balls of her feet, still crouching down.

"To pretend to be my mother," Ashlynn muttered, "I would think that you would put more energy into knowing me."

"Why, weakling? Why should I know more about you when I am going to devour your soul?" it asked.

It studied its long, decayed nails, clicking them together. The sound was reminiscent of bones tapping each other. A fire burned inside of Ashlynn. She could feel the tendrils of smoke reaching every part of her. She knew how she would get away, and she would make it count.

"Because if you knew more about me," Ashlynn said, feeding the fire inside of her with desire and courage as she heated her crescent necklace, "then you would know that I don't give up easily. Not anymore at least!"

She called the heat out of her as she screamed those last words. A whirlpool of fire exploded from Ashlynn's mouth, reaching out to the being. It singed part of the creature, making it flee from the fire. Ashlynn released the fire, not caring if the woods burned to the ground or not. Drawing on her last reserves of strength, she put all of her energy into escaping. The trees ahead, as if sensing her plan, closed to block her in, shaking free their bare branches with loud moaning creaks.

CHAPTER TWENTY TWO

She had grown overconfident in her desire to figure everything out, and now she was paying the price. The knarke, now in the form of a pewter grey and seaweed green floating specter, charged her. The change in appearance didn't surprise Ashlynn. Once again, her time to question her reaction, connection, and what these tests meant would be later. She dashed through the forest, over roots and under low hanging branches, and back into the little space of protection.

"Sebastian! Barcinas! Wake up!" she called, ploughing through the barrier. They jumped, alarmed to see Ashlynn sweating and crazy-eyed over them. Sebastian took one look at her and jumped to his feet, whacking Barcinas in the mouth with his elbow as he did.

"Ashlynn! What in the name of the Goddess did you do?" he bellowed, stuffing the blankets and mat into his bag. Barcinas grunted in pain as he climbed to his feet.

"Would it have something to do with that floaty being hovering right outside the moonlight?" he asked calmly.

Sebastian swerved around and yelped.

"Yes. That thing pretended my mother. Then it attacked me. So I ran. And now I am here waiting for you two snails to *pick up the pace*!" The image floated around the outside of the moonlit circle, as if it could not penetrate the space.

"At least Sebastian has his clothes and shoes on this time so we don't have to wait for him to remember where they go," Barcinas snickered.

"Very funny, Barc. Why can't it get in?" Sebastian asked, throwing his bag on. "Wait, did you say your mother?"

"I think I placed a spell of protection over you when I left somehow—don't ask how because I don't know how I did it. We must be protected while we stay here, though," she said.

"Then why are we leaving?" Sebastian asked wearily.

Barcinas nudged him. "Because it is waiting for reinforcements, and the longer we wait, the chances of us getting out alive grows slimmer."

"Reinforcements?" he asked.

Two new knarkes approached and Ashlynn felt her inner fire extinguish. She knew these beings and what they were capable of.

"Ashlynn, did you say you saw your mother?" Barcinas squeaked.

"Yes, Barc. Why?"

"Because right now I see Daia," he whispered.

Ashlynn checked but could only see the ghostly specters in the same form as her knarke.

"And I see Odessa. How could Odessa get here?" Sebastian asked.

"They are from our memories! I just told you I saw my mother, Sebastian!" she called out. "You only see the true form of my knarke because I was able to snap out of the illusion. They are not real."

"Knarke?" Barcinas asked, still studying the floating Daia.

"Yes!" she yelled. Her declaration had the desired effect on Barcinas who shifted his eyes away from Daia. Sebastian, however, was drawn to Odessa. He could not tear his eyes away from her, continuing to look as if it might be the last time he would see her alive again.

"Daia is dead. Of course! Barc, you are able to see through the knarke because of that," she whispered to him. "But Odessa is still alive. So Sebastian must be fighting with his brotherly instincts." She paused, then gulped. "At least, she should be. We have to leave now. Barcinas, be sure to grip Sebastian's hand. He hasn't seen the knarke as an illusion yet," she whispered. "When I yell, I want you to follow me. My eyesight is more in tune than yours, so you have to trust me entirely. Do not stop. No matter what is said or what happens. We run together."

Barcinas grabbed Sebastian's hand, who barely noticed it from the spell placed in his mind by the knarke.

"Are you ready?" she asked them, still eyeing the original knarke as it drifted back and forth taunting her.

Barcinas nodded, but Sebastian continued to stare off.

"Now!" she yelled. Ashlynn dashed through the open space between the two oncoming beings. Each screeched in fury and launched after them. Barcinas pulled Sebastian along with him. Sebastian could only see his little sister and resisted the forward motion.

"Barc! Let go! I have to help her! I promised I would protect her!" he cried out, working against Barcinas.

Barcinas continued to pull him, ignoring his demands.

"He is hurting her, Barc! We were wrong! Father doesn't care about her! He will kill her!" he yelled.

Ashlynn turned around to check on their progression. "Sebastian! No!" she screamed as Sebastian lunged for a rock. Barcinas turned at Ashlynn's voice, but was not fast enough to avoid being hit. The rock connected with Barcinas's head, and he fell to the ground hurt. Sebastian took his chance to race after Odessa. He grabbed and held her tightly, yelling at an invisible attacker.

The knarke cackled. "You think you can save me, brother? You left me to die, and now you will suffer the same!"

The knarke reached through Sebastian, as if it were grabbing his heart to stop it from beating. Sebastian froze, his mouth agape in silent terror.

"No! Sebastian! No!" she screamed, unable to move to protect him.

A rock went hurling through the air, aimed directly at the being holding Sebastian. Ashlynn was sure it would make contact, and she was right. Except it made contact with Sebastian instead. The rock knocked Sebastian in the back of his head. The knarke backed away, alarmed. Sebastian fell to the ground, and Barcinas ran over to him. He bent down to listen for his heartbeat.

The other being flew at Barcinas. "You would save him, but send me to my death?" it shrieked.

Barcinas gazed up, his cheeks wet and streaked with dirt. "I did what I thought I was supposed to do. I did not kill you, Daia," he whispered back, full of confidence. "Get out of my memories!"

"No, I breathe in your fears. I can smell them on you. You sent me to my death at the hands of your master, and you worry daily how you will ever make it right," it spat back. "You can't. You will suffer for your decision to betray me, son!"

Sebastian opened his eyes and stared up at the being above them.

"I will not give into your taunts, you wicked being. I know my path, and I will live with my decisions. Now, leave us be!" he exploded. The strength of his words sent a ripple of power at each of the knarkes. They floated away in fear. As they disappeared from view, their collective voice spoke one last warning.

"You may have lived through us, but you will die at the hands of your companion who is not strong enough," they snickered.

Once they were out of sight, Ashlynn ran over to Sebastian and Barcinas.

"I am sorry, Barc," Sebastian murmured, rubbing his head. "I thought it really was Odessa. I couldn't see past the illusion."

Barcinas nodded, helping him to his feet.

"I am more concerned with their warning," Ashlynn said, surveying the area around them.

The three took in the space, trying to figure out where to go next. They had run from their spot of rest, but everything still looked the same. Each tree matched the next, with vines and roots covering the ground.

"I think we need to cover Sebastian's ears," she

whispered.

"Why?" he asked.

Ashlynn stared straight at him. "You are more susceptible to their tricks, Seb. If we cover your ears, then you can still follow us through the woods without hearing them. You will just have to stay focused on us."

His gaze shifted down with embarrassment.

"And we have to do it now," she continued. "Because the thing the knarkes warned about is almost here."

Sebastian and Barcinas were terrified—eyes wide, mouths slightly agape—at the idea of something approaching them without being able to hear or observe it. Once again, they couldn't see anything except the dark night against a backdrop of shadowed trees.

"It is a shadow," she mouthed. Her necklace was their only source of light and illuminated her lips as she accentuated each word. "I only know this because it bragged about taking us to our deaths. I think only I can hear its voice. It will be here soon, so let's cover his ears and go."

They stuffed his ears with moss right as a blood curdling howl pierced the night.

CHAPTER TWENTY THREE

Ashlynn glanced behind as they ran through the unknown, unsure of where to go. An outline moved in the dark, wet terrain blending in among the shadows. It blurred into the sway of the trees and only seemed to exist on the outskirts of Ashlynn's mind. If she stared at the spot she had seen it, then the image disappeared, leaving her confused and disoriented.

The farther they ran from their safe meadow, the foggier the forest became. She scanned the horizon to establish the best path out. The figure hid in her peripheral vision and Ashlynn turned her neck to face it head on. The moment she did, it vanished again.

Sebastian rubbed the back of his head and surveyed the area, as if expecting to get attacked the moment he dropped his guard. Barcinas continued to hold his hand, pulling him along like a mother tugging at a child. His confidence in Ashlynn was absolute. He kept his eyes on her at all times without bothering to scan the landscape.

Ashlynn's thoughts circled in confidence around the idea that Sebastian would stay safe if he kept his ears closed. They had to find a way out eventually, and she counted on her two companions to follow. Focusing on the path ahead, she remained in tune with her thoughts and movements.

"I don't see anything. I think it has left. Ash, is it still around?" Sebastian whimpered. Ashlynn's lack of answer caused him to remove the moss from his ears. The moment it was out, Sebastian screamed.

The shriek of agony and fear attacked Ashlynn's mind. She jumped as she was mentally pulled back to reality, unaware of the danger.

"What is wrong?" Ashlynn yelled over his screams. She searched around for the attack, but saw nothing. The shadow following them had disappeared entirely. "Barcinas! What happened? Why is Sebastian screaming?"

Barcinas's hollow look of regret caused the color to fade from her face. His words placed the final nail in the coffin. "He took out the moss.

Realizing the full intent of what he had said, she cried out, "Barc! Grab him! The Shadow has seeped into his mind. It has taken control of his fears!"

Barcinas switched hands for a tighter grip, while Sebastian slipped out of his hold. His eyes turned red mixed with his brown to create the effect of lava swirling throughout him.

"I have him now," came the voice within Sebastian. "He has accepted his fate and his death awaits."

"Sebastian. Can you hear me?" Ashlynn begged. "Sebastian, fight back. He is only showing you what you fear most. It isn't real, Seb. Follow our voices out of the darkness."

Sebastian didn't respond but gaped at her in confusion. Without warning, Barcinas slapped Sebastian across his face. The impact and surprise caused the shadow to slip in control long enough for Sebastian to regain his composure for a few seconds.

"I'm sorry," he muttered, his voice hoarse. As if he were being burned, he screamed in agony. He thrashed until he was free from their grasp and sprinted between the trees.

Ashlynn and Barcinas took off after him. His talent for running and new knowledge of the forest gave him the advantage. Barcinas sped past Ashlynn, but stumbled as a root rose to trip him. She leaped over the roots and ducked in time to miss a branch swinging down.

"The forest is against us!" she called. "It is trying to keep him in its grasp."

Barcinas picked up his speed and lunged at Sebastian. Sebastian leaped out of the way, dashing around a tree as Barcinas slammed to the ground. Ashlynn jumped over him to catch Sebastian. Up ahead the trees opened to a clearing. Sebastian increased his speed as Ashlynn pushed herself with every piece of energy and determination she had. Her recent sprints for safety had increased her stamina, and she couldn't help but grin at the thought. Beside her she could hear Barcinas making his way past her, but she didn't glance away to check. As they got closer, Ashlynn noticed that the receding trees were pushing them toward the end of the forest.

"Barcinas! The forest ends up ahead," she yelled out.

As she hurled those words, she noticed that not only did the forest end, but so did the ground. A cliff awaited them, and Sebastian was headed straight for it.

"Barcinas! Stop! It's a cliff!" she screamed.

But Barcinas showed no signs of slowing down. When he made it to Sebastian, he reached out to grab him, but Sebastian leaped off the cliff without a second thought. Barcinas's fingers grasped the air as he slid off the cliff. He held onto the last bit of ground left. Ashlynn ran to tug him back onto land. Below lay an ocean with jagged rocks and enraged waves beating against them. The same water her mother must have drowned in.

"He jumped," Barcinas said, dropping to the dirt. "I tried to grab him, but he jumped. He laughed at me, Ash. He knew that I was trying to save him, and he wouldn't let me!"

"Barc," she soothed, "it wasn't him. It was the being inside of him. It controlled every form of fear in his head. He didn't see a cliff."

She glanced over to the edge, eyes wildly searching for Sebastian. Dread and apprehension washed over her as she realized their next move.

"What are we going to do, Ash?" Barcinas cried out.

"We are going to jump," she replied calmly.

He glanced up at her. "What? We are going to jump? We will die!" His eyes showed a fear she hadn't seen before.

"Barc, we have to go after him. It is the only thing that feels right," she explained.

In pure trust, Barcinas stood shakily and held out his hand. "Okay. I will do it. To save Sebastian. But promise me you won't let go," he begged.

She smiled on this gesture of mutual friendship between them and at how far they had come. "I promise," she whispered.

They stood at the edge of the cliff, hand in hand gazing over.

"Let's get a running jump," he suggested.

She nodded and walked back with him.

"Are you ready?" she asked.

"No," he admitted, "but I would do anything for Sebastian."

Ashlynn tore her gaze from the ocean in front of them to Barcinas's face. She knew in that moment that the Barcinas of her past was a façade. This man holding her hand held much more value than she ever expected.

"Me too. I would also do the same for you, Barc."

He squeezed her hand tighter. They let out a breath and then, as if their souls were connected, they ran in sync and jumped off the cliff into the treacherous sea, falling seventy or so feet into the water below. Ashlynn swore she heard a maniacal laugh right before her feet broke the surface of the water.

Submerged, Ashlynn struggled to keep hold of Barcinas's hand, a wave forced them apart. She reached out to find him but grasped only water. Swimming to the top, she broke through the surface in time to catch a giant wave as it tumbled over her. Ashlynn had a brief second to breathe before being sucked back under. She opened her eyes and swam against the current, knowing she had to find them before they were lost in the endless waves.

Her lungs cried out as she fought to swim back up for air. She burst through the water as the final wisps died in her lungs and watched the sky darkening above her. A powerful current swept her closer to an enormous whirlpool.

"Dammit! I am sorry, Great Goddess, for whatever I did to anger you!" she called out in desperation.

She saw a flash of black hair with a single hand reaching up out of the water to her right. She locked on to his position right as a wave crashed over him.

"Sebastian?" she screamed.

Gulping in the biggest breath she could manage, Ashlynn dove back down. In front of her, she saw a body gradually drifting to the bottom and watched as the current tossed it back and forth as if rocking a child to sleep. Except this was a sleep Sebastian would never wake from. Ashlynn struggled to make it toward him. She was pushed back with every stroke. The waves held her in place as she slowly ran out of breath. In her final moments of clarity, she gazed up out of the water to the dark sky.

She begged the Goddess to hear her plea and keep them safe. Ashlynn closed her eyes and let go of her breath. The water rushed in as she forgot to struggle. The ecstasy of painlessly floating took over. Her body went numb and everything around her felt cold, as cold as the deep ocean around her.

CHAPTER TWENTY FOUR

Don't give in. Push through the water. Swim up.
Though she wasn't sure she wanted to. Too tired of
fighting. That wasn't what she wanted either. These
words flowed through her as she struggled to move her
fingers and wiggle her toes. The desire to fight was still
there. She pushed with the last bit of strength she had to
clumsily swim her body to the surface. Right as her hand
broke through the water, claws grasped her tightly
around her shoulders and flew her over the ocean with
such speed that Ashlynn could barely hold on to her
thoughts. This felt familiar, yet she couldn't place when
she had last been pulled from the water by a giant beast.

She glanced at the being above her, but her vision was
blurred. All she could make out was a dark gold blob in
front of the sky blue background. The storm dissipated
as the sun broke through the clouds to shine down on
them. Ashlynn closed her eyes and breathed deeply. The
roar of a beast could be heard in the distance as
everything turned black inside of her. She flitted into
unconsciousness. Her fervent friend welcomed her with

an embrace of darkness.

The sun shone on Ashlynn's face as something pinched her cheek, causing her to open one eye. The sand felt warm and wet beneath her face as she lay to one side. A crab as big as her hand snapped at her with its small claw. She sat up abruptly which sent the crab scurrying away. The blood rushed through her body as she pushed up, causing her to fall back down dizzy. Ashlynn rolled onto her back and let the sun warm her face as she breathed in salty air. The smell cleansed and purified her inside and out. She opened her left eye, then her right as they adjusted to the brightness. She sat up slowly. Her mind was still hazy from the events that brought her here.

The image of a massive beast soared through her mind. She closed her eyes to focus and gasped.

A dragon had saved her.

Just like in her dream. Could this be the same dragon?

Ashlynn searched for the beast but spotted Sebastian on the sand instead. She took another breath and gently pushed herself up. Her whole right side was numb from lying down for so long. Her left knee burned from a gash, and her arm was still cut and swollen from the knarke's attack. The wound on her knee was deep, but not nearly as severe as the claw marks in her arm. She sensed poison swirling around inside of her, attacking other parts of her body. Ashlynn thought it was odd that the infection hadn't spread, but she attributed that to her ability to heal herself. Feeling a numbness and blinding pain throughout her entire body, she realized that those individual wounds were inconsequential to her overall state.

With as much intention as possible, she hobbled to Sebastian. It took everything she had to not run and hug him, but she knew doing so would only hurt herself more. A few more steps. Her knee pulsed with pain as she slid it across the rough sand. The grains had formed a crust around her cuts, and she mentally prepared herself for the inevitable cleaning process that would later come.

Ashlynn studied Sebastian who was flat on his back. His hair was knotted and his right cheek was red while the other was covered with seaweed. She peeled it off as his body rose and fell slowly. Each breath seemed to be forgotten then remembered at the last moment. Once she was sure he was okay, she tried to rouse him.

"Sebastian," she whispered. "Can you hear me?"

She reached for her water to pour over him, only to find it wasn't attached to anymore. Ashlynn searched in each direction, hoping to spot Barcinas. Silence emanated all around and inside of her. Even the gulls hushed and the trees paused their swaying in respect. She lowered herself back down and put her head on Sebastian's shoulder. On a strange beach, without water and near exhaustion, Ashlynn was unsure of what to do next.

"Look what I have found here!" came a voice so unlike her own that she squinted her eyes in intrigue.

A shadow hid her in shade as the silhouette of a man approached. Standing over her and staring down at her with an amused smile, was a dark eyed man with coarse black hair. His hair was tied like tiny ropes all over his head. Ashlynn had never seen that style before. She tried to speak, but her throat felt as rough as the sand beneath her.

"Don't talk. We have plenty of time for that later. Drink some water first," cautioned the enchanting man.

He carefully lifted her head and poured cool water down her throat. It burned and soothed at the same time. She wanted to drink more but coughed from the pressure building inside as she chugged it.

"Not too much. Let your body get used to it," he said. She sipped slower. "There. Much better. Can you sit up?"

She nodded and lifted her arms to push up. He helped her without asking. When Ashlynn was seated, he moved to check out Sebastian.

"Your friend looks better on the outside than you, but I am not sure about his insides. I will need to take you both back to the other human we found," he said, muttering the last part more to himself than to her.

The joy on Ashlynn's face showed because the man smiled in response.

"He is fine. Not a scratch on him, either. He is already coherent but silent. He won't talk to us except to ask about you two. If you can walk, I will take you to him as I carry this one."

Ashlynn nodded so he helped her up, steadied her, then bent down and picked up Sebastian like a bag of hay, placing him like a log across his shoulders.

"We will go slow, but be sure to stay alert. There are many secret traps here. I wouldn't want to get you off the beach just for you to fall prey to one of those," he said, smiling as if the thought were amusing to him. "My name is Kristopher, by the way. Welcome to the Queendom of the Elves."

Ashlynn felt tears form as she walked behind him. She grinned. They had made it. Somehow. She breathed out a sigh and struggled to respond, "Ashlynn. And thank you."

Kristopher didn't turn around, but she could see a smile playing at his lips. As they walked, Kristopher told her a story of the past day. She listened intently with each step, reveling in the knowledge that she had come to the end of her travels.

"Last night, we had an unusual storm appear. A waterspout fell from the sky and thunder crashed around my cousin and I. Curious to see it up close, we rushed to the other side of the beach and saw a huge beast flying, carrying something in its claws."

He paused and peeked at her, gauging her reaction. Ashlynn smiled, unsure of what to say or do.

He continued, "My cousin, Niko, and I have experience with unique beasts. When we got to the water's edge, the storm vanished, and we found your friend face down on the sand. We brought him to a hut outside of the queendom gates. He awoke earlier this morning and the moment he did he pressed us about you two." Once again, his smile betrayed an amused reaction, and Ashlynn had to stop herself from rolling her eyes.

She questioned his intentions. Everything he said sounded like they were already indebted to the Elves for saving them. If that were true then she would have to play by their rules to find the answers they needed. A small piece of her questioned if she even wanted to go back to Levander. To fight with the king and struggle to save him from himself. Instead of letting her mind run in circles, she studied the area as they walked. The beautiful, tropical landscape gradually shifted into a dense forest of the most ancient trees she had ever encountered. Ashlynn held her breath each time she passed one and even thought she imagined a face staring back at her when she glanced at them.

Fascinated yet terrified, Ashlynn craned her neck to find the tops of the trees. Doing so caused her to bump into Kristopher, who had stopped to talk to the guards. He bowed slowly and nudged her to do the same. She did, uncomfortably, and he rose with a signal of his hand. The gesture looked personal and secretive, but stirred a knowing inside of her. His hand traveled from his brow in a semicircle to his cheek, then from his lips back up. He glanced at Ashlynn. She tried her best to mimic him, earning a feral, teeth exposing grin.

The guards repeated the same gesture but added a few embellishments. Ashlynn tried to pay attention to their response, but got lost when the guards differed in their movements. They were in sync while their meanings varied. The result was an emphatic promise and warning. Ashlynn wasn't sure how she knew this but quickly passed through the white aspen wood and silver glowing gates as it magickally swung open to allow her through. Ashlynn felt the warning inside of her, almost as if it had been meant specifically for her. Yet she wasn't sure it had any other meaning than to open the gate. Hopefully their journey's end had led them to a place safer than Levander, but she wasn't entirely sure, and she shivered at the thought.

The gates shut behind them inaudibly, and Ashlynn released a breath she didn't realize she was holding. Around her, elves shopped, traded goods, and conversed. They were living their life right here and didn't give her an ounce of attention. She focused on Kristopher as she walked through the town, trying not to gawk at them. She didn't want to attract any attention until she knew what was expected of her. Their skin seemed to radiate pure light, as if the sun shining down on them were only a tool to activate their magnificent beauty. Most she saw had long, hair that hung down their well built, slender bodies.

A certain female caught her eye. She was the most ethereal being Ashlynn had ever seen. Her skin was as pale as a swan with the softest blonde curls falling around her face. She had them pulled back into a long braid, which highlighted her sky blue eyes and pointed ears. Her face was delicate and full of life.

"That is Iseult," Kristopher whispered. "Stay away from her. If you want to survive this trip."

Ashlynn glanced up, expecting to see an amused face, but instead noticed a seriousness in his eyes that shocked

her.

"She is the second most dangerous elf in the land," he warned.

He didn't continue, which itched at Ashlynn. She knew he was pulling her along and wanted her to ask. Feeling the familiar game of cat and mouse, Ashlynn realized the role she was to play with him. He started walking again, and she had to push herself to catch up. He stopped in front of a hut that was covered in vines and tree branches. It looked more like an overgrown shrub than the type of mud huts she had seen in the rural outskirts of Levander.

When she reached him, she asked, "Who is the first?"

He smiled with his teeth bared, but the answer didn't come from him. It came from behind him.

"The Queen is the deadliest being in the land and throughout the world," replied a voice. The sound triggered a reaction in her body as she recognized its resonate tone. "If you didn't know that before, then you better learn it now."

He appeared from around Kristopher, and Ashlynn gaped in surprise. In front of her stood the shadow who saved her at the party. The sun blinded her view of him, but his deep sapphire eyes and voice gave him away. His hair was as dark as his eyes, and he stood just above

Kristopher. Ashlynn took a breath to steady herself as she wondered if he remembered her and their encounter at her birthday party. He had stayed hidden in the shadows though, so she couldn't be sure.

"I take it you are the Ashlynn he won't be quiet about? Well, go on inside. Kris, put the other one on the mat. Soon we will have answers, and then we will know what to do with you," he replied, directing that last statement at her. Without a hint of recognition, he charged through the flap, without bothering to wait for her.

Ashlynn snorted. Either he didn't remember her, or he didn't know her because the man that night was nicer than this brute. She brushed the sand off her skirt and followed them into the hut. A candle sat near Barcinas, lighting the back of the space as the sun shining through gave the most coverage. Seeing him alive and whole gave her such joy that she couldn't help but run to hug him. He seemed surprised but embraced her back, his warmth and steady heart beat calming hers. She scowled over at her new captors and took seat. Kristopher glanced back at her and shrugged a cocky grin before studying his companion. The shadow from her dreams glared at him and then at her.

"My name is Nikolai, and I am the diplomatic emissary for the Queen," he said, his eyes holding hers as if testing her. He peered down at Sebastian and murmured to Kristopher. Ashlynn couldn't hear what he said.

An elf had saved her that night, which was something she had not expected. A sigh through her nose helped to release her pent up tension. She rolled her eyes, then straightened her stance. Barcinas sat beside her and reached a hand to hold hers. Ashlynn gripped it tightly, noticing that Nikolai carefully watched them.

"I know," Barcinas whispered to her. "He is a brute, but his eyes are as if the depths of the ocean have grabbed my soul and is holding it for ransom. Don't fall too hard."

Ashlynn ignored his words as he squeezed her hand for reassurance. She would never have believed that being in Barcinas's presence could be comforting.

"It's good to have you back," he muttered.

She leaned her head on his shoulder in response. "We made it, Barc."

"Yes, we did," he replied. "But will we make it out?"

Ashlynn didn't respond, because she was wondering the same thing. Doing so felt too real, and she wanted to relish in having time to rest before unpacking what was to come. It was hard enough to get here. The thought of going back stifled her.

Breathe. One breath at a time. We have found them. The Queendom of the Elves. It was crazy to think that after all they had experienced, they were finally here. Surely, the rest would be easier now. Ashlynn continued to breathe as the control she acquired on the journey quickly dissipated around her. She had to remind herself, yet again, that her control was only a desire and an illusion.

Kristopher situated Sebastian on a mat and grabbed a wet cloth to wipe him down. The damp rubbing roused him.

"Ashlynn? Ash! Where are you?" he called.

Ashlynn and Barcinas stooped down to reassure him, but their presence didn't calm him. "Ashlynn! Barcinas! Where are you? Please answer me!" came his frantic voice.

Ashlynn froze, unable to breathe or answer him. Barcinas grabbed her hand, squeezing it as a reminder to be present and trust.

"Sebastian, we are here," she replied, trying to keep the emotion and fear out of her voice.

"Ashlynn? I can't see you! I only see black! Can you light a candle?" he asked.

Ashlynn could feel the hope in his voice and recognized the fear on his face. She knew he wanted her to confirm that it was indeed dark around them, because denying that would mean something even scarier. Ashlynn held her breath and turned away.

CHAPTER TWENTY FIVE

Seb, it's me," replied Barcinas in a steady voice. "A candle *is* lit, and the sun is shining through." He scooted beside Sebastian and rubbed his hand gently. "Something has happened to your sight. You've been through a terrible accident, and may have gone temporarily blind. Let's give your sight time to come back."

Ashlynn hoped he was right and that this change was not permanent.

Sebastian stared up, trusting the direction of their voice and shook his head. "No! Barcinas, this isn't funny! I am not playing one of your games right now! Ashlynn! Tell me Barcinas is joking!" he demanded.

Ashlynn did not know how to respond. Her affirmation would only cause him more pain. But in her silence, Sebastian knew. He touched his open eyes and placed his hands over them, rotating them in hopes of seeing something. Tears rolled out of his open eyes and down his cheeks. She had never seen Sebastian show such sadness and despair. His tears and silence were deafening.

"Seb," Ashlynn tried, "we have made it to the Elves. We are in their queendom. They brought us to this hut after we..." she paused, unsure of how to address their last encounters, "after we woke from that horrible experience."

She wanted to go on but didn't know what to say. Sebastian kept his hands in front of him, as if repeating the movements would replace his sight. Ashlynn noticed his wounds again and reached for a rag to wipe him down.

"I can rub him," Barcinas said, reaching to take the cloth from her.

She let him take it from her hands, unsure of what to do next.

"No, let me," Kristopher said, intruding on their space. "You both need to rest, and it is a sign of hospitality from the Elves to nurse someone back to health." He took the cloth from Barcinas, ignoring his outrage and sat to rub Sebastian's face. "Sebastian, my name is Kristopher, and I am here to help you heal," he said, gently combing through his hair as he rubbed his cut.

"Can you heal my eyes?" Sebastian said, almost too quiet to hear.

"No, Sebastian. Not yet. That is a possibility for later on, but right now there is other work that must be done.

More important work, if I am correct," he said, almost sounding sincere.

Sebastian nodded. Ashlynn wasn't sure if he heard Kristopher's response. Barcinas sat at Sebastian's feet, while his eyes stayed on Kristopher, watching his every move and gesture.

"Ashlynn," came a voice behind her. She turned around and saw his ever flowing eyes. "Come sit down and tell me what you remember as I bandage your knee and arm, if you please." He tacked on that last piece as if it were a forgotten thought.

She frowned at him, unsure of what to say and or how to feel.

"Please, Ashlynn. Your wounds are getting worse, and there are some things I would like to know before the queen's guard arrives," he said, gesturing impatiently to the mat in front of him.

She hobbled to the mat and sat on a cushion, ignoring the searing pain in her body. He wet the wound on her knee. Being this close to him made her skin crawl, and she wasn't sure if it was from fear or excitement. She breathed through her mouth, so she wouldn't inhale his scent, and held it while he meticulously cleared out the sand. Ashlynn released her breath and pent up aggression toward him. The scratch of his calloused hand on her leg distracted her from the smell of the ointment and herbs he used, some of which burned and caused her to gag.

As Nikolai cleaned, he barreled through a series of questions. "How did you make it here? Where did you come from? How did you survive the storm? Are there any more of you?" he asked, avoiding eye contact with her.

She gawked at him as the questions poured out. "Oh, is that all?" she retorted.

"No," he said, "but those are the most pressing."

She glanced around the hut and responded without looking at him. "You said the queen is sending men here? For what?"

He put the herbs on her cut, causing her to wince, then blew on her knee to flatten them. Peering up at her, he responded, "Trust for trust. She wants to know exactly what I ask and more, except her way isn't as gentle or kind. It is invasive, but to gain access to the inner realm you must submit to her methods." His voice was tense and rushed.

"Why are you informing me ahead of time?" she asked, stalling. Nikolai didn't respond but held her gaze. "What will they ask? And how?" she tried again, but he continued to stare.

Breathing out another sigh, she nodded. He went back

248

to laying the herbs on and wrapping her knee as she answered. "We come from Levander. There are only three of us. We arrived through a barrier in the desert, and it took us to a rainforest. We leaped into the ocean after we were chased by knarkes, and Sebastian was attacked in his mind by a shadow," she said, releasing it like waves tumbling over her body before she found her desire to live again.

He finished wrapping her knee and gave her a curious look with one eyebrow raised. His eyes softened a bit, but his body was still rigid and full of control which accentuated his tense jawline.

"Your responses are appreciated. I will answer your questions before they get here. Heed my warning, you are only allowed in this area, the trading village. You are mostly free to come and go from here. If you submit for the questioning from the queen's men, then whatever they find will be used against you," he said, conveying the benefits and shackles possible. "So if there is anything that could incite them to hold you prisoner, I need to know." He paused for an answer, but she stared back at him waiting for him to finish. "They will ask if you concede to questioning and when you say yes, they will search your mind." Ashlynn sat back alarmed, but Nikolai went on as if he didn't notice her response. "It isn't usually painful." He said this last part to all three of them.

"Consent must be given, though, because it is forbidden to enter another being's mind without permission. The result is catastrophic to the invader. Now, your arm is in worse damage. It has become infected and will take more than just herbs to heal." As he said this, he placed his hands over her wound, covering it entirely. She winced at his grip but held still. After a few seconds, her arm burned. She cried out and pulled back, but he held on tight. Staring at his face as his eyes remained closed and focused, Ashlynn calmed herself, trusting that what he was doing was for healing and not torture. A few minutes passed before he released her.

"What was that about?" she asked, glaring.

Nikolai studied her but didn't answer. Scowling at him, she glanced at her arm and blushed when she realized he had healed the poison. The gashes were still visible, but the infection had vanished. Nikolai reached over to bandage it, while Ashlynn sat back in surprise. "How did you do that?" she whispered.

He gazed at her, eyes twinkling. "Magick," he whispered back, with a slight smile that he quickly hid.

She just stared at him, unsure of how to feel or react now.

"What about Sebastian?" Barcinas asked, trying to

ease the awkwardness. "He can barely sit up." He paused before continuing, "Won't the mental questioning tire him out? What if it is too much?"

Sebastian didn't act as if he heard Barcinas's words. He had placed his hands next to his body, clearly giving up on his mission to see them.

"Yes, it will tire him out, but it won't incapacitate him in any way he isn't already experiencing," Kristopher responded.

"What if we say no," Barcinas asked right as a silhouette appeared in the doorway.

"Why would you say no?" responded the figure.

They each gazed up as a tall elf strode in. His voice was stern but had a low vibration that held your mind captive. The sunlight hit his face and features, causing her to take note of his long, dark blonde hair tied up into a knot at the back of his head. The rest of his hair was shaved underneath, which made his intense eyes stand out against his light skin.

His eyes searched around the room, taking in the three new visitors and halted on Ashlynn. She peered into his forest green eyes and noticed a movement of gold swirling around his pupil like a snake mesmerizing you. The elf in the doorway chuckled and headed to Nikolai. They clasped hands with a brotherly gesture and then turned to face them. The room grew thick with silence and tension as they waited to hear his declaration.

Nikolai announced him instead. "This is Kaenon, the queen's commander. He is here to conduct your questioning."

"Actually, I am not. I am here to arrest the one who flew. I am here for the dragon," he said, studying each of them.

Kristopher glanced at Nikolai, who was trading stares with the new elf. They seemed in deep concentration, as if they were having a match to see who could stare the longest. After a few minutes of their intense exchange, Nikolai nodded and sat beside Ashlynn.

"Now, which of you can transform into a dragon?" Kaenon asked.

None of them answered. Ashlynn didn't know if she was more confused or stunned. "Sir, none of us..."

Before she could finish, a howl echoed from the tall elf. "I am not a sir. Only the queen's commander. You may call me Kaenon."

Trying to hide her embarrassment as her entire face and neck reddened, she swallowed. "Okay then. Kaenon, none of us can turn into a dragon. The being that saved me from the water, I have never seen before."

Kaenon eyed each of them. Ashlynn held his gaze,

while Sebastian looked around the room, trying to understand what was happening. Only Barcinas shifted in his seat, uncomfortable.

"The Dragons died out in the last war. They no longer exist," she finished quietly.

"Well, that is laughably false. But if you say none of you are the dragon, then I have to take all of you into our custody until we are able to figure out who crossed into our territory," he declared, still studying each of them. "Dragons must have permission to enter this realm, just as any other area in which they don't live. It is part of the agreement with Queen Elspaeth and the Dragons of old. Even if a new dragon doesn't know this, they are subject to obeying the rules of their ancestors. We all are."

The room fell silent. Ashlynn felt guilty as she thought about her ability to somehow breathe fire. The thought of Sebastian locked up in his current condition made Ashlynn cringe. She wasn't sure what it entailed, but she would rather admit to something that wasn't true than to subject him to more uncertainty right now.

Ashlynn cleared her throat, and each person turned to her. "Well, I guess...,"

"No, Ashlynn!" Barcinas interrupted. "I won't let you take the fall for it. I am the dragon you are seeking."

CHAPTER TWENTY SIX

Ashlynn's eyes widened.

Sebastian scoffed. "The truth finally comes out."

Ashlynn could barely process Barcinas's confession or Sebastian's response.

Kaenon smirked. "Welcome, young dragon. We are pleased you have graced this queendom with your presence. In your ignorance or disregard for our customs, you have entered without consent. Please follow me."

Barcinas hesitated, looking back and forth between Ashlynn and Sebastian. "I respect that I have unknowingly violated the old agreement, and I agree to come with you, but I would like to be here for their procedure."

Kaenon glanced at Nikolai then nodded to Barcinas. "You can stay until Niko..." he paused as if something had caught his attention. He kept eye contact with Barcinas, but his mind seemed elsewhere as his eyes darted back and forth. It looked like he was mentally reading a book. "I stand corrected." He coughed. "You can stay until I search everyone's mind. Then we will leave."

Only Ashlynn noticed Nikoali releasing an inaudible breath. He acted like his life had hinged on what Kaenon almost said.

Kaenon faced each them. "If any of you give consent, which I highly recommend you do, then I will touch your mind and navigate through your thoughts and intentions. Understand that you won't be able to hide anything from me and doing so could be extremely painful. Now," he asked with a smirk, cracking his knuckles, "who will go first?"

Kaenon, still shadowed with the sun at his back, glanced around at each of them. His eyes landed on Barcinas. "We could always do a piece of your investigation here," he said, smirking.

"No. I do not agree. I will not let you wander through my mind," Barcinas announced.

Kaenon grinned, enjoying the challenge. "You will have to consent to leave our lands, young dragon. You chose to enter without approval from the queen, so now you must follow her rules to leave," he explained. "The rest of you are free to stay in the outer realm but to enter, you must submit. However, we can definitely handle yours back in your cell. So, I ask again. Who is first?"

"Me," Ashlynn said, before her voice could give out. "I have nothing to hide." She sent Barcinas a kind smile, and he dipped his head to her in gratitude.

"Alright then. The female first. What is your name?" the elf asked.

"Ashlynn."

He nodded, dropping his smile. Kaenon stepped forward. "I will put my fingers on you like this," he explained, carefully positioning his thumbs on her temples and his two pointer fingers coming up to a triangle at the top center of her forehead, resting right below her hairline. "You will feel a slight jolt," he warned. Ashlynn breathed in and noticed a buzz spinning through her head, sending pulses down to the pit of her stomach. "Good," he said. "Now, breathe through your nose."

Ashlynn focused on her breaths, intentionally drawing her deepest ones while using the knot on top of his head as a focal point. Tears formed around her eyes as the intensity continued to permeate inside her skull.

"Relax, Ashlynn," Nikolai's voice came beside her. "He will sweep through and be done. Right, Kaenon?"

Ashlynn took her eyes off of Kaenon's hair and glanced at him. While Kaenon didn't respond to Nikolai, his face held a smile that he tried to hide. She studied Nikolai, who gave her the same raised eyebrow she distinctly remembered from the night at the ball, and she closed her eyes.

A few moments later, Kaenon stepped back out of her mind and her space. "You are cleared, Ashlynn. And I have to say, you have quite the history."

She held his stare, ready to defend herself and her story. His eyes bore into hers, and she saw, deep down, sympathy and understanding. While she couldn't be sure, she got the impression that Kaenon would do his best to not share everything with Queen Elspaeth.

"You are next," Kaenon announced, speaking directly to Sebastian.

Barcinas's head peeled up to look at Kaenon and then at Ashlynn. "Are we sure this is the right thing to do? We don't know what is going on with Sebastian, and it could make his wound worse. Maybe we should give him a few days."

Ashlynn wanted to respond, but didn't want to speak for Sebastian. She shuffled to him. Sebastian, somehow knowing she was near, reached his hand out to hers. She grasped his tightly, relishing in this fleeting connection with her cousin. Before she could get the words out, Sebastian moved his head closer to hers. She leaned into him and took in his face as he got closer.

"Ash," he murmured, "I need to do this. Maybe he can help, and if he can't, then maybe someone closer to the castle can. Trust me. I may have lost my sight, but I haven't lost my mind."

Ashlynn admired his strength and determination—he knew something was off and he was ready to commit to mending it. She just hoped his resolve would blend from his internal struggle to their outward one. She gave her support by kissing him on the cheek, which made him pull back. She chuckled at the normalcy of his movement, remembering the past few days. Sebastian nodded his head and closed his eyes. Kaenon placed his hands the exact same way on Sebastian and prepared him.

"Sebastian!" Barcinas called out. "Please, just wait a few days!"

Sebastian ignored his request, keeping his eyes closed and focused his breath. Ashlynn glanced at Barcinas, hoping to send him comfort, yet Barcinas's face was plagued with doubt and fear. Anger rolled off of him at the betrayal and lack of trust.

"You will feel a slight jolt," Kaenon informed Sebastian, "and now breathe."

Sebastian's hand started to shake from the interaction, but his face stayed serene with his eyes closed. Ashlynn counted his breaths, and by the time she reached thirty, Kaenon was done.

"You are cleared, Sebastian. Your experience was faster since you seem to be too weak to fight me from your trip to Varjo," he revealed.

"What is Varjo?" Ashlynn asked, still gazing at Sebastian. Kaenon's response had jolted him. He did not like to be considered weak.

"Varjo," Nikolai responded instead, "is where you were sent when you left the oasis and arrived in the rainforest."

Ashlynn gaped at him. "The forest we arrived in after walking through the portal is called Varjo? That treacherous place, with fear sucking Knarkes, has a name?"

The three companions were silent as they waited for Nikolai or someone to answer.

"It is where we send travelers who wish to enter the realm," Kaenon said. "It is their test to see if they are true hearted and able to connect with us through an honest and open energy."

"You subjected us," Barcinas called, "to danger just to see if our energy was open?"

Kaenon turned to Barcinas, who was gazing at Ashlynn and Sebastian with sadness. "Yes. It is a requirement of Queen Elspaeth's."

"I wondered if the Elves had opened the portal for us to arrive there, but doubted it after the atrocities we faced. Such a traumatic experience just to enter this land," Ashlynn muttered.

Kaenon studied her with his mouth shut about the topic. "Are you ready to leave now?" Kaenon asked.

He glanced between his companions and the elves. She could see the cogs working in his mind, and she couldn't sit by and not do anything while he was taken away.

"If Barcinas lets you into his mind, would you still have to take him?" she asked.

Before Kaenon could respond, Barcinas answered for him. "No, Ashlynn. I will not let them. Even if it means I am taken away."

She nodded, tears forming as the feeling of uncertainty swarmed her. Barcinas had become a dear friend during their trek here, and not knowing when, or if, she would see him again was terrifying.

"I would like to talk to them privately before we leave," he said.

Nikolai and Kristopher left without another word.

"I will wait for you out here. If you choose to escape instead of come with me, then your companions will be imprisoned in your place. Do you understand?" Kaenon asked.

"I understand," came Barcinas's response, not bothering to raise his voice since Kaenon had already disappeared.

Ashlynn faced Barcinas while holding Sebastian's hand. "What are you thinking? Let them look into your mind. They might release you!"

"No, Ashlynn. Marcus taught me to never relinquish the vulnerability of your mind to anyone unless there is no other option. Here, we have options," he explained.

Ashlynn wanted to speak up against the plan, but she knew she couldn't change his mind.

"He is right. Barcinas has lied to us enough for now. We will talk with him when he has his story straight," Sebastian said.

Ashlynn glared at her cousin like he had lost his mind, remembering at the last moment that he couldn't see her as she shifted between her two companions. Split between her cousin and her new friendship, she stood. Barcinas didn't defend himself or contradict Sebastian's accusations. Instead, he looked at Sebastian with sad eyes and put a hand on Ashlynn's shoulder.

"Come on, young dragon. It is time to go," Kaenon announced, standing in the doorway.

"I will see you soon, Ash. I am tough. Don't worry about me." He gave her a lopsided smile, squeezed her hand, and followed after Kaenon without another glance at Sebastian.

CHAPTER TWENTY SEVEN

She stood in silence for a few minutes. The air between her and Sebastian felt stilted, and Ashlynn wasn't sure she wanted to have the hard conversation about his time with the Shadow being and decision to turn his back on Barcinas.

Instead, she took a few calming breaths and said, "I'll let Nikolai and Kristopher know we are ready to leave." Without giving Sebastian time to respond, she walked out. The two cousins stood a few steps from the entrance and paused in mid-conversation to notice her.

"We are ready to go. Would someone help me carry Sebastian through the gate?" she asked, glancing around the square instead of having to experience their eyes again.

"Don't worry about him," Kristopher said with a smile. "I'll take care of him. You go on ahead with Nikolai, and I will bring Sebastian up."

Before Ashlynn could process his comment, he hurried past her back into the hut. She glanced at Nikolai. "Well, lead the way, I suppose," she said, putting more confidence in those words than she actually felt.

Nikolai bowed and escorted her through the outer village to a gate made of birch, vines, and silver. Ashlynn could sense a vibration coming from it that set her on edge. He signaled to the guards with a gesture so fast and specific that she couldn't replicate if she tried, which she did attempt behind his back after he walked past the gate. She followed him up a little path and stopped beside him in awe of the land she surveyed.

"Welcome to the Queendom of Miras, the land of the Elven folk and stronghold of Her Majesty, Queen Elspaeth," Nikolai formally announced.

A chill circulated through her body as he said those words, like a spell had been incanted over her. She stepped ahead of him, and her breath hitched. The inner realm was the most magnificent place Ashlynn had ever seen. Below stood a castle made of stone, mixed with different types of metal and wood. The arches flowed up to the sky and back down, moving more like a river flowing through the land than architecture. The doors shimmered, and the windows were cut through the stone to reveal an openness among the people and the queen. Surrounding the castle was a land rich of laughter, dancing, food, and wares that paled in comparison to the outer realm. A few shops stood out toward the edge of the water, but most of the homes and businesses were clustered around the castle.

"This is one of the only spots in Miras where you can see the castle and the surrounding area in totality. The only other spot that displays all of Miras is on top of the mountain of Pyr," he explained, pronouncing the mountain as a guttural purr.

Ashlynn held back her giggle as she imagined him as a mountain lion. While she caught her breath, Nikolai jogged down the slope with ease, unaware that the path ahead was a long trek for someone with a hurt knee. But Ashlynn was not willing to show any weakness in this foreign, beautiful land. The main thing she had learned from her uncle was to never show fear. She was unsure of what to expect when it came to the Elves' customs and expectations, but she held her head high and wobbled down the slope with tiny steps.

With each purposeful step, she kept her goal in mind. They would find what they needed to know to save King Theodore. Then Barcinas, Sebastian, and she would head back. Yet again, she questioned if she wanted to go back and face it all.

This time, she didn't have an answer.

They arrived at a little house near the water's edge after traveling for about an hour. The sun had descended behind the mountains in the distance. Being found on the beach this morning seemed like such a long time ago. Even the thought of leaving Levander six days ago sent her mind spiraling. Her path was now in the control of a race she hadn't known still existed.

Ashlynn surveyed the water around her and noticed a beautiful cascade of stars and swirls hovering over the sea. The intensity of this pure moment with the vast sky overhead brought her immense joy. She closed her eyes, reimagined the image in her mind, and breathed in the celestial goodness. When she opened her eyes, the vision had forever shifted. Ashlynn realized her place on this planet was small compared to all that was out there, but that didn't make her feel insignificant. A grin emerged at the insight and peace she had received. Turning from the magnificence of the scene, Ashlynn spotted Nikolai studying her with a strange expression. For a moment, they stared at each other in a way that felt as if they were laying their souls out in the open.

A cough interrupted their connective exposure. Both turned to see Kristopher standing with Sebastian leaning on him. Kristopher had his amused smirk covering his face, obviously giddy at their interaction. Sebastian didn't ask why they had stopped or make any other noise. He appeared to be resolved to silence on his new path toward healing.

"I can see we are interrupting something, although I had no idea silent stares could be so vulnerable and revealing," Kristopher commented, helping Sebastian walk into the house.

Nikolai cleared his throat and gestured for Ashlynn to follow. She stepped through the door and saw a comfortable place with cushions and rugs all over. Ashlynn expected a table and chairs, or even a lounge, yet every room she was led through showed a humble homage that evolved from living close to the ground. It reminded her of Marcus's apartment that day she had sat with Daia.

"Why are there so many cushions? Don't you have chairs?" she asked.

Nikolai gazed at her in silence, judging her statement. He took a breath, heating the fire in the stove. "Elves are close to nature. They believe they have descended from a great tree as Nymphs, while some evolved even further into the ethereal beings you see now. There are still many Nymphs, but they were the ones who chose to be a direct part of nature instead of removed," he explained.

The fire from the stove heated the small room. "It doesn't get very cold in Miras. Nights can be a bit chilly, but that is why you won't see any coverings on the windows. We let in both the warmth and the cold, because we are a part of all of it."

Ashlynn glanced around the space, taking in this new culture.

"You will stay here," he continued, "with Kris and I. Technically you are our guests, although you are in the realm of the Elven Queen."

"What will happen to Barcinas? Will we be able to see him?" she asked, studying the tapestry behind him. It was streaked with red and woven with fury. Large shadows flew in rage, breathing out fire while a distant, glowing figure sent other shadows flying in fear. Ashlynn tried to dissect each area, but she knew it would take months to fully see and understand each component.

"That depends on how he responds to the queen. Since I am the diplomatic emissary for the Human realm, you will stay with me and possibly get a chance to see Barcinas in his cell. We are the only humans in this realm." He paused. "Well, almost, but the queen's consort doesn't count."

When he finished stoking the fire, he glanced at Ashlynn. Her face showed shock. "Did I say something wrong? I can find you a different place to stay if this doesn't suit what you are used to in the Human realm," he commented, narrowing his eyes and rubbing his temples.

"No! This is perfect. It's fine. We don't require more. I just, well, I," she stuttered, "I thought you were an elf."

Nikolai gaped at her dumbfounded then guffawed. His voice warmed Ashlynn from embarrassment through the vibration that rang out from him. He stopped laughing and stoked the fire, still chuckling every few moments.

"Well, I didn't find it that funny," she remarked, feeling her temperature drop back down.

He turned his eyes back to her and smiled, genuinely. "I wasn't laughing at you or your remark. It is the thought that I have lived here so long that the human aspect of me is almost cut out. I can understand your uncertainty though. Even I have wondered if my ears are sharpening or my skin radiating."

He poked at her kindly, in a way she hadn't seen him do before. In a human way was how she could explain it to herself.

"I am part man part beast," he replied, winking at her.

Ashlynn smiled at his attempts to make her feel comfortable. "So you, Kristopher and the queen's consort?" she asked.

"Indeed. The queen's consort led Kristopher, myself, and his mother to the Elves after the war with the Dragons. He protected us on the way here and created security for us when we arrived. So, here I am trading my position for safety, and a life for Kris and I," he finished, giving her a half smile. "If you follow me this way, then I will show you where you will stay."

She trailed behind him, taking in every detail he had just revealed.

"This is where Sebastian is staying," he said, pointing to the first room on the right in the hallway. "Kris's room is connected to his so he can care for him if he needs something while he heals. His wounds on the outside were minimal, but Kae informed me that his mental field is torn to shreds. I am amazed he is keeping it together so well. Something got into his mind and tried its best to obliterate him."

Ashlynn stared at the door and heard laughter behind it. She wanted to go in and hug her cousin, who fought against the Shadow in his mind while running through the woods. Beside her, Nikolai took in the silence and motioned her to follow him up stairs that led off to a back area of the house.

As she ascended them, there was a little balcony directly in front of her. She headed straight out onto it to take in the celestial ambiance again. Nikolai came out after her and stood silently. She could feel his skin touching hers. Allowing herself to finally study him, she glanced sideways. His hair was as dark as Kristopher's but much longer. Where Kristopher kept his twisted like ropes, Nikolai encouraged his ringlets to flow down without any restrictions. Ashlynn felt a desire to touch his locks but clasped her fingers together instead. He gazed at her gently as the moonlight shone down on his smooth, creamy cheeks and his dark eyes that were full of waves and smoke.

"What are you thinking, Ashlynn?" he asked softly.

She gazed back at the moon. "I am thinking that I have never seen such a beautiful sky. The sky in Levander is bleak compared to this. I have never seen the swirls of light or the different colors mixing together like I do here. Why is that?"

Continuing to study her, he answered, "The sky is different here than in Levander because we are in a different realm. While still on the same planet, our minds are more open to the variances all around us."

"That sounds beautiful," she whispered. "The thought of such an open environment seems foreign to what I am used to."

He turned back to the night sky. "It isn't perfect here either, Ashlynn."

They stayed silent for a few more minutes. Right as she was about to ask where her room was, Nikolai put his hand on hers.

"I haven't forgotten about the night we met at your party," he confessed.

Confusion and questions coursed through Ashlynn's mind at his reveal, but she stayed silent to let him talk.

"That night I was out for part of my research of the Human realm. I had been to Levander a few times before, but the king specifically requested I come that night. When I arrived, I realized why. He wanted to show off in front of me. I was disgusted at the grandeur and expense that I left without acknowledging him," he said.

Ashlynn released a gasp. "You actually did that? You disrespected him, Nikolai. He will never forget or forgive your act," she whispered.

He studied her carefully and said, "I know, and I don't care about him at all. He is not worth the queen's time," he paused, "or yours."

She glanced away at the comment and his attempt to reach across the gap of their experience.

"I do not pretend to know what you have gone through, Ashlynn. If stopping that bastard that night was any indicator, then I have a fairly good idea. But you are free now, from him and his control."

Ashlynn wanted to be anywhere but here having this vulnerable conversation with him. She refrained from looking directly at him for fear of crying or exposing herself further. "You can call me Ash," she replied instead.

Nikolai took the hint and walked to the door behind her. "This is your room. Mine is right across from yours since we don't get many human guests in the realm. If you need anything, call out. There are only the four of us here, so everything is cooked, cleaned and tended to by us." He opened her door, and she walked into her room.

The bed, which was on the floor, was covered with pillows, while sheer wrappings flowed like vines off the pyramid shaped dome above it. The fire place was lit and a wardrobe closet stood near a full length mirror. A rug covered the floor in front of the fire, with cushions in every corner. She could study the night sky from outside the large open window across from the door. While this space would be considered bare in Levander, it gave her a sense of comfort that she had never experienced before. Rose gold walls completed the ambiance, making her feel more at home here than she could ever remember being in the kingdom she grew up in.

Still in her thoughts, Nikolai slowly closed the door. Ashlynn twirled around. "Thank you, Nikolai, for the space and your protection while here. And during that night in Levander."

He nodded to her, backing out but leaving the door open as she followed him. "You can call me Niko," he said.

"Niko," she whispered, his name flowing from her lips with ease. "Why is the queen so strict about Dragons entering her realm? Do you know anything about them?" she ventured, right as he touched the knob to his room.

Without turning around, he replied, "Yes, I do. Goodnight, Ash."

Nikolai crossed into his room and closed the door. Ashlynn stared across the hallway, perplexed by her host and rescuer. She shut hers and sat on a cushion near her bed. The sea breeze blew in, cooling her hot, tingling skin from the warmth of her interaction with Nikolai. Yawning, she crawled into bed, falling asleep the moment her eyes shut.

CHAPTER TWENTY EIGHT

Scratching awoke Ashlynn from her restful sleep.

A high pitched, girlish giggle permeated through the darkness. "Hello, Ashlynn. Welcome to Miras. I knew you would make it," announced the little voice.

Ashlynn turned over in bed to see yellow eyes staring back at her, the same that had guided her for half of her journey. Except this time, the face was different. On the window sill, as the cool breeze played with her short, twisted, blackish-brown hair, sat a girl in place of the panther. Her catlike smile grinned down at Ashlynn.

"Are you the panther?" Ashlynn asked.

The girl nodded.

"But how are you a girl now? And how did you get into Miras?" The questions tumbled out her mouth before she could process what she was asking.

"My name is Whendy. But if you want any more answers, you must first catch me," Whendy said.

"Catch you? What do you..." but she didn't get a chance to finish. Whendy jumped off the ledge of her second floor window. Ashlynn scrambled over to the opening, not sure what to expect. What she saw exceeded her wildest imagination.

When Ashlynn peered over the ledge, she didn't see a panther on the ground, or a little girl staring up at her. Instead she saw a magnificent dark, shimmery dragon. The eyes were still yellow, but her color was a resonate blue, as dark as the sky and the ocean mixed together. She blended into the night and Ashlynn wouldn't have known she was there if she didn't feel little tufts of wind with each flap of her wings. Although she could only compare to the dragon in her dream, Whendy seemed small, barely bigger than her bed.

Come along, Ashlynn, came the girly voice in her head. *You have been waiting for answers for a long time. Are you going to let this stop you?*

Ashlynn was sure Whendy was teasing her. "Where are we going? I won't be able to keep up with you if you fly!"

You never know what you can do until you try, she responded with a giggle. *Who knows, maybe you will transform into something too!*

"Well, I can apparently breathe fire so maybe I can fly, too!" she muttered.

Glancing at the dragon with wonder and still in her dirty travel clothes, Ashlynn pinned her hair back and crouched on the ledge as Whendy had. "Now what?"

Now, jump! giggled the voice in her head.

Ashlynn gawked back, took a weary glance down, breathed deeply, and closed her eyes. Something about being in Miras and seeing a dragon in front of her was enough to enchant herself to believe.

Ashlynn, you have to open your eyes. And believe. If you jump out of this without believing you can fly then you will just fall to the ground. You have to believe in yourself, Whendy instructed, soaring in little circles above Ashlynn with excitement.

Ashlynn released her breath and jumped, still keeping both eyes closed. She flapped her arms like a bird, waiting for something to happen. The more she flapped, the faster she fell. Yet she still kept her eyes closed and waited for the hard thud she expected to come from hitting the ground. Except, it didn't come. Instead her body floated up. She opened one eye to peek out and saw the night sky around her. Ashlynn opened her other eye and glanced around her. On either side she saw massive wings.

"Wee! I'm flying!" she called out.

No, Ashlynn. I am flying. You are riding, came the high-pitched voice.

Ashlynn checked around again, and blushed as she waved her arms. Whendy was indeed carrying her.

"Why did you catch me?" she mumbled.

Because we have much to talk about and only a few hours before the sun shows his face again. We need the cover of darkness for our journey.

"Where are we going? And how can I hear you?" she asked, glancing around at the inner realm at night. The multitudes of stars created a galaxy swirl above her head, which shined enough light to see the tops of the trees and houses. The moon was perfectly positioned above the castle and poured her glorious, soft rays on the shimmering, magickal fixture. The castle created an ambiance of peace and protection. It signaled that the queen would protect her people and home at all costs.

To my home. No one can hear us up there. Her voice whispered, as if she were worried someone could still hear her inside of Ashlynn's mind. *I can speak in your mind because you have finally opened it enough to the energy of mental communication. If I had tried that as a panther, you would have been too overwhelmed and weary to trust me.*

Ashlynn sat on Whendy's back and took in the forest around her, pondering what she had revealed. They had left the beautiful sanctuary of houses and shops to fly further north. It were as if the queendom grew in size the longer they travelled.

"Where do you live?" she wondered aloud.

I live at the top of Pyr Mountain. The mountain is in the realm, but since Elves do not claim nature as their own, they do not limit those who choose to embark on the treacherous journey up it," she explained.

"Is that why you are taking me up there now? To talk? And how can you fly around as a dragon? Kaenon said Dragons aren't welcome in the queendom."

Dragons are allowed in the realm. But only if they get approval from the queen and work out an agreement. Also, she giggled, *I was born here.*

"How were you born here and how can you change into so many—"

No more questions, Ashlynn. We are about to arrive. Now get ready! she instructed.

Before she could ask why, Whendy spun over and dropped Ashlynn off her back into a canyon.

"Whendy! Help!" she screamed out, barely hearing herself over the wind rushing around her. She tumbled through the air, wind piercing her face as it forced open her eyes.

"Help yourself, Ashlynn," came Whendy's voice.

CHAPTER TWENTY NINE

I'm scared! I can't do this, she yelled back to the voice in her head.

Stretch yourself, Ashlynn. You can do anything, she soothed.

Ashlynn reconnected with her breath and closed her eyes. She could feel the air moving past her like an arrow soaring. Her heart flew into her throat. She swallowed and tried to breathe.

"I don't know how, but I believe in myself. I believe I can save myself," she muttered.

I believe I can save myself. Crack, went her arms as they flapped. *I can save myself.* Heat warmed her entire body. *I am more powerful than I know.* Her necklace burned her skin, yet she still didn't give up. *I choose to save myself.* Her body felt heavy. *I believe in myself.* The wind died around her. She no longer felt as if she were free falling into a ravine below. Instead, she noticed her body floating up.

She peeled open her eyes and glanced up to see massive wings full of sparkling silver light poking through a dark pink background. These definitely weren't

Whendy's wings. Ashlynn surveyed the sky around her and saw the tiniest rabbit at the very bottom of the field below. She took a deep breath and laughed at the miracle of it, but instead fire came flowing out. Ashlynn screamed, sending out a massive roar that sounded like a whip cracking across a canyon.

You did it, Ash! laughed Whendy as she flew up next to her.

Why did you do that? Ashlynn demanded.

Sometimes we need a bit of fear to push us grow. Or transform more like it! she said, letting out a magnificent roar.

Transform? Does that mean...

Yes, Ashlynn. How do you think you are flying right now? Whendy asked.

Ashlynn stared down at herself. Her tan skin had morphed into the creamy mauve dragon of her dream, with scales that shimmered in the moonlight. This was who she had imagined herself as that day in the forest as she soared above the trees. *What is going on?* Trying to breathe out in an attempt to calm herself resulted in fire that scorched the tips of a tree instead. *Whendy! What do I do?*

Follow me to the cottage, Whendy replied.

Ashlynn flew behind, hearing the laughter rolling off

Whendy like the air that caressed her new body. Her chest still felt warm from the fire she had expended. As in her habit, she reached for her necklace, only to find it was gone as her claws scratched her new, itchy scales. The heat she had associated with her crescent moon pendant blossomed as her chest fell and rose in confidence. Fire. Breathing to calm herself. Breathing fire. Her power. It was all connected. Fire poured out of her as she realized that she had this power all along. She only needed to trust in herself.

Whendy paused, her iridescent wings flapping effortlessly. *We will land by the large tree near the cottage.* Her raspy laugh echoed as she dived down. She swerved around the tree and landed on the ground, transforming back into a girl right before she landed. Her shift happened so fast that Ashlynn didn't have a chance to blink.

"Come on, Ash! You have to come down sometime!" Whendy called up to her.

Yes, but it won't look as fancy as that!

You can do it, little one, came a strong, confident voice inside her gut.

Wait, is there another voice inside of me? Ashlynn had always wondered where her deeper intuition came from, but never imagined it was the voice of a being living inside of her.

Yes, and Whendy will explain it more. But first, we must go down, she resounded as ancient memories and knowledge stirred to the surface.

Ashlynn exhaled for a momentary pause and dove down. She could feel the wind rushing up around her like when she had fell, except this time it was exhilarating. She closed her eyes to take in the freedom.

"Ashlynn, no! Open your eyes!" Whendy called up.

Ashlynn did, right in time to see the massive tree she was supposed to land beside. She jerked around it, hitting a branch with her tail. It flew off and landed a little ways from the cottage as Ashlynn circled around to land. Yet, she didn't decrease her speed. By the time her feet were near the ground she was still going too fast. Stiffening her legs, she tried to stop herself but skidded instead, creating rivets in the dirt. The tree progressed toward her and Ashlynn didn't know how to stop herself. She attempted one final method and sat her dragon butt down with a thud. The reverse action lifted her front legs off the ground and caused her to face plant with such intensity that she transformed back into her human self.

"Well, that's one way to land," Whendy chuckled.

The door to the cottage blew open, and a tray flew out with tea on it as Ashlynn shook off the dirt and confusion. It bumped into her until she took her cup.

"How is it doing that?" Ashlynn asked, taking a sip of her tea. It was very hot and tasted of vanilla, jasmine, cinnamon, and rainwater.

"I control it with my magick," Whendy said, sipping hers.

"Whendy, what is going on? Why did you come to Levander to guide me, and how did you know there was a dragon inside of me?" Ashlynn asked, letting her tea warm her hands. Nikolai had been right about the cool breeze from the water chilling the night. "Wait! Am I going to get taken away like Barcinas for transforming into a dragon while in the queen's realm?" She shivered at the thought.

Whendy grinned. "Hm, it is possible. *If* the queen finds out. We just have to act like you don't have the knowledge of this ability yet, until you are ready to face her and explain it."

"But *how* do I have this ability?" She pushed.

"As you now know, you have a being inside of you, a dragon of old. This allows you to transform into a dragon yourself. When your mother agreed to help Daia. Yes, I know about Daia," she said with a smile. "When she agreed to save the Dragon race, she took on the energy of one. That voice you heard was once a dragon living in

283

this world named Hatta. She was a fiery, fuchsia colored beast with fierce intuition and a kind countenance. When she found out that her race would be destroyed, she chose to fight in a different way—by giving her life force away. It transferred to you since you were in Sabah's womb at the time. That is how she now lives inside of you. I have been waiting to share that with you."

"Hatta?" Ashlynn whispered in reverence.

Yes, my Ashlynn. I have been here your whole life, guiding you. I waited for you to wake to your power and own intuition, came her passionate yet loving voice.

"Wait! Does that mean that Sebastian has a dragon inside of him too?" she asked, mouth agape.

"That is not my story to tell or yours to know quite yet. When Sebastian is ready to learn about his own past and future, then you will know too," Whendy replied, with a smirk.

"So, that's a yes," Ashlynn laughed, sipping her tea. "How will we keep this from the queen?"

Whendy gazed out at the water, which reminded her of Oren back at their meeting in Mount Fermont.

"The queen does her best to know and see all. Her pride gets in the way though. For now you should be safe. She has the information from Kaenon searching your mind. Since you didn't know, she will have no reason to inquire about it now. Just be sure to work on your transformation up here, away from the prying eyes and ears of her spies," she advised. "Now, no more questions. I have something to show you. Our fates are so closely connected that I have seen glimpses of your future almost as much as I have seen mine."

Before Ashlynn could ask, Whendy grabbed her hand. A spark shot through Ashlynn, except it wasn't painful like the one that came from Kaenon. This one was comforting like an old friend she hadn't seen in a while. Then, images and sensations appeared in her mind.

She was flying high above the clouds with the sea below. The sun warmed her back. She went in for a dive and noticed Nikolai in front of her. Right as she was about to land, the image morphed into another large tree except this time she landed in front of it. The tree bent toward her, so she bowed back. Ashlynn walked up to it when a fight broke out all around her. Dragons were flying around in an organized attack. There was fire and blood everywhere. She glanced back at the tree and saw that it had turned black and putrid.

Ashlynn snapped back to the present. Whendy was staring at her, excited at the future she just shared.

"How does that connect us?" Ashlynn asked, still thinking over the events she was shown.

"I have no idea," replied the child wonder with a grin, "but I am thrilled to find out."

"So you knew I had a dragon in me from this? What was that? How did you do it?"

"I am a seer!" Whendy said. "I was born with the sight, and ability to shape shift into a panther and a dragon," she giggled. "Quite a lot for a little girl to learn as she's growing up alone, wouldn't you say? But no, I knew from my dragon, Brynn. She was the twin sister to your dragon."

Ashlynn studied Whendy, her large eyes and jovial smile seemed true and serene. Whendy didn't give the impression that she faked any of it. She was happy and carefree. "This is a lot to take in. How can you be happy and full of joy growing up alone?"

"I know my parents love me, and I have the answers I need for the time being. Even with the ability to know pieces of my future and the future of others, I am not meant to know everything. So I accept what the Great Goddess shows me and enjoy the rest of what I don't with a sense of spontaneity." Whendy drank a sip of her tea and smiled. The top of her lip had a thin layer of brown. She licked it off and sighed. "Mmmm. Hot chocolate. My favorite!"

"Our drinks are different?" Ashlynn asked.

"Of course!" Whendy cried. "Do you think I would give both of us the same drink? No! We have different tastes, just as we have different hair and dragon hide."

They sat in silence as the stars disappeared and the moon had her meeting with the sun to trade places. Ashlynn had many questions to ask Whendy, she could feel them buzzing in her mind, but instead she chose to enjoy this moment of peace. She had been rushing on this journey for a week, and even before that time she had never felt this sense of freedom and serenity. There would be time to learn and ask all she wanted.

Whendy broke their silence with a sip. "Also, know that you can trust Nikolai. You may need his help while you are here. He is the most trustworthy male I have ever encountered. I consider it a blessing from the Goddess that the queen's consort brought him here from Levander for safety."

Levander. The kingdom. King Theodore and the sickness.

"Whendy! The sickness that flows through the king! Oren said we would find the cure here. Do you know what it is or who to talk to?" she asked, excited that answers were so close.

"Oh, Ashlynn," came her regretful voice, "I do know of the sickness you mention. And I do know the cure which you seek."

Ashlynn's eyes grew wide with joy, yet she couldn't understand the sadness in Whendy's voice. Jumping up, she exclaimed, "What is it, Whendy? Is it a tincture? Or maybe it is a magickal incantation, since you know how to weave spells! This is wonderful! We have found the answer to saving Levander!" Whendy stayed quiet, as Ashlynn prattled on. "Sebastian and Barcinas will be thrilled! Oh, do tell me! I can't wait any longer!"

"Ash, it isn't what you think," Whendy muttered. "The cure isn't something to take or say or apply externally. The answer to curing the king lies within you, within your dragon. Only by connecting with the knowledge of your dragon can you help the king defeat the evil inside of him," she explained.

"Wait, I don't understand," she said, shaking her head. "We came here for a cure. You're saying there isn't anything I can give the king to make him better?" she begged. "Nothing? Couldn't I have known this earlier?"

Whendy shook her head. "It is a journey he will have to figure out. Only by taking steps to learn from and accept your dragon and yourself can you navigate him through the process. If he chooses to, that is," she remarked. "And you had to grow in your intuition as you travelled here to experience the understanding that comes from connecting with your dragon. Only then would you be able to lead others."

"But Oren said," she stuttered.

"Oh, my father enjoys his riddles. While he spoke truth, he also knew you would need to venture to Miras to undertake this task of safely uncovering what you hold inside yourself," Whendy revealed.

"Oren is your father?" Ashlynn asked, shocked by all she had revealed.

Whendy nodded, but stayed silent to let Ashlynn process. All she wanted, in this moment, was to cry. It was all pointless. The journey. Barcinas taken away. Sebastian losing his sight. Odessa and Aunt Arya in danger. Daia murdered. What was the point of it all if she couldn't leave with a cure and save them? She lowered herself to the ground for stability and sat in the beauty and stillness around her, choosing to be present with her tears as they fell into her tea. She was without hope, and for once Ashlynn did not care her despair showed. It poured from her freely as she heaved to unbind her constraint on her emotions in front of her new friend.

CHAPTER THIRTY

After Ashlynn dried her eyes and took a few sips, Whendy went to her with an outstretched hand. "I want to show you something," she said.

Enough light poured in from the rising sun for them to see to the winding path ahead. Ashlynn followed her up a steep, rocky path as she led them to the highest point in all of Miras. The strain caused her leg to throb, so she sat on a rock near the drop-off. The view in front of her caused tears to bubble up again, but this time from the beauty she saw all around her. Not only did she see the castle of Miras, but she also saw the forest of Varjo when she turned to her left. This spot displayed all of the inner and outer realm, and Ashlynn had to remind herself to breathe from the sheer magnificence of the view.

Here she could feel the Goddess's power of creation by honoring all that had been birthed forth from her womb. It quieted the ache inside of her and soothed her quest for answers. Hatta stirred within to reassure her they would figure it out. Together. She was not alone, and that thought made her smile in the midst of her turmoil.

Ashlynn spotted the sea in the distance as the sun rose from the water. It gave the beach a bloody appearance. In front of the sun she saw a flock of birds approaching. The more she stared at them though, the more she realized that the flying beasts were too large to be birds.

"Are there other dragons that are welcome in the realm?" she questioned.

"Why do you ask?" Whendy eyed her.

"There is something flying down there by the beach that looks too big to be a bird," she said, pointing to the little dot. When she looked again, the dot had grown even bigger. Her eyes focused, and she gasped.

Whendy had already started to run down the mountain toward the outer gates.

"We have to go!" Whendy shouted back at her.

Without explaining, Ashlynn ran after Whendy as she weaved back and forth following the trail. Her knee burned with pain as the wound tore open again, while her body ached from the impromptu flying in the chilly air.

Ashlynn wanted to yell after Whendy to wait for her, but she had to breathe with every step she took. The pain throughout her body grew. Her feet, her hands, even her eyelids swole with heated exhaustion.

"That was a dragon with a cluster of beasts following

close behind. But it is not one that is allowed to enter," Whendy yelled. "An army approaches, and they are headed for the inner realm. You must have been followed to Miras, Ash. We are all in great danger."

Ashlynn accelerated through her dread to keep up with Whendy. She led them to the inner gate to warn the guards.

"Sound the alarm! An army is approaching!" she cried out.

The guards at the gate shared glances. Ashlynn ran behind her. Her knee dripped with blood, making her wound look even worse. Stopping was more painful than running. It caused the pressure to build, and she toppled to the ground. The guards ran over to help, but she shooed them away.

"There is an army approaching! We saw them flying in over the beach!" she said.

Her entire body was covered with sweat, and she trembled. She had almost nothing to eat the previous day, and she vowed she would never be this weak again.

"Why are you just standing there?" Whendy demanded.

"Highest apologies, seer. We trust you. However, your sight might have been seeing many years into the future, so we just want to be sure before issuing an alarm," one of the guards on duty stuttered.

"My sight? I know the difference between the extended future and right now, Ian!" Whendy yelled, cutting her eyes at him. "Ashlynn saw it as well, and she can't tell the future! Now sound the alarm!"

Ian bowed to her. "Whendy, while you are highly revered you know the queen's orders. We have to hear it from someone... uh," he paused unsure how to phrase the rest.

"Fine! I will get Nikolai then. But know that this is your fault for not believing me! We will see who the queen punishes later when her realm is burned to ashes!"

The guards exchanged worried glances and bowed to her again. She rolled her eyes and focused on Ashlynn. "Stay in the shadows. I will be back soon." With one more cut of her eyes toward the guards, she changed into a panther. One moment her hair was at her ears, the next her ears had shifted above her hair, with the entirety of her body covered in dark fur. Her eyes were still the same, but fangs grew out from her mouth. She hissed at Ian, who jumped back, knocking the other guard off his feet. They stumbled over each other as Whendy sprinted toward the castle.

After regaining his footing, the guards shared a look and muttered to themselves, as if second guessing their choice in sounding the alarm. Ashlynn walked to a nearby rock. She took a few breaths, holding her stomach. She stayed on the rock and clutched at the only part of herself that remained calm and focused, her necklace. Her fear rose at what was coming, and she glanced up to see the sky lighten with the rising sun, while simultaneously blacken with clouds and dark pulses that rumbled like thunder from hundreds of wings. Ashlynn stared at the dragon-like beings, trying to make sense of them. They were thinner than she expected most dragons to look, and they had a harshness about their stature and energy.

"Wyverns," came Nikolai's voice behind her. "They are related to the Dragons in a way I have not yet figured out. They do not have the capabilities to converse or think for themselves. They act first, usually harshly, and then fly off before their consequences can be dealt."

"So you've seen them before?" she asked, keeping her eyes locked on the assault.

"No," he said. "But I have read about them. I have a deep distrust and dislike for them."

"Where do they come from?" she muttered.

"Only dark magick can spawn them. They are born of evil and deceit. Someone with immense power has come out of hiding. The question is, where did they get this knowledge?" he wondered aloud, his brow furrowed.

"Where are Sebastian and Kristopher?" she asked.

"Kristopher is watching over Sebastian at the house. He heard what Whendy told me and said he would keep him safe." He surveyed the sky in front of them. Their perch overlooked the beach below as it transformed to black. Its pure sand now clouded with evil intent. "I am going after them. Do you want to fight or stay back?"

Ashlynn glanced at him and then down at her knee. She bit her lip trying to decide the brave choice. Nikolai took a step closer to her. The wyverns started to burn huts and attack elves. She heard wisps as arrows flew toward the beasts. The wyvern's screeches of pain blended with the screams from the children as they woke to fire and destruction. One brave child, about eight years in age, ran out of his hut and chanted, weaving words full of magick and protection. Yet with every wyvern that was hit or killed, another took its place. This was not a battle. It was a massacre. All around them, elves bravely fought, not once doubting their ability or chances of winning. Yet in that moment, it was just the two of them.

"You will not be judged for whatever your decision. It is yours and yours alone," he whispered.

She took a breath in. The smell of smoke wafted through the air, reminding her of the Tuhka village. She wanted to help, but knew that she would only be in the way, and this realization of her inability to protect others made her even sadder. Her leg still ached and every step sent pain to her chest. Breathing out, she mumbled her answer, "I think.. uh... I think I will sit this one out. I would only do more harm with this leg. I can go back and stay with Sebastian so Kristopher can help."

Nikolai nodded at her response, accepting it without judgment or anger. "Stay there until I come get you."

She peered up at him, but he had already disappeared. The pain in her chest grew as she watched him run to fight with the Elves. Confused by her attraction and fear for his safety, Ashlynn turned and hobbled deeper into the inner realm. She still had to walk up the hill and back down toward the castle, so she took her time, breathing intently with each step. Making it to the top of the hill, she surveyed the sea and realm below. She could barely see Nikolai's place. The shops were dark and quiet.

"I should've gone to fight," she mumbled to herself.

"If only you weren't such a coward," attacked a voice from behind her.

She froze and gulped. "You aren't here. I am imagining this," she said aloud, hoping to convince herself.

A familiar laugh echoed around her, telling her she was indeed lying to herself. Her blood chilled, wishing

Nikolai was still beside her. She turned around slowly to face the voice, except this time the voice didn't match what she expected to see. Standing in front of her was a creature with Tiberius's face and voice, but it stood on all fours with lion fur, massive feathered wings and a dragon's tail.

"Tiberius?" she whispered. "Is that you?"

The laugh she had grown to love and hate came out of this beast. "Oh, Ashlynn. How I've missed you," Tiberius said. "It is still me, but this is my true form. I am surprised you never saw me in it. But you were so content to believe the lies and tricks fed to you. You are truly awake now, aren't you? How does it feel knowing you brought destruction to the majestic Elves?"

Ashlynn gasped. Every moment with him flooded her mind as she replayed each kiss, laugh, orgasm, and beating. As she rewatched them all, she noticed a fabric tear in each memory. Her moment under the tree with Tiberius no longer showed him in human form, but showed wings with some fur. Each of her memories morphed into that half-human half-beast-like being. It was as if her mind tried to fill in the gaps.

"What are you, Ti?" she asked.

The beast in front of her strutted around, enjoying his new freedom and radiating from the attention. His entire body was covered in fur, with wings protruding from his shoulders. His golden locks had transformed into a glorious mane that fell from his curls. The back part of him was a rich honeyed-brown with his skin transforming into mahogany scales as it flowed to his tail. Only his face was the same, making his fierce new body even scarier.

"I am a manticore," he said, circling around her like a beast watching its prey. "I am the only one of my kind. My father fought during the war as a winged lion loyal to the Dragons and their cause, but he and my mother were killed because they were too weak. I decided to commit to Marcus and King Theodore's agenda the moment I could and received even more power and strength than my parents could have ever imagined possessing." He grinned at himself. "The tail is a beautiful new addition, don't you think?"

Ashlynn continued to flip through her memories. All of the kind gestures, loving chats, and silly moments cut sharp when she realized it had been fake.

"You tricked me! Was any of it real? Did you care for me at all?" she yelled at him. Tears started to build, but she choked them down, remembering her promise to never show him her emotions again.

"Does it matter, Ashlynn? I am here to take you back. King Theodore's orders," he said. "I did warn you to be careful."

"You are sick, Ti!" she screamed. "Stay away from me!"

Another shriek echoed as an elf was snatched up and hurtled across the sky. Something closed around her neck. She reached to pull it off, only to realize it was her own panic closing off her airways.

"I can't go back, Ti. You won't catch me," she whimpered, backing away.

"You know I love a challenge. I can't let you go this time, Ashlynn," he growled, when a black flash came from the bushes and attacked him.

Ashlynn took off as fast as she could push herself toward safety. She didn't know where to go. Tiberius would find her anywhere. All she knew was that she had to try. She would not go back on a leash. She would rather die than become someone's object again. So Ashlynn ran, groaning in agony from the pain of her wounds, those on the outside and the ones that had begun to heal on the inside. She didn't stop until she reached the shops. She checked back at the hill, trying to find the black blur and Tiberius, but it was empty.

A gush of wind behind her made her turn to see a giant sage dragon swerving with Sebastian in his grip. The dragon gave her a smirk, something she didn't know dragons could do. It reminded her of Kristopher and she gasped.

"You're a dragon too? Keep him safe, Kristopher!" she yelled at his back. He dived out of the way of wyvern that barreled toward him. Roaring, he swung his tale and knocked the beast into a massive tree. The tree wrapped its branches around the wyvern and squeezed until the beast stopped moving. Eyes wide, Ashlynn took a step back. With Sebastian safe, she could better focus on hiding until Tiberius gave up looking for her.

"Don't worry," said Tiberius's voice behind her. "Your panther friend is gone."

"What did you do to Whendy?" she screamed and waved her arm around to hit him. He didn't expect her to react. She whacked him across the face. Doing so caused her arm to ache, but she took the opportunity that came from him pausing to escape.

"You. Little. Bitch! When I get you back, I am going to show you just how pathetic you are!" he screeched.

Tiberius approached, his tail flicking like a lion hunting before that final jump to capture and subdue. He lunged into the air, claws swinging to make contact with her soft shoulders, and knocked her down. Ashlynn rolled onto her chest, her heart pounding. She took a breath and pushed her body off the ground with wet hands. Her shoulder dripped blood down her arm and onto the sky blue stones below.

Sharp nails dug into her shoulder sockets as he lifted her from the ground. Tiberius had grabbed her with his front paws and was carrying her up over the inner realm toward the outer gates. Squirming only caused his claws to cut in deeper. The passing trees and huts below were sure to kill her if she made him let her go. But she wasn't ready to give up. Tiberius may have her in his grasps, but that didn't mean she would make it easy on him. He carried her out toward the beach. The soft sand was a perfect place for her to fall. If she could get free of his clutch. Wind whistled in her ears as he led her over the outer gate and approached the open waters, heading toward Levander.

CHAPTER THIRTY ONE

Something crashed into Tiberius. She jerked violently in a moment of self assurance before he released her. Last time she fell, the dragon within her exploded out with massive wings. Except this time, she couldn't call forth her dragon. She couldn't even focus on that power inside of her, much less her own breath. The trick to transforming was lost in her scrambled brain. If only—but her vision turned black in her desperate attempt to save herself.

Ashlynn. Wake up! a voice called into her mind, piercing through her unconscious fog. *Ashlynn!*

Ashlynn peeled open her eyes. She could feel the sand underneath her and saw the sun at the top of the sky as she scanned the horizon. Her knee was numb, and her shoulders stung. She hauled herself up, her leg past the point of feeling pain. Near the water's edge, she spotted two beasts circling each other. Ashlynn rubbed her eyes and looked again.

One was Tiberius in his beast form, hunched and snarling. His face dripped with something wet, but she couldn't tell if it was blood or spit. The other beast was a dragon, but not one she had seen before. Its color a mix of azure and sapphire with scales that shimmered like sea water and the midnight sky blended together. Ashlynn was transfixed by the beauty of its movement as it prowled like a pendulum in front of her, intentionally placing its body between her and Tiberius.

Ashlynn! came the voice again. A vibration resonated in her head as the words connected like an ever-flowing river. The sound was much deeper than her dragon within. She stared over at the two beasts still facing each other. Neither seemed to pay her any mind, but there wasn't anyone else around.

"Where are you?" she asked.

I am in your head. I need you to wake up and run. They want you, Ash. Get far away.

"Nikolai? Is that you?" she asked.

Just go! it yelled.

A roar came from the two beasts as the manticore advanced. Tiberius swung his razor sharp claws at the dragons snout, missing him barely as fire exploded from its mouth. Tiberius had already backed away, but the tip of his tail, which flicked without intention, had been in the crossfire. A wail sounded from the ferocious lion as he dashed for the water to soothe his raw, aching scales.

"You are going to pay for that, Nikolai!" he roared.

"Wait! You are a dragon too?" she asked.

Leave now! Run for Whendy's hut, he reiterated.

"But you are so... enchanting," she whispered.

His roar startled her, which made Tiberius's sound like a kitten in comparison. *I am not fighting him for fun!* he gritted out. *Move your ass!*

Tiberius leaped for Ashlynn and Nikolai slammed him with his tail and roared. The strength and raw emotion behind it made Ashlynn shake. Tiberius jumped back, shook off the hit, and prowled around.

"Oh, I see, Ashlynn. You are gone for a week, and you find a new toy," he snarled. "You accuse me of lying and being fake, yet you are the one already moving on."

"Go back to Levander and warm the king's bed! It's what you are best at!" Ashlynn retorted. Her voice came out rough and quiet, but Tiberius heard every word.

He snickered. "Does Nikolai know that you like it rough?" he asked, cocking his head. "Not sure you can handle the beast in him! He is worse than me, Ash."

Ashlynn laughed. "How would you know? You barely know him!"

Nikolai roared again and swiped at him, but Tiberius expected the move this time and jumped away. As Nikolai turned to face him, Tiberius bounded on top of him and dug his claws in. "I have known him my entire life," he spat. Nikolai shrieked and reached his neck around to knock Tiberius off his back. "And if you can't trust me then don't expect honesty from this backstabber!"

Nikolai roared again but didn't deny Tiberius's truth. She could only watch. It took every ounce of her strength to stay standing. Her leg was entirely numb and it spread to her hip, while her head pounded from the deep punctures in her shoulders. That, in addition to her lack of food, made her have to balance on a rock to stay upright.

Every time Nikolai reached his head to grab at Tiberius, he missed. Tiberius could maneuver easier than Nikolai on the ground. Realizing this, he took Tiberius to the sky. He ran and jumped, pumping his wings with intensity as he propelled into the sky. Then, he twirled and spiraled back down toward the water. Tiberius turned with him, trying to detach his claws. After a few spirals, Tiberius plummeted into the water.

Ashlynn searched but couldn't find him. As Nikolai headed back to the sand, a horn sounded across the beach. The army of beasts departed as quickly as they had attacked. There was a large, putrid green dragon racing away from the outer gate carrying a little girl—dark hair wildly waving, body dangling in the beast's talons as it cut into her shoulder blades. Something about its color reminded Ashlynn of someone she knew, but she couldn't place them in her mind. All that mattered was that the dragon had Whendy.

"Nikolai! They have Whendy," she called out.

Ashlynn gazed back to the wretched dragon carrying her and noticed two dragons fighting each other behind it. One was a skinny, sage colored dragon who fought with confidence and zeal. Ashlynn recognized him as Kristopher, except this time he seemed to be in his element. The other was an old, gold colored one that shined in the sunset. He was much bigger than Kristopher, but fought with the uncertainty of a beginner.

"The green one is Kristopher," came Nikolai's actual voice beside her. He had transformed back into his human self. "He must be fighting the other to get Whendy back."

The wyverns swarmed together and headed away from the realm. Their mission seemed to be complete with Whendy subdued.

"Where is Sebastian?" she asked. She scanned the horizon but couldn't find him.

Kristopher took a swipe at the other dragon, knocking him down. He grabbed someone who looked like Sebastian and flew off.

"Our work here is done," a voice said behind them.

Ashlynn turned around to see Marcus and Tiberius holding an unconscious Whendy, her limp body looking more dead than alive. Her chest faintly rose with each breath, and she was covered in scratches and blood.

"Give her back, Marcus. You don't want to make an enemy of the queen," Nikolai said.

Marcus stared Ashlynn and responded. "Your uncle was beside himself when he found out you left. He had so many plans for you, and you abandoned him," Marcus sighed, still ignoring Nikolai. "What kind of niece ignores the handouts of her family by turning her back on them? It's time to go back, Ashlynn, to answer for your actions."

"My actions? I have done nothing wrong! And I didn't turn my back on them, Marcus! I was never part of the king's family. He only wanted a toy," she said, "and I am no longer anyone's toy." She directed her last statement at Tiberius. Taking a breath, she stepped toward him with courage, ignoring the pain that shot through her body. "Neither is Whendy. Why the hell do you want her anyway?"

Marcus smiled. "You have no claim on her or yourself for that matter. You are the king's subject and you will never escape him. It was awful of you to leave your aunt and cousin, whom miss you dearly. Arya has been

307

dreadfully sick, and Odessa has had to nurse her back to health all alone," he said, moving toward her with each word. "They have locked themselves in the Queen's suite. How dreadful of you to inflict such pain on those you supposedly love. The king wants you back to help them recover. Then you will agree to his offer to never leave Levander again."

"You are a liar! I will never agree to his offer, no matter what it is!" she yelled, shaking.

"Tiberius grab her! I am done with this charade," Marcus muttered.

"Happily," he said, grinning and stepping over Whendy's limp body.

"The queen will not be happy that you have attacked her realm and took her people," Nikolai said, steering the conversation away from Ashlynn's family as he put himself between her and Tiberius once again.

"The queen had a powerful seer and chose to keep it from her allies." Marcus sneered, finally acknowledging Nikolai. "The king and I got tired of your queen's little games. We came to get her and his son back, with the seer as a guarantee," he said.

"They are under my protection now, thus the protection of this realm. You have no authority over any of them!" Nikolai announced. He studied his nails casually but his jaw was tense.

"Ah, of course they are. But if she chooses to leave to protect Odessa then you have no claim over her," Marcus replied, with a sly smile, as Tiberius took a step closer.

"The king would never hurt her!" Ashlynn assured.

Marcus's eyes twinkled. "We have different definitions of that word. But if you are willing to risk her safety, then by all means stay here. You trust people you don't even know over those who have cared for you your entire life. You trusted my son, yet he did a marvelous job leading us here."

"Your son?" she asked.

"Ashlynn clearly chooses to not go with you. I can't speak for Sebastian, but if you leave Whendy here then you can leave safely," Nikolai said, his eyes narrowing.

"That is not something you can promise. Only your queen can, and she is no where to be found. I will take Sebastian back to his father, and Whendy for good faith."

"Good faith? You attacked her realm. That is laughably stupid of you, Marcus," Nikolai smirked. "You will regret your decision when she finds out."

Tiberius had worked his way to Ashlynn's left as Nikolai balanced between keeping both him and Marcus away from Ashlynn.

"We will meet again soon, Ashlynn, and when we do,

you will regret your decision," he announced, transforming into a dragon and grabbing Whendy. Ashlynn recognized his putrid coat and grimaced. He flew off laughing.

Tiberius growled at Nikolai, and hit him with his tail. Nikolai took the hit full as a human and was thrown back.

"Nikolai!" Ashlynn screamed, taking a step to run after him.

Tiberius's tail blocked the path as he sauntered closer. "I told you I wouldn't let you escape," he snickered.

Remembering the knarke's attacked in Varjo reminded her that she was no longer helpless. Knowing this would be her final chance to get away, she glared at Tiberius and said, "And I promised you would never take me back."

He laughed. "And what can you do? You are beaten and bloody. Even when you aren't hurt you couldn't save yourself from a bug."

She waited one more moment as the fire inside grew with intention. "I wonder how you will be able to fly when you don't have any feathers," she thought aloud.

"What are you going on about?" He took one more step toward her and lifted his claws to swat her down.

Without another word, Ashlynn called her final breath of fire out of her and blew it at Tiberius. His mane sizzled as the fire grew toward his wings. He roared in pain and ran to the water. Ashlynn had held her balance for as long as she could, and now fell to the ground after her final piece of energy had been expended.

"I will take good care of Whendy for you," Tiberius yelled back and retreated after Marcus.

Nikolai ran to her but, she cried out, "Leave me! You have to go after them. You have to save Whendy!"

He gazed at her a moment and then shifted course. "I'm on it." As he ran for the water, Kristopher flew up. They glared at each other for a moment, and then Kristopher soared after the swarm while Nikolai jogged back to her.

"Where is he going? What are you doing?" she asked.

"He's going after Whendy. He said to keep you safe," he responded.

"Then where is Sebastian?" she asked, confused.

"Ashlynn! There you are!" Barcinas called. He ran across the beach to get to them. "I thought they had grabbed you too."

"You! You lied to me! You led them here! I never should've trusted you again!" Ashlynn cried out, struggling to stay conscious.

"No, Ash, I didn't. I swear!" he said.

"How can I trust you? Marcus even called you his son!" She screamed.

311

"But I'm not his son. He has never called me that! Ash, listen to me, please. They took Sebastian. I tried to stop them, but I was overpowered," he said.

Barcinas was covered with scratches. There was not a limb on his body that did not bleed.

Ashlynn's heart dropped. "What do you mean too? Barcinas, where is Sebastian?"

"Kristopher is on the way to get Whendy. If he sees Sebastian, then I am sure he will grab him too," Nikolai soothed.

"Kristopher?" Barcinas yelled. "It was him I fought! He lied to you! He grabbed Sebastian. He was the one to lead them here! All he could do was brag about it while we fought."

"You were the other gold dragon that I saw fighting him?" Ashlynn asked. Barcinas stared past her and nodded. "How did you get out of your cell, then? I'm sure the guards didn't just let you go!" she said.

"I transformed into a dragon when I heard the screams. I had to be sure that you and Sebastian were safe," Barcinas said.

Nikolai joined him. "If what you say is true, Barcinas, then Kris lied to me. Why would he do that?"

"Niko, if he lied and led them here then that means..." Ashlynn came up behind him.

Nikolai didn't turn to look at her, but continued to face the water where his cousin had flown off a few minutes prior.

"Yes, Ash. That would mean that Kristopher is Marcus's son," he said, still focusing on the water.

"You have to get them! Barcinas, Nikolai, please! Don't let them take Sebastian back. Save Whendy! Please!" she cried. No longer caring who was around, Ashlynn screamed. She feared for Sebastian's life and for the chains they would inevitably place on both him and Whendy. The three of them stared out across the sea as the sun bore down on them.

"You know we can't go, right Ash?" Nikolai whispered, his voice raw. "They will already be out of the realm by the time we reach them, and we will be outnumbered."

Ashlynn didn't want to believe him as she sobbed into the hard, wet sand. She punched the ground, giving the last of her strength and pain to the impenetrable, dense cluster of sand in front of her. She raged at the betrayals and at the king's triumph. Ashlynn hit the sand until her knuckles were red and torn, and yet still she attacked. She only stopped when she heard someone approaching behind her. Pulling herself out of her anger, she turned to find Ian and the other guard from the gate.

"Whendy was right, wasn't she?" Ashlynn said to them.

She narrowed her eyes at the two soldiers who looked fuzzy from her exhausted eyes.

"Barcinas. Queen Elspaeth has sent us here to arrest you. Again," Ian announced, avoiding Ashlynn's eyes and comment.

"He didn't bring them," Nikolai informed.

The other soldier gripped Barcinas's hands, and a bright red circle of light appeared around them. "He broke out of his cell and transformed into a dragon, again, without permission from the Queen to do so. We will mention he helped save her people, but the decision rests in her hands," Ian proclaimed.

"Ian," Nikolai said stepping forward. "I can vouch for Barcinas. Tell Queen Elspaeth that I claim he is innocent."

Ian gazed down at the sand, not meeting Niko's eyes.

"I do not mean to offend, Nikolai. I trust you entirely. But the queen has given a specific order to bring him in. Not even you can overrule her. Not this time," he said.

Nikolai rubbed his hand through his hair. "Yes, Ian. I understand and do not put you at fault," he said facing Barcinas. "I know that I have not given you many reasons to trust me, but I trust your word here. They will take you to the prison and subject you to many tortures before taking you to the queen."

Barcinas nodded to Nikolai as if he expected this, but

Ashlynn could barely focus as she swayed.

"Before they start, you must say this sentence explicitly. It will grant you a reprieve and possibly save you," he explained.

Once again, Barcinas nodded. Nikolai walked to him and whispered the phrase into his ear. Ashlynn saw Barcinas's eyes go wide, but he nodded again to Nikolai when he was finished.

Ian and the other soldier led him away. Ashlynn could only watch as they took away her final companion in this journey. She had failed them. Her entire body felt numb. She had released the bulk of her pain, betrayals, surprises, and whirlwind of emotions inside of her at the ground moments earlier. There was nothing left to give. A few tears rolled out and down into the sand. Her hand was shaking as she wiped them off her face.

Nikolai's warm, steady hand came on her shoulder. She winced as he touched her wounds, causing them to seep out more. His gesture was the only reminder she had that there was still kindness in the world—her world. She tried to reach up to grasp his hand, but cried out at the pain and crumbled to the ground. Nikolai pulled her torn blouse back to see her injury and picked her up without another thought. He held her tight to his chest, and sprinted back to the realm, his beating heart the last sound she heard as her vision blackened.

CHAPTER THIRTY TWO

The fireplace blazed in her room, and the moon was shining her light when Ashlynn awoke. She stretched out her leg and noticed her knee no longer hurt. Pushing the blanket down, she found a new scar where her soft skin had once been.

"I tried to heal it fully, but I am not a healer," Nikolai said. She glanced over to see him standing in the doorway.

"How long have I been out?" she asked. Her body felt weak. Everything ached, and her head still pounded.

"Three days. I saw you stirring earlier so I brought some food. You're probably hungry," he said. He put a tray of food down next to her. She reached to grab a bite of bread, but her muscle seized.

"Let me help you, Ashlynn," he insisted.

Ashlynn noticed a tinge in his jaw when he said those words, but she chose to process it later. Nikolai grabbed a piece of bread, dipped it in a honey like substance and put it to her lips. It smelled as sweet as honeysuckle. The bread was still hot and melted in her mouth as she chewed.

"Did you make this?" she asked in between bites.

He nodded, but seemed intent on feeding her without talking. So she ate in silence, savoring each bite. He gave her a few sips of something warm and spicy.

"This will help heal the aches," he said.

"Do you have anything for the memories?" she mumbled.

Nikolai gazed at her, his eyes sad with his own memories. "Ashlynn, I would not take that from you if I could. I understand the pain you feel, but because you are able to feel pain, you can also understand love, joy, and compassion. Taking away one would take away the others," he whispered.

She sighed and laid her head back down. "Usually I heal in a few hours. I must have been drained this time," she mumbled.

Nikolai studied her before answering. "Well, you had emptied yourself entirely from your journey here. The wounds you received when arriving and flying, not eating for the entire day, then being grabbed by Tiberius were cutting into your very core. Then you spit fire at Tiberius, which was unexpected. Add to it that a manticore has poison in its claws and you were fighting for consciousness," he said, his voice careful and thick. "I am surprised you were able to stay present through the entire fight."

"I did have someone yelling in my head," she muttered.

He smiled at her. "Yes, you did, Phoenix, but you are stronger than you give yourself credit for!"

"Phoenix?" she asked, eyeing him.

He smiled was so large that it reached his eyes. "Well, you can breathe flames. Plus, it sounds better than Ash. You rose from the ashes of your own pain and attacked back! To me, Ash is your past. Not to mention, I hear you can fly," he smirked with a raised eyebrow.

"How did you—"

"Whendy told me when she came to find me. You don't need to worry. I won't spill your secret to the Queen," he said, putting a hand on her arm.

"Does the queen know you have a dragon inside of you?" she wondered, aloud.

"Yes! She was the first we told so I could grow up in safety. That's another reason I am part of her retinue."

Ashlynn peeked up at him, cheeks red. "Phoenix. I like it. Thank you."

They sat in silence for another moment as she took another bite of the bread. "What else should I know about Dragons?" she asked after swallowing.

Nikolai held her eyes. "There is a lot I have to teach

you, but first you should rest."

"I have rested enough. We need to figure out how to save the others and cure the king. He is sick, in many ways, and I have been tasked with healing him. His evil will only spread, and I can't see another person I love hurt," she said, listing them out on her fingers as she projected her fear into each task.

"Well, that is a long to do list upon waking up," he announced. "But after you rest, we can talk with Barcinas. He is downstairs right now," he revealed.

Ashlynn pushed up on her arms, nearly falling back down from black spots and dizziness.

"What are you doing? You cannot go see him in this state," Nikolai said, helping her back down.

"Thought you weren't going to tell me what to do," she said, continuing to get out of bed. She paused, realizing that her statement had been rude after all of the care he had provided. "I didn't mean it like that," she said.

Nikolai held up his hand.

"I know. I just meant that you are still naked and need to recover."

Ashlynn put her head down on the pillow and closed her eyes. The crackling of the fire soothed her nerves and anticipation of seeing Barcinas and hearing his tale.

"What about getting the others back?" she asked, her

eyes still closed.

"We could talk about it now, but I would rather wait until we are all together to discuss it. Then we can have the best strategy and won't have to repeat what we decide," he said, deterring her at every path.

Ashlynn laid there listening to the silence around them. It was comforting. She used to fear the quiet. Her mind rambled too much, or she was worried someone was always listening if she talked too loud. This silence didn't feel forced. It felt right.

"Will you tell me your story while we wait?" he smiled.

She stuck her tongue out and pushed a strand of hair out of her face. His request about something so intimate to her was kind and respectful. She felt like he genuinely wanted to know more about her instead of gleaning information to use against her like most of the people she was used to being around in Levander.

"Yes, but only if you promise to tell me how you know Tiberius."

He nodded but stayed silent as he waited for her to begin.

"There isn't much to tell. My dad disappeared right after the war, and my mom believed him to be dead. Then she gave birth to me in the castle with my aunt, who had just married the king. He hoped she could prove useful, but she thwarted him at every turn. When I was about two, he killed her," she paused, taking a sip of warm water. "I lived with my aunt and cousins after that. I was mostly protected until I started to bleed. That day the king decided I was his property. And labeled me as such. I received whippings for messing up, a slap for saying the wrong thing, or was locked up for making a slight mistake. I constantly lived in fear. The night of the ball was the worst. I have to cure the king. It's the only way I can be free— that everyone can be free. But Whendy said the answer lies within me, and I don't even know what that means."

She took a breath. It was a lot to release, even if there were holes in what she revealed. Some things she wasn't quite ready to say aloud, especially to someone she had just met—no matter how breathtaking his eyes and energy were.

"I am honored to know part of your past. I don't judge you, and I will never lie to you or hurt you. Now, I give you part of mine. I am very open about who I am. I have had a long time to come to terms with my past. There is old magick that keeps certain secrets safe, so I can't tell you the facts I am not in control of. It isn't because I don't trust you. I do." He paused. "I cannot share what isn't mine to share."

"And how do you know you can trust me?" she asked.

He smiled. "Whendy told me about your dragon form before running off because she knew you would need support during this time. A friend. But she didn't say anything to Kristopher. She has always mistrusted him. I knew then that I can trust you." He smiled

"Niko, we just met. How can you promise those things?" she asked.

"Phoenix, that is the base of what I can offer as a friendship. And I have a feeling that we are going to become exceptional friends," he replied.

The name gave her tingles and made her face warm. She looked away to breathe but smiled. "I had someone else say that to me many years ago, except he became the one who inflicted the most pain on me," she replied.

"I am not other people and I am certainly not Tiberius. I always keep my promises, even if he no longer believes me. What I promise to you will never be broken if I can help it. And there is very little that I cannot help. I am not asking you to trust me right now. I am asking you to give me a chance."

"Why, Nikolai? Why do you care so much?" she muttered.

"Do I have to have a reason?" he whispered back.

She stared at him for a few minutes, their eyes

connecting to that spot deep within their souls again. Ashlynn didn't know how he was able to crack her open so easily, yet every time he did was gentle. She never felt forced to talk or judged by what she had said. "So how do you know Tiberius and why doesn't he trust you?"

Nikolai cleared his throat before beginning. "His father was an emissary to the queen for all winged lions. I met him when I was around five years old. His father brought him along on all of his visits. We became close since we were different from the Elves. One day when we were older, I made a mistake in trusting someone with information he had shared with me. Since that day, he blamed me for the consequences that came and has chosen to believe that I meant to hurt him." He swallowed and ran his hand through his curls. "But the Tiberius I saw today was not the one I knew years ago. Something has happened to him. I fear it has to do with the king's sickness." He studied her eyes. "I can't tell you anything else. It is more his story than mine."

Ashlynn sighed and nodded. Ashlynn twirled the blanket in her hands to help her mind stay focused. Nikolai shook his body, and Ashlynn could feel the tension that rolled off him. Then he continued his tale.

"When I was still in my mother's womb," Nikolai stared into the fire as if it were the source of his memories, "my

324

father tried to kill my mother. She had gone against him many times in the past, but this time was different. She lied to him about the dragons and ran away before he found out. When he did find out, he chased after her. He caught up with her then beat her. My aunt finally got him to stop, but by the time he did she was close to death. He walked away without a care. My aunt knew that my mother had a special relationship with the Dragons, so she ran to a certain dragon to ask for help." Nikolai paused as if recalling the story took great effort.

"When her dragon friend arrived, he recognized that she had little life left. He had grown to appreciate her passion, kindness, and love. He offered his life force to keep her alive. He sacrificed himself so that my mother would live. Since I was inside of her, his life force transferred to me also. This is how I am able to transform into a dragon, and how I am able to tell you this story. I am accessing his memories, even though they are tattered from the divide of the life force."

Ashlynn put her hand on his and smiled. "What was his name?" she asked.

"Samen. His name is Samen," he said.

His name made Ashlynn—no, her dragon—warm in remembrance, but she kept it to herself as he finished his story.

"I was born a few months later. My mother hid me from my father. He suspected that she was dead without knowing that she was pregnant with me. Soon after I was born, the Humans attacked the Dragons. She realized that she had to get me out of Levander. I had already started to show the ability to transform. A few dragons came to her and said they had organized a way to get me to freedom, but they needed her help. They needed her to choose three other women to take on their life force to preserve the Dragon race."

Ashlynn gasped. She had heard this story before, except from a different perspective.

"It is strange, I know. But I promise it happened. And that is how I think you have a dragon inside of you," he continued. "So my aunt brought me here with our guide. She was pregnant with Kristopher and was the first woman after my mother to accept the offer. The others were..."

"My mother and my aunt," Ashlynn finished. "My aunt told me this story, Niko. I didn't realize that it was your mother who was the leader. Daia was your mother!"

Nikolai laughed. "I suppose that would fit her. Yes, I only ever heard her name. My aunt gave me that but wouldn't tell me much else. She said it was to protect me."

Ashlynn gaped at him, feeling the truth inside of her

yet unable to release it.

"But," he continued, "what I can't figure out is how Barcinas can transform into a dragon."

His comment surprised her, causing her to forget about her secret. "What do you mean?"

"My aunt told me that the other two women were related. Since you have a dragon within you, that would mean Sebastian's mother is the last one. There were only four women though. So, how did Barcinas get a dragon inside of him?"

Ashlynn sat back thinking of Barcinas's orphan story and where he actually came from.

"Maybe he took on the life force as a child?" she said, thinking aloud. "But that doesn't make sense either. He was born after me. The Dragons were supposed to be gone by then. It doesn't make sense."

"Who are his parents?" Nikolai asked.

"He was orphaned. Marcus took him in and raised him as his own. No one, not even he, knows who his parents are," she said.

"What about Marcus's wife?" he asked.

Ashlynn stared at her hands. "She didn't know. But even if she did, we can't ask her." She glanced up at him with tears in her eyes. Before he could comfort her, she climbed out of bed.

"What are you doing, Phoenix? Where are you going?" he asked, helping her stand.

She grabbed a robe and tied it around her. Then, she hobbled out of the room. Ashlynn felt stiff everywhere, but the pain was mostly gone. The food Nikolai fed her had given her more strength. "I am going to Barcinas. We need to talk to him, and this can't wait," she said, stomping down the stairs.

Ashlynn paused on the next step before proceeding down. She thought back to every moment with Barcinas on the trip, playing through each of them like she had when she noticed the fabric tear in her interactions with Tiberius. Ashlynn searched for them in her memories with Barcinas. They were not as noticeable but were clearly there. It was odd, though, because they seemed to be expertly woven into the very being of her mind, whereas Tiberius's had stood out once her senses opened. It was as if Tiberius choosing to deceive her made it easier to locate, and Barcinas was the one being deceived on top of his own deception. One specific instance stood out.

Ashlynn knew Barcinas was keeping a secret, one even deeper than hers about Daia. She had to know what his was before she could spill hers to Nikolai. She glanced back at Nikolai who was wide eyed and amused at her little expedition and attire. Ashlynn gazed into his eyes, which were full of understanding and companionship, and knew that she could trust him.

"It matters," she said, "because the truth matters. The only way to find the cure is by revealing and releasing any deception, so we can know what is being hidden from us. So I can uncover the secrets inside myself and find the answer to ending the king's sickness. And his reign."

CHAPTER THIRTY THREE

She arrived at Barcinas's door to see it wide open with Barcinas staring across at her.

"I could hear you coming down the stairs. You're louder than twenty cannons sounding at once," he said with a smile.

"Barcinas. It is good to see you," she said, giving him a hug. He stiffened as her arms went around him, but relaxed into her as she continued to hold him. She whispered, "I was worried about you."

He gave her a crooked smile. The cut from Kristopher had left a deep gash that could not be healed entirely.

"It is good to see you too, friend," he replied.

Ashlynn smiled at the word.

"Ashlynn said it was important to come down and ask you a few questions. Do you feel up for it?" Nikolai asked.

"Of course not!" he grinned. "What do you want to know, Ashlynn?"

"Barc, how did you change into a dragon? Where did that ability come from?" she asked. "And does Marcus know?"

Barcinas glanced between them and sighed. Rubbing his face with his hands, he replied, "Sit down, please. Both of you."

Ashlynn and Nikolai sat down near the fire, and Barcinas moved to sit near them.

"Sebastian was right in his accusations," he began, gazing into the orange glowing flames for strength. "Years ago when Daia disappeared from our house, Marcus asked me to spy on Sebastian, Odessa, and you. He told me it was for the safety of the kingdom. He said King Theodore needed to know what his son was up to in his free time. I did it eagerly because it meant I had friends. Or what I thought were friends. I quickly learned that spying made me a bad friend, but I couldn't give it up."

He paused to glance at her. "I know you didn't consider us friends. I was always mean to you. But that was how I coped, and I understood it was wrong. I just didn't have another reference."

Barcinas paused to take a breath. His hands were shaking, but he held them tight.

"My senses were starting to open as we journeyed up the mountain to Oren. After that, I followed you, and I trusted you. Every time you saw or heard something, I adjusted my senses to yours. I believed in everything you

331

told me." He paused, but she could no longer wait to ask.

"What actually happened with the soldier that night on the cliff? We were in the cave and you were beaten down. I know you lied," she asked.

Barcinas lowered his head. "You are right," he said, covering his face with his hands. "I lied to both of you. I didn't know the warrior I fought, but it was because he was no longer the man I trained with. He has transformed into a beast similar to the ones we fought a few days ago. He had wings and a tail, and his eyes held the same malice and disease as the king. I had to silence the warrior I fought, that part was true. But it was because I was scared he would tell you that I had lied again. He didn't actually seize and fall away like I said. He morphed into a wyvern. Marcus knew you would leave after the party, and told me to go with you to keep him informed. It wasn't until the Tuhka village that I realized the evil I was serving."

Barcinas paused again, swallowing a few lumps in his throat. "I realized I had been played and had in turn played each of you. I didn't feel worthy to continue on this journey, but I knew I had to. You finally trusted me, even after all I did to you. So, I knew I had to be better. I killed him because he was going to out me, and also because he was going to kill both of you. So in those moments, I stopped fighting for Marcus and started to fight for myself. I didn't tell either of you because I was scared. I apologize for that, and I have been honest since then. I promise."

He whispered the last part, as if he were a child asking for forgiveness which he felt he didn't deserve.

All of her wanted to yell at him for lying. To rage at his mistakes and blind acceptance. She finally understood Sebastian's anger at him that day in the hut. Yet the more she thought about his actions, the more she saw herself in them. How she thought her mistakes were the cause of her beatings. Even after she begged for forgiveness, her pain wouldn't stop. The king would laugh or beat her harder. As much as she wanted to hold it against him, she knew that this was the beginning for her to not only forgive him but to also forgive herself. To begin the long process of loving those pieces that she had blamed for her abuse. To heal. "Barc," Ashlynn said, reaching out to hold his hand, "I choose to forgive you."

That was all she said, because it was all that was needed. Barcinas released a sigh. "In the forest, before the shadow showed up, I heard a voice in my head saying, 'You have more in you than you know. Trust only yourself. Look deep inside yourself, for only then will the fog clear, and you will be able to fly freely.' As I trailed behind you in the forest, I started to dig inside myself. I hadn't focused on keeping Sebastian safe and beat myself up over it as we chased him. When he ran over the edge, I was on the verge of breaking. I had lost the last person I truly cared about.

"Sebastian had leaped to his death because I was more concerned about figuring out more about myself. I fell to the ground and was about to give up forever. But there you were, willing to fight for him and urging me along with you. I saw you as the friend I had always wanted to be. There was a bright light in you, so I stood up and grabbed your hand. Your desire to include me sliced open the veil blocking the beast from emerging within. And I awoke to my power."

He stopped and Ashlynn smiled up at him. His face was raw with emotion as tears poured down his cheeks. He stared at her, letting his raw vulnerability run free.

"You helped me open what was locked inside. When we fell into the water, I knew that I had to overcome my fear of dying to save us. I gave into my fear by admitting my weakness and failures. The dragon inside of me saw it all and loved me for being myself. I begged for his help, and he came forth, pulling me from the water. I saw you and Sebastian and no longer cared if I died or not. I saved both of you because you had saved me from myself. But while I was comfortable with this new part of me, I didn't know how you would both feel. So I hid."

He finished talking, but his tears still poured. Ashlynn reached over to wipe away his tears, then held his shaking hands in hers.

"That is why I didn't want Kaenon to look inside my head. I didn't want someone else finding out and learning more about something inside of me that I hadn't had time to figure out," he said, finishing his tale and sobbing with each breath he took. "I am sorry for all I ever did to you and Sebastian."

Ashlynn took his face in her hands and smiled. "Thank you for being raw and confident enough to share that. And I am proud to call you my friend." She hugged him and let him cry onto her shoulder. They stayed in this moment until his sobs turned to careful breathing. Finally, he pulled away.

"I don't know where the dragon inside of me came from. My dragon knows, I can feel that, but it is as if he thinks I am not ready to know that answer. The time isn't right. I believe the answer will come one day," he said.

Nikolai was still sitting across from them and gazing at the fire. "Barcinas, who was Daia to you?" he asked.

Barcinas peered up at him. "She was my adopted mother. She took me in when my own mother didn't want me."

Nikolai continued to stare at the fire. "I heard you mention her name, but I wasn't sure I heard you correctly."

Ashlynn faced him while still holding Barcinas's hands. "That is why I rushed down here. Daia was married to Marcus. They raised Barcinas."

Nikolai nodded as tears formed in his eyes. "That means Marcus is my father?"

"Wait, what did I miss?" Barcinas asked.

"I'll tell you later," she mouthed to him as Nikolai stared into the flames.

"I had never wanted to meet him for what he did to my mother, and I will keep that secret until the day I die. I will never consider such an evil person my father." Nikolai took a huge breath, swallowed and wiped his face. "Daia, my mother. Where is she?"

Barcinas stared down at his lap while Ashlynn held Nikolai's eyes. "The king and Marcus had her killed. She is the one who was brought forward for trial during my ball," Ashlynn answered.

Nikolai put his face in his hands. He breathed a few times, fighting with his control over his emotions.

"Her death was my fault, Nikolai. I thought at the time it was best to divulge Ashlynn's meeting with Daia to

Marcus. Now I know I always had a choice." Barcinas glanced up at Nikolai. "I killed her. I sent her to her death. The only mother I ever knew. And I am so sorry."

"Barc, you didn't kill her. Marcus and King Theodore did," Ashlynn said. "Don't take their blame, or there will never be justice for her death."

Barcinas nodded, but stared at Nikolai. They sat in silence for a moment.

"So, Marcus doesn't know about me, Kristopher is my cousin and brother, and Barcinas was raised by my parents." Nikolai peered up at both of them and chuckled. She glanced at Barcinas who began snickering as well. Ashlynn was surrounded by two emotional, adopted brothers who were guffawing so hard they could barely breathe. All she could do was smile at the thought and laugh with them. They would need a lot of laughter to get through the coming days.

"Only crazy people would think this is funny," Barcinas said, breathing out as he tried to calm himself.

"If this is crazy, then I don't want to be normal," Nikolai announced barely holding in his laughter. "That sounds boring. I gained two brothers in one night!"

Ashlynn looked between them and snorted, which caused everyone to fall into a fit of laughter again. It was exactly what each of them needed in this time of doubt, fear, and revelation to feel less alone. Her new task was to learn about the secrets she held inside, and that was daunting.

"Niko, why do you think Kris would lead Marcus here?" she asked after they paused their chuckling. "Did he even know Marcus was his father? And how would he even meet up with him to give the information?"

"I don't know. It doesn't make any sense to me. I just have to trust that Kris didn't mean to hurt us," he said, still gazing back at the swirling tendrils of smoke.

"Why?" she demanded. "He betrayed us all and took Sebastian. I barely know the jerk and I am furious at him."

Nikolai sighed. "Because imagining the cousin I grew up with turning against me to intentionally hurt me is much harder to stomach. And I have no way to prove it either way. So, I choose to have faith in him. What I want to know is why the king wanted Whendy," he said.

"Oh, that's easy," Barcinas announced, standing up to stretch. "He has been paranoid about Dragons still being alive. Marcus has repeatedly told him over the years that there were dragons who escaped. He wants her to tell him where they are and to warn him if someone is out to get him."

Ashlynn sighed, realizing how time sensitive figuring out the cure was now that Whendy's life was at stake.

"What is our next step? Saving Whendy or figuring out how to access this knowledge inside myself? I don't know if I can do it," she whispered. "Assuming Whendy is still alive."

"She is," Barcinas comforted. "The king needed her alive to predict the future for him. If she plays it right, then she can lead them along for a while. I would rather believe that than the alternative," he said.

Nikolai gazed at her with a strength she struggled to find in herself at times. "Whendy is clever. She will have outwitted them many times before we recover her. And I have no doubt you can, Phoenix. We are fighting for a better world. A world where every being is accepted and appreciated without fear. We are fighting for people who have been cursed without even knowing it. We are fighting an old system. But old doesn't mean wise. It means decaying and stagnant. It isn't meant to be easy. We see how that breeds laziness and led to this sickness. It will take time, but I know you can do it."

His words reminded her of the spark inside, and she caressed her necklace. "Thank you, Niko."

"Kaenon and I were talking," Nikolai continued, "about what he saw in your minds. The Shadow, as you each call it, is not something the Elves put in Varjo. At least not that he and I know of. He sent me images and the sensations of what he saw in your minds, and it feels darker. This is something we need to keep an eye on as well. Especially if the Knarkes are doing its bidding instead of the queen's."

Barcinas shivered at the memory as he stood near the hearth.

"He called himself Syren," Ashlynn explained. "It wasn't announced, but when I think back to that moment there was an energy that conveyed more than what we felt during the intense escape. I will feel more into it over the next few days to see if I can glean anymore underlying energetic knowledge it exuded."

"Hmm. I will have to bring that up to Kaenon," Nikolai murmured. "Another mystery to add to our list. I would like to know what my mother would say about all of this. She set it up, so I wonder what she would say after we all found each other."

"Niko, I never had a brother, and learning that you are Daia's son makes me feel even more connected to you. They weren't my parents, but I feel like you are the brother I always wanted. It would be an honor to share Daia's memory with you. I know this is what she would've wanted," Barcinas said with a shrug.

Nikolai stood and walked to Barcinas. The two hugged each other tightly. Seeing them hug struck a chord in Ashlynn.

"Nikolai! I have something from your mother!" she shouted and hugged him. "Daia asked me to give this to you. I didn't know who she meant at the time, but now I know that she must have realized that I would be meeting her son soon," she whispered in his ear as she held him tight. "Daia gave me a note from my mother. It was in my clothes when you took them off to care for me. Did you find it?" she asked.

Nikolai reached into his pocket and pulled out the letter. "I held onto it because it felt important."

Ashlynn barely heard his response as she snatched the letter from him. It was in the exact same condition as when she pulled it out of her pocket in front of the Tuhka village that day to honor their memory. She couldn't help but wonder how it survived the ocean water without a tear or stain. She held it close. "Thank you, Niko. I think it is finally time to read this."

Walking out of the room, she climbed the stairs to the balcony. Her mother's scents— vanilla and cypress— filled Ashlynn's nose and memories. She smiled at the love behind them and froze in that moment, imagining her mother's arms around her again.

As Ashlynn stood there in her mother's arms. Her hands clasped the letter for fear of it being snatched away. She knew that her mother had imbued this letter with magick and love. The mixture of the two had protected it, and Ashlynn figured it would always protect it, from weather, aging, or life's mishaps. In this moment, she realized her mother had sent her love and protection that would be with her for as long as she lived. She hugged it to her heart and held it there for a moment, cherishing this gift from her mother.

Both the idea of her mother's words between these pieces of parchment, and the effort she took to protect it gave Ashlynn a sense of awe and reverence for this moment before its contents were revealed. Then, with her fingers trembling, she unwrapped the smooth edges of the paper— in pristine condition despite its age. Ashlynn took a deep breath and sighed it out. Holding onto her necklace for comfort, she started to read.

☾ ☾ ☾ ☾ ☾ ☾ ☾ ☾ ☾ ☾ ☾ ☾ ☾ ☾ ☾ ☾ ☾ ☾ ☾

My dear Ashlynn,

Oh, my child. How I wish I could be there to see you grow up. My death is imminent, and I fear that this time I cannot avoid it. But if you have this letter then my greatest fear has come to fruition. Do not let that sadden you, sweet girl. I thank the Great Goddess that I was able to see you grow for the first few years of your life. I want you to know that you are my greatest joy. You were your fathers' unknown gift to me, and he would've adored you, as I do. You are my life, Ashlynn.

I am so sorry for this path I have put you on. I wish for a much easier life for you than the one I expect you will have. However, I know that these difficult years ahead will not harden you. Instead, I believe you will grow into a kind, loving, and understanding person because you have had these struggles. But I want you to know, my girl, that those struggles do not define who you are. They will only help shape who you will become. Trust in yourself. Fight for yourself. Most importantly, love yourself. You have an extraordinary journey ahead of you, and the kingdom's safety is in your hands.

Don't lose hope, my dear Ashlynn. For when all else fails and despair sets in, hope will remind you that anything is possible. You will find the answers you seek by going inside yourself. Let your power and knowledge guide you. You are proof that a better world exists.

Stay strong, my world. I love you.

Mother

⟨ ⟨

Ashlynn hugged the letter again and sobbed. All of the pain she had endured over the years, the loneliness and despair, felt like a wound that had started to be stitched back up with her mother's words.

"Mother, what would you think of me now? I don't know how to love myself. I can't love myself because I don't even know who I am. I fear that I haven't been that kind person you dreamed of. So, what now mother? What

343

do I do now?" she begged aloud.

Ashlynn gulped down breaths while releasing all of the confusion and pain. Deep inside a little child was hiding, unsure of who she was. The beast inside of her curled around this little girl, protecting her and loving her.

We will do this together, Ashlynn. Trust me. You are no longer alone, came Hatta's voice within.

Those words gave her the peace she needed to take it one step at a time. She curled up and hugged herself, knowing that her next journey would be the biggest and most painful one yet. But this time she was ready to figure it out, one step at a time, one foot in front of the other.

END OF BOOK ONE IN
HER STORY

PRONUNCIATION GUIDE

Characters

Odessa: Oh-dehs-suh

Barcinas: Bar-sin-us

Daia: Die-uh

Sabah: Sah-bah

Aurik: Or-rick

Elspaeth: Els-peth

Kaenon: Kay-nahn

Iseult: Is-ult

Place

Levander: Leh-van-dur

Pyr: Purr

Tuhka: Tu-kuh

Varjo: Var-ho

Miras: Meer-ras

Reis: Reys

Fermont: Fer-mon

Other

Magick: Magic (Meaning that which we have inside of us)

Knarke: Nark

Syren: Sigh-ren

BONUS CONTENT

"Tell me, Nikolai. What do you think of our guest?" the Queen of Miras asked.

She sat on her violet wooded throne, looking down at her two spymasters. Her long silver curls swirled in braids, forming a circlet upon which her crown of purpleheart wood, rose gold, and black obsidian crystals rested. Her slender, yet muscled body was adorned with a light pink flowing blouse attached with a high collar. She wore tight black pants, which connected to a shimmery silver fabric that hung around her waist to create a ruffled skirt. Her face was stern with a mischievous smile.

Nikolai and Kaenon were kneeling in front of the dais in her private throne room. The intense eyes of the Queen of Miras gazed upon them as they supplied information about the attack on her realm. Her queendom. Anger burned inside at the assault as her icy power threatened to melt under the intense ire. She rubbed her brow to soothe the rage that coursed through her.

"From the small amount of time I have spent with her, Your Majesty," Nikolai responded, his voice neutral, "she seems," he paused, as if to taste the words on his tongue before saying them. "motivated. She is determined to save the king from his sickness."

The queen studied her favorite emissary. He had risen to the challenge of intercepting a hidden message at the king's ball a few weeks back and had fought bravely against the intruders. His loyalty toward the Elves was welcomed.

"I see. And Kaenon, do you think your brother is biased," she asked, using an elven term to describe the two males who had completed a blood ritual that tied them together as battle brothers for life.

"Yes, Your Majesty. I do," he murmured. "But I think he has good reason to be. What I saw in her mind was unlike any I have ever searched."

Nikolai gave him a side glance and kept his mouth shut.

"Yet she was weak during the attack. Helpless as a babe. It caused our Nikolai to get sidetracked. She seems to be a liability," the queen thought aloud.

"Possibly, but I believe there is much she has to offer," Nikolai countered, keeping Ashlynn's fire a secret. "Once she figures out how to access her power, that is."

"You have fallen for her, haven't you, Nikolai?" she mocked, her eyes narrowing.

"You know I'm not allowed that luxury, Your Highness," Nikolai remarked.

"Yes, I do. But I wanted to see if you remembered our deal." The queen looked across her queendom through the open window next to her chair. "She will come to trust you, Nikolai. Be sure she has no reserves in doing so. She can't have any doubts as we move to execute our final plan." He nodded and kissed her hand in allegiance, then walked toward the door to wait for permission to leave. "Keep an eye on her, Kaenon," she murmured. "Train her. She must be ready when we need to utilize her. And if she isn't," she said with a pause as a sly grin spread across her face, "then I'm sure the king would pay handsomely for her return."

Kaenon followed Nikolai's lead as he kissed her hand and walked to the door. The two bowed and closed it behind them, leaving the queen alone with her thoughts.

ACKNOWLEDGEMENTS

I am so thankful for everyone who has supported me and loved on me during this time! I had an amazing team help me with this book.

Above all, I want to thank Spirit for pouring these words, intentions, and magick into me as I wrote this story. All that you have read was connected to Spirit and meant for you to read because there is something here for you! I am thankful that I was chosen to write this story and forever grateful that I listened to what poured out!

To my Kara Sevda, my forever mate- Justin. My dearest, words will never be enough to express the love and appreciation I have for you as you supported my dream by washing the dishes, watching the kids, cleaning the house, and just being you! You gave me the time to create, and this book is able to reach others because you believed in me. I love you and thank you!

Dominic, Thomas, Elias, Rose, and Ruby... my sweet ones. Each of you inspired me in specific ways, and because of you I had the courage and drive to do this! Our dreams are in our reach. Thank you for that reminder.

Hannah, my dear! Thank you for being my first reader and the person I could call at random times to weave crazy additions to the story. I am so thankful to have you in my life and call you my best friend!

To my illustrator, Darcy! You made my vision of Levander and Ashlynn a reality! Your unique artistry helped me see her more clearly and her world as vividly as our own! I cannot thank you enough for believing in me and my story!

Clari, you constantly made me smile while going through my book! Your comments and first edits solidified that this was beautiful! Thank you for your love and your videos of excitement! They made my day every single time!

Lilly, my twin flame! Your poem was divinely inspired and connected through our portal. I am forever grateful that we found each other and can love on each other the way we need and deserve!

My editor, Nicolette Beebe! Thank you for believing in me and in Ashlynn's story. You're edits, encouragements and jumps of excitement made the last editing processes much more enjoyable! You have helped create the easy flow in this novel, and I am grateful to have met you!

Mom, I love you! Thank you for helping and believing in me when I wasn't sure. I am blessed to have the most supportive mother! You are a lesson and an inspiration.

Dad, thank you! I appreciate your love and dedication to me by reading something you never would've picked up and by telling everyone you knew about it. I am blessed to have you as my father. I love you!

To my friends who read the book ahead of time and gave me feedback, Katie and Kathryn, or cheered me on during this endeavor! Please know, if you are reading this section and wonder if I mean you—yes, I am talking about you! Thank you!

Finally, my readers! This story has been in my heart for a while but now it is on the page for you. You get to determine what you see, what you hear, and what you take away! I made this for you! Ashlynn has a few lessons for us, but what they are is totally up to each person for interpretation.

THE TEAM

Hannah Peden (Support)
@library_of_velaris

Clarissa Vera (Support)
@clarivcrystals
www.clarivcrystals.com

Alyssa Lilly (Poet)
@beautifulandcourageous
www.beautifulandcourageous.com

Darcy Farrow (Illustrator)
@darcy.farrow
www.darcyfarrowdesign.com

Nicolette Beebe (Editor)
@33nbeebe
https://33nbeebe.weebly.com/newsletter.html

About the Author

Tara Webb works at home while homeschooling her three boys. She also has a coaching business, Pandora's Labyrinth, where she works with women to discover their creative passions by helping them feel empowered to publish themselves. She thrives on connecting with other women and lifting them up. She is devoted to creating her dream life, which is to live in the woods with her family, grow her own garden, and supporting women in their pursuits without fear or doubt! She believes in magick, Dragons, Fairies, Elves, and more, and wants to rekindle your knowledge and love of them too.

Want more of Ashlynn's story? Follow Tara Webb on Instagram, @iamtarawebb, and sign up for her newsletter for updates about the next three books in this series.
www.iamtarawebb.com

If you enjoyed this novel, a review on Amazon & Goodreads would be greatly appreciated! Submit a copy of your review to tara@iamtarawebb.com to receive a special thank you gift.

Made in United States
North Haven, CT
24 January 2022

15244216R00221